Harrison Jones

THE
PILOT
CLASS

A Novel

ISBN 13: 978-0692371510
ISBN 10: 0692371516

Published by Av Lit Press
Contact the author at www.harrisonjones.org

DEDICATION

For all there is
For all there will ever be
For Diane

Acknowledgments

When I sat in new hire pilot class many years ago, I was most certainly not thinking about writing a novel. After six weeks, the only thing more paralyzed than my brain was my posterior. I was most fortunate to have six outstanding classmates to help me get off the ground. You know who you are, gentlemen. Thank you!

Thank you to all the flight attendants who suffered my bad landings and bad jokes with equal patience and tolerance. A special thanks to Lee Heath, flight attendant extraordinaire, who exposed the humor and irony in the profession by authoring the book *How To Do A Stew*. Lee's musings remind me that a career in aviation doesn't build character, it reveals it.

An apology to all the crew schedulers who rang my phone at three in the morning and endured my half conscious babbling until they could be sure I was on my feet and moving toward the airport in an airworthy condition. When the late Carl Smail retired from crew scheduling, I believe the on time performance at Delta Airlines suffered a drop of several points.

I am indebted to my friend Richard Smith, author of *Airship* and *The Boys With Wings,* for creating the cover art for *The Pilot Class*. I am indeed most fortunate to have his multi-talented collaboration, not only for cover art, but for editorial advice as well.

Lastly we should all be reminded that there is never a moment, no matter what time of day or night, when airline personnel are not on duty with safety as their first concern. Pilots, flight attendants, dispatchers, mechanics, crew schedulers, meteorologist, agents, ramp personnel, and so many others are plying their trade 24/7/365. All should be acknowledged with gratitude.

Chapter One

Clear skies and light winds were the best news Captain Robbie Jenner had heard all day. His four-day trip had been like a safari along the east coast with landings at fourteen different airports. He was returning to his domicile in Atlanta, like a homing pigeon, and eager to begin five days free of duty. Draining the last of the coffee from his Styrofoam cup, he tossed it into the plastic garbage bag hanging on the aileron trim knob at the back of the control pedestal. Turning to the copilot, he said, "Do you think we could work our way through the approach checklist one more time?"

The reply came with a smile, "Your wish is my command, boss. Not only that, it's in the rulebook."

"Really? I need to get a copy of that."

"Please don't, you'd make me carry it in my brain bag and its heavy enough already."

"When you're done whining, inform the flight attendants that we're returning to earth and read the checklist."

Joyce Hoffman walked down the narrow aisle in the tourist section of the MD-88 holding a garbage bag open for passengers to discard whatever trash they had accumulated during the flight. Along with plastic cups, napkins, and peanut bags, she had collected one barf bag and two baby diapers. The glamor of being a flight attendant had escaped her long ago. As she neared the aft galley, the 'No

Smoking' light flashed and the chime sounded. No one had been allowed to smoke on the airplane for years, but the light and chime were still used for the captain to signal final approach and time to prepare for landing.

Reaching the rear of the airplane, Joyce disposed of the garbage bag and secured the loose items in the galley. She checked that the aft lavatories were unoccupied and then joined the other flight attendant on the crew seat for landing. Stretching her legs out in front of her, she wiggled her toes and tried to relax her aching feet. After twelve years of flying the line, she had yet to find a pair of shoes she could love.

Sitting at the rear of the MD-88, between the twin jet engines, made conversation difficult, and when the landing gear extended, the noise level made it hardly worth the effort. The landing announcement over the PA system competed for attention as it echoed through the cabin. Joyce knew she now had about five minutes to relax before touchdown, and she planned to enjoy every second. That was before she saw the toddler slip from her mother's lap and stumble down the aisle toward her.

Joyce uttered an expletive as she released her shoulder harness and lap belt. The child's mother had also stood to retrieve the runaway, but Joyce was faster and had just cradled the girl in her arms when the explosion ripped through the cabin. The airplane lurched to the left, sending the mother sprawling across a row of passengers and leaving Joyce on the floor with the child underneath her.

The airplane seemed to stabilize, and Joyce attempted to stand as panicked screams assaulted her ears. She choked back a scream of her own and checked that the child was uninjured. The toddler's mother was back on her feet and grabbing for her baby as Joyce hustled them back to their seat and fastened the seat belt.

Turning her attention to the back of the cabin, she could see blue sky through an opening in the fuselage and smoking debris scattered everywhere. Other than shock and panic attacks, the passengers appeared to be unharmed, and there were no visible flames in sight. *Thank God the cabin was almost depressurized. Are we going to crash?*

As she made her way aft, the roar caused by the gaping hole in the fuselage was so loud she could no longer hear the passenger's screams. Her heartbeat was just beginning to slow when she saw the jump seat she had occupied a minute before. A smoldering piece of metal was impaled in the back of the seat, and the other flight attendant was slumped forward beside it, still held in place by the shoulder harness. Blood pooled in the seat and on the floor at her feet.

Captain Robbie Jenner jammed right rudder to stop the airplane's unexpected turn to the left and cranked in rudder trim to keep it there. The sink rate increased dramatically, and he pushed the throttles up and raised the nose to gain control.

The copilot's voice elevated an octave in pitch, "Left engine fail!"

Robbie was correcting back to line up with the runway, "We're gonna land, declare an emergency."

Before the copilot could trigger his mic, the tower called, "Tri Con Twelve Sixteen you have smoke from the left engine."

The copilot answered, "Yeah, we're declaring an emergency."

"What's your intentions, Twelve Sixteen?"

"We're continuing to land, and if we have to go around we want a straight out departure."

"Cleared as requested and I'll scramble the equipment for you."

The copilot turned to Robbie, "The normal checklist is complete, and you're cleared to land."

Robbie estimated less than a minute to touchdown, "Pull the fire handle on the left engine and do the best you can with the emergency checklist. Standby to roll the rudder trim out when I call for it."

"Confirm the left engine fire handle."

Robbie glanced to see that the copilot had his hand on the correct T-handle and wasn't about to shut down the wrong engine, "That's the one. Pull it!"

Pulling the handle, the copilot disregarded the remainder of the checklist and said, "Three up and seven down," informing Robbie that they were three hundred feet above ground and descending at seven hundred feet per minute.

Red and amber warning lights dotted the instrument panels, but they were not telling Robbie anything he didn't already know. He ignored them all to concentrate on the landing. At thirty feet above the runway, he pulled the throttles to idle and said, "Roll the trim."

The copilot centered the rudder trim to ensure the nose wheel was straight for touchdown. The main landing gear met the concrete with a thump and the flight rolled out with smoke still trailing the left engine and fire trucks arriving to join the chase.

Joyce had just reached the flight attendant in the jump seat when the wheels touched down. The airplane decelerated rapidly, and she slipped on the blood soaked floor. With nothing to hold on to, she slid forward into the galley and hoped the airplane didn't explode. As she regained her feet and once again approached the girl in the jump seat, fire-fighting foam began to cascade through the hole in the fuselage.

Chapter Two

Molly Jackson glanced at her watch as she walked into the Tri Con training center's cafeteria and noted that she had twenty minutes to enjoy her morning coffee. Molly's flight attendant uniform was tailored to perfection, and she projected an image suitable for a magazine cover. Shoulder length red curly hair framed her attractive forty-year-old face. Molly did not normally perform the duties of a flight attendant and only wore the uniform for official occasions. Her title was *Manager of in Flight Service,* and she was responsible for the supervision of all 15,000 Tri Con cabin crewmembers. Molly's first fifteen years with the company had been as a flight attendant, and she sometimes regretted accepting the offer to join the management team four years earlier. She would go to war with anyone who mistreated one of her flight attendants. It was rumored that she had unofficially informed more than one abusive passenger that they were welcome to try another carrier for their travel needs. On the other hand, she was not as subtle with flight attendants who did not perform to her professional standards and, therefore, did not object to being called *Mama Molly* behind her back.

With steaming cup in hand, Molly walked into the crowded cafeteria and smiled when two pilots in uniform stood and waved her over. The taller of the two captains greeted her, "Please join us, Molly."

"I'm not sure I should be seen associating with you two. Might set a bad example for all the flight attendants in the room."

The second captain pulled a chair out for her. "Just pretend you're chewing us out about something. Raise your voice and call us something rude."

She sat down with a sigh, "Colt, are you ever going to grow up?"

Colt Adams was the Chief Pilot for the Atlanta base, "Charlie was just asking me the same thing, but I haven't formulated an appropriate response."

Charlie Wells, Vice President of Flight Operations, shook his head, "We all know the answer regardless, so just try not to color outside the lines. Molly, are we all in costume for the same reason? Are you here to talk to the new pilot class?"

"I am. All my assistants are traveling, so I'm stuck with the duty."

Colt chuckled, "We're going to tell them how gorgeous the ladies are, and you're going to tell them to stay away from them."

Molly smiled, "Not in so many words, but I'll make it clear what will happen if they don't give them the proper respect."

Charlie's expression turned serious, "Have you talked to the cabin crew from Flight Twelve Sixteen?"

"Two of them walked away uninjured and I met with them in flight operations right after the accident yesterday. The third girl is in critical condition with lacerations and burns on both legs. She probably wouldn't have made it if the other two hadn't slowed the bleeding until help arrived. I went to the hospital, hoping to talk to her, but she's still sedated."

"Let us know if we can help," Charlie offered. "I've never seen an uncontained engine failure that catastrophic. It seemed to just start throwing fan blades for no apparent reason. We're lucky there were not a lot more injuries. Hopefully, maintenance can tell us what happened before the FAA decides to ground the entire MD-88 fleet."

"If that happens you won't need the new pilots you just hired. How many are in the class?"

Charlie answered, "We hired eight, but there's been one casualty already. Some people just can't stand prosperity. This guy had a few drinks during the flight to Atlanta yesterday and tried to impose himself on the lady sitting beside him in First Class. He evidently thought that telling her he was a Tri Con pilot would cause her to subordinate herself."

"What happened?"

"She told the flight attendant she wanted to change seats, the flight attendant told the captain, and when they landed the captain called me. Last night, Colt went over to the hotel and escorted him back to the airport with explicit instructions to sit down and shut up or he could walk back to Los Angeles."

"Good riddance. Are you going to replace him in the class?"

"We were just talking about that. You know ground school is like drinking water from a fire hose, and if I start someone a day late, he will never catch up. I've got a few applications from local people, and Colt and I are going to look at them after we talk to the class. We'll see if anyone is acceptable and if they can be here by noon."

Molly paused to take a sip of coffee with a thoughtful look on her face, "Can I see the applications?"

"Sure, I haven't had a chance to look at them myself, but they're here in my briefcase."

Molly shuffled through the stack of paperwork with a hopeful expression and paused to look at one of the forms. "Charlie, I may be way out of line here, but do you remember this application?"

She handed him the paper, and he glanced over it. "Oh yeah, I remember you requesting that I do the interview several months ago, and I did. The weak point on this one is the low multi-engine time. I recommended continuing to build time with an emphasis on multi-engine and instrument experience."

"I don't know what that means, but she's been with Tri Con for six years and she's an excellent flight attendant. I can only vouch for her character and work ethic if that means anything."

Colt had been looking at the application, "Character sure didn't mean much to the idiot we sent home yesterday. Charlie, all these applications have a minor weakness, or we would have hired them already. She doesn't need the company orientation class this morning so she could start this afternoon without a problem. As I recall, the day I met you was the first day of ground school. When Tri Con hired us how many multi-engine hours did you have?"

Charlie looked at the application again, "Do I get to vote on this?"

Colt took a sip of coffee, "Of course, you're the Vice President, but Molly and I have you outnumbered, so somebody needs to get this girl on the phone."

Charlie stuffed the papers back in the briefcase, "You call her, Molly, and if she washes out, you'll have to decide what to do with her next. If she can't be here by noon, the deal is off."

Molly took out her cell phone and speed dialed her secretary, as Charlie spotted a man in the coffee line and waved him over. The man wore a sports coat and tie with a name badge on the lapel with the words *Phil James—Pilot Ground Instructor.* His bald pate was surrounded by reddish-blond hair, and he held coffee in one hand while pushing his glasses up the bridge of his nose with the other.

Charlie shook hands and said, "I was hoping to see you before the class started, Phil."

"Always a pleasure, Charlie. How you doing, Colt?"

"Fine as frog hair as long as you don't start asking me questions about lift over drag ratios and all that other stuff that nobody but you understands."

Phil chuckled, "Don't worry, I never do math before coffee. I hear you've already sent one of my students packing."

Charlie said, "He'll be replaced later today—you'll still have eight to contend with. It should be a good mix—four former military pilots and four civilians."

"Is it true that one of them has a bit of notoriety?" Phil asked.

Colt said, "You mean Senator Walker's son?"

"No, I mean the other one."

Tri Con Flight 386, en route from New York's JFK to Atlanta, had just passed overhead Washington, D.C. when the company datalink chime sounded. The copilot glanced down at the ACARS screen to read the message and then hit the print button. The captain frowned, "If that says we're being re-routed, don't acknowledge it. I've got an afternoon tee time with a chance of winning back some of the money I lost last week."

Tearing the message off the printer, the copilot handed it across for the captain to read.

> TC 386, please relay following msg. to
> D. Daniels F/A employee #304656.
> "Imperative you phone M. Jackson at
> 898-686-3420 immediately upon arrival
> ATL." THX C. Smail ATL crew sked.

The captain sighed, "D. Daniels, M. Jackson, and C. Smail, don't anybody have a first name anymore?"

"Too much information, boss. Uh…what was your name again?"

"I asked for a copilot and they send me a comedian. See if you can find D. Daniels and pass the message."

The copilot chuckled and typed *ack* at the bottom of the screen and hit the send button. "That would be Denise, the blond flight attendant who brought your coffee a little while ago… right before the turbulence began. I'm guessing M. Jackson is Mama Molly and C. is Carl Smail in crew scheduling."

"Thank you for your interpretation and the editorial. If D is in trouble with M, I hope I don't have to write letters of explanation."

✈

After serving the twenty-four first-class passengers their breakfast snack and doing a second beverage service, Denise Daniels stood in the forward galley enjoying a moment of peace and quiet and a glass of orange juice. She removed her serving smock and made a mental note that it was due to be laundered. Her hotel wake-up call had come at five a.m., and the departure from JFK was delayed almost two hours due to a mechanical issue. She and her crew would have to hit the ground running in Atlanta in order to make the next flight on their schedule—a four-hour leg to Los Angeles, with a full meal service. She felt grungy already, and it was barely ten a.m.

The cockpit call chime ended her pity party, and she picked up the phone, "This is Dee, what can I get for you, gentlemen?"

The copilot remembered that she didn't like to be called Denise because she said it sounded like someone sneezing. "Hey Dee, we've got a message for you from crew scheduling, and when you come up, could we get a couple of coffees?"

"If you guys keep drinking coffee, you'll be awake for the entire flight."

"Don't bet on it."

"What time are we landing?"

"The magic box says touchdown at 11:33—we should be at the gate by 11:45 unless they make us hold."

It was actually 11:52 when Dee Daniels disarmed the emergency evacuation slide and cracked the entrance door to wait for the gate agent to position the Jetway. She had read the message from crew scheduling several times and had a sinking feeling in her stomach. The call to Molly Jackson would undoubtedly be bad news, and she could only guess that some passenger had written a nasty complaint letter that required her explanation. The tension was increased by the fact that the Los Angeles flight was already on delay and awaiting the flight attendants. The passengers could not be boarded until the cabin crew arrived to ensure their safety.

It seemed to take forever for the agent to position the Jetway, and when he finally opened the door, Dee was alarmed to see that he wasn't alone. The tall redhead standing beside him had a serious look on her face, and Dee knew the situation must be much worse than she had imagined. More proof came when Molly said, "Dee, I want you to get your bags right away—I'm pulling you off the trip. Your replacement is already on the L.A. flight and waiting for the crew. Give your paperwork and reports to one of the other girls to complete and come with me."

Dee did as instructed and racked her brain to think of what offense she could have committed. As she left the cabin, she took a quick look around and considered that it might be the last time she saw it as a Tri Con employee. She had given her best effort, but life can be so unfair. She felt embarrassed and humiliated when Molly said, "We're taking the outside stairs, there's a van waiting for us on the ramp."

Balancing her shoulder bag with her left hand and carrying her heavy suitcase in the other, Dee navigated the steep stairs. She wondered how she would explain being fired to her uncle, who had taught her to fly and given her a part-time job with his air taxi service. She loved her mentor dearly and had vowed never to disappoint him.

As the van sped across the airport, Molly handed Dee several sheets of paper and asked her to read and sign them. The first form began with the words, "Dear Ms. Daniels...We are happy to offer you a transfer to the position of first officer..." She fought back tears of joy as she scribbled her name in all the blank spaces. The last form she signed was a ground school attendance record. Molly took the form, and glanced at her watch to note the time was 12:32. She wrote 11:55 in the appropriate space as the van stopped in front of the training center.

Chapter Three

It had been a hectic morning for the pilot class. They had signed several employment forms without regard for what they had agreed to, and then listened as Charlie Wells and Colt Adams welcomed them to Tri Con and the Flight Operations Department. The two captains explained in no uncertain terms what they expected of them. The highlight of the morning was when the tall, red-headed flight attendant explained the importance of the cabin crew and the working relationship with the pilots. They hoped all the female flight attendants were as attractive as Molly Jackson. At mid-morning, they were given a coffee break and the first opportunity to get to know their classmates.

After handshakes all around, the four former military pilots launched into a debate about the jets they had flown, thus excluding the three civilian pilots who had no clue what they were talking about. The most verbose of the three civilians introduced himself as Lindbergh Walker and declared that he had gained his experience flying copilot on a corporate jet owned by his father. His father was also the senior senator from the state of Pennsylvania. He was the only student who wore a coat and tie. The class had been previously informed that the appropriate dress for ground school was business casual. His wavy blond hair contrasted nicely with the dark sports coat and blue tie. After holding forth for several minutes, he allowed the other two to speak.

Without comment on Walker's dissertation, the next student spoke with a soft southern accent, "My name's Cameron Horner from North Carolina. Most of my flying time has been in old cargo planes flying freight overnight. Call me Cam."

Walker gave a little sniff and looked to the other pilot who had been quiet with little to say all morning. He was taller than the other two with short hair and an athletic build. The cowboy boots he wore probably added another inch to his height. Words rolled from his lips like thick syrup on buttered pancakes. "Glad to meet you both. I'm Kyle Bennett from Corpus Christie, Texas. I'm a flight instructor and fly charters for a living. Mostly single engine stuff."

Walker looked down at the boots and then asked, "How did you get a job with Tri Con with that kind of experience?"

"Just lucky I guess. I must have been in the right place at the right time."

"Have you ever flown a jet?"

"I got a couple of hours in the seat, but mostly just observing."

"Well, you're in for a big surprise, cowboy."

Cam could sense the conversation deteriorating and said, "Lindbergh is an interesting name. Does it have some significance?"

"It's my mother's maiden name, and yes Charles Lindbergh is an ancestor."

"I'd say that's significant. I don't have much jet time either, but we'll have to survive six weeks of ground school before we worry about flight training."

Walker sniffed again, "Ground school's just a formality, so you better start worrying about flying the simulator."

Kyle looked at Cam and smiled, "Couldn't be any worse than riding a bull."

Lindbergh shook his head and walked away.

Kyle said, "Reminds me of a jackass braying."

"I never saw a blond jackass," Cam said.

"They must be indigenous to Pennsylvania."

Cam laughed, "Lots of weird things up in Yankee land."

Returning to class, Phil James issued aircraft manuals and training outlines and then launched immediately into a barrage of facts and figures that had their head spinning by noon. The lunch hour gave them a chance to relax, and they gathered at the cafeteria to find a table big enough for the seven of them. The four military pilots had sorted out their posturing and joined the conversation. Foster, Baker, and Smith were ex-air force pilots and had flown transport aircraft. Stark was an ex-navy fighter pilot. Now that Lindbergh had a captive audience, he elaborated on the virtues of flying the Gulfstream corporate jet for several minutes.

When no one encouraged him, the conversation lulled and he changed the subject. "Did you guys know that Captain Wells was the pilot on the Tri Con jet that ditched in the Atlantic a couple of years ago?"

Stark said, "I did a little research on that. There are not many pilots who could have pulled that off without killing a bunch of people. I read the NTSB accident report, and they heaped praise on him. That doesn't happen very often."

"At least it got him promoted to Vice President," Lindbergh smirked.

Stark continued, "Here's something you may not know— Molly Jackson was on that flight too, and credited with saving a lot of lives."

"You mean the redhead who spoke to us?"

"Take better notes, Lindbergh. That's the only Molly Jackson I know."

Kyle continued to eat as he listened to the gossip.

Stark added, "Captain Wells is also the guy who talked that 767 down a few months ago after the captain got shot. The guy's a legend."

Cam said, "So is the light airplane driver he talked through the landing. It's hard to imagine landing an airliner if you've never flown anything but a Cessna."

"If you don't think you could do that, Horner, you may be in the wrong class," Lindbergh gloated.

"Yeah, but I've got six weeks to learn—he had to do it with the first try. Besides that, I've got your vast expertise to guide me. I wonder what happened to that guy. The FBI was investigating and then the story seemed to fade away—I think there was a big cover up."

Stark said, "The story never lasts, unless a lot of people get killed. There wasn't even a crash, just a shooting. What happened to the captain that got shot?"

Foster chimed in, "I heard he's out of the hospital and will be flying again soon. You can ask him all about it when you're his copilot."

Stark pushed his chair back, "Kyle...you don't look so good. Is this talk about crashes and shootings giving you second thoughts about an airline career?"

"No, but I'm thinking we better get back to class."

The seven students crowded into the elevator and waited for the doors to close. Kyle pushed the door open button when he saw the blond flight attendant hurrying across the lobby, pulling her bag behind her. She rushed aboard with a smile, and a, "Thank you."

Lindbergh Walker grinned, "Wow, we get a stewardess for our flight to the second floor. Honey, can I get a coffee with cream?"

She turned slowly and smiled at him, "Does your mommy let you drink coffee?"

He blushed as everyone snickered. The doors opened, and she exited pulling the bag behind her. After the group had stopped at the restroom, they made their way back to class for the afternoon session. Phil James stood at the podium and seemed to be enjoying his conversation with the flight attendant from the elevator. He surveyed the group as they took their seats, adjusted the glasses on the bridge of his nose, and said, "Welcome back, gentlemen. Did everyone get fed and watered?"

Lindbergh rose to the occasion and said, "Yes sir."

"Glad to hear it. Let me introduce you to Denise Daniels. Until about an hour ago, she was a Tri Con flight attendant. Now, she's an ex-flight attendant and will be joining the class for first officer training. Denise, take a seat, and we'll get started."

Dee found an empty seat at the table with Kyle and Cam as Phil began, "We have one item to cover and then we're going to take a field trip. Tri Con currently has almost nine thousand pilots on the seniority list, and you are the bottom eight. Your seniority number will determine what equipment and what seat you can hold, as well as which trips you fly and your choice of vacation.

"That brings us to the important question of how we assign numbers within the class. Seniority is normally determined by birth date, with the oldest person receiving the first number. The exception is in the case of a company transfer. Denise is already a Tri Con employee and is, therefore, awarded the first number. Kyle Bennett is the oldest of the remaining seven and is number two, followed by Cameron Horner..."

He continued to read names until he announced Lindbergh Walker as the most junior pilot of the nine thousand at Tri Con. When Walker realized he had been reduced to the lowly status of bottom man on the seniority list, his shoulders slumped, and his gaze lowered.

Phil continued, "Your number will change every time someone retires or dies so you may want to encourage the captains you fly with to take skydiving lessons and ride motorcycles."

He didn't smile, and no one laughed. "Now for the field trip. We have an appointment at corporate security to have photos taken and to have your company ID cards issued. We'll walk over to the headquarters building and trade those ridiculous visitor's passes for permanent ID cards."

As Phil led the group down the hall, Lindbergh locked step with him and bombarded him with inane questions as they walked. Kyle found himself walking with Dee in the back of the gaggle and introduced himself. "Denise, I'm Kyle Bennett."

"Call me Dee, and I know who you are, Kyle."

"I'm sorry, have we met before?"

"No, I saw your picture in the Atlanta newspaper."

Chapter Four

The Tri Con corporate security offices were on the third floor of the headquarters building. Ed White was a no-nonsense gentleman who had taken an early retirement as a special agent with the FBI in order to join Tri Con as Director of Corporate Security. When his secretary entered his office, she found him with his sleeves rolled up, and his stocking feet propped on his desk. She was accustomed to the Director being shoeless and thought nothing of it. "Here's the initial accident report you wanted, boss. The photos are printing, and I'll have them for you shortly."

"What would I do without you? Would you ask Harry to come over, please?"

Harry Dade was the assistant director and occupied an adjoining office. Tall and lanky, the former police officer was Ed's go to guy for everything but coffee. He had joined Tri Con twenty-five years earlier after a gunshot wound to the knee had rendered him unfit for patrol duty.

When Harry entered the office with his distinctive limp, Ed looked up and waved the file. "Harry, what do you think about this Flight Twelve Sixteen accident? Why would an engine explode like that?"

"I've been talking to the maintenance guys and they're scratching their heads. It was a low time engine...overhauled just a month ago. They're still taking it apart and inspecting what's left of it."

"Well, it almost killed a flight attendant and it could have been a lot worse. I want to make sure we eliminate any possibility of sabotage or some deliberate act. Am I being paranoid?"

"Of course, but no more than usual."

"Let's get the passenger list and see if anything jumps out at us."

"I've already requested it along with the crew list."

The secretary stuck her head in the door, "The new pilot class is on the way over for credentials. Are the background checks complete?"

Ed replied, "There's one incomplete, but she already has an ID. Just issue her a new one, and we'll update her security check."

Harry asked, "Did you notice Kyle Bennett's name on the class roster?"

"Yeah, I want you and me to have a little talk with him. We have some unfinished business."

Harry chuckled, "You never give up do you?"

"It's not over till the fat lady sings, and she's not even warming up yet."

When the photographer set the camera up for the ID photos, Phil said, "Denise, this is your first opportunity to exercise your seniority. You're first in line. Gentlemen, you know the drill. Get used to it."

Lindbergh sulked in the back of the line and waited his turn. He barely managed a smile for the photo. Phil announced, "The hard part's over. Now we wait for the paperwork to be finished and the ID's to be made. Let's adjourn to the break room down the hall and evaluate the coffee. Denise, you may lead the way."

"Everyone, please call me Dee."

Lindbergh said, "Just lead the way, Dee. We need caffeine."

As they lined up at the vending machine, an older gentleman limped into the room and greeted Phil. "I see you found the coffee, Phil. Would it be possible for me to borrow Mr. Bennett for a few minutes? The director would like a word with him."

"No problem, Harry. We'll probably be here thirty minutes while the ID's are made."

"I'm sure we'll be done by then. Mr. Bennett, would you come with me, please?"

Kyle didn't speak, but he followed the man from the room. Phil's cell phone buzzed, and he went into the hall to take the call.

Lindbergh broke the silence, "Well, it looks like the cowpoke might not make it through the first day. I thought there was something strange about him. I predict everyone but Dee is about to move up a number in seniority."

Dee asked, "Why do you think that?"

"Well, it's never good when the director of security calls you on the carpet. Not only that, I saw Captain Wells having a word with him before class this morning too. I think he's done."

Dee laughed, "I wouldn't count on moving up in seniority, Lindbergh."

"Just wait...I've seen it before. They'll probably announce that he resigned for health or personal reasons."

Dee laughed again, "If they want to fire you they don't need an excuse, believe me."

"You'll see. I know what I'm talking about."

"Actually you don't. You don't have a clue."

Lindbergh folded his arms, "Why do you say that?"

"Look...I probably shouldn't explain this to you, but you're going to find out eventually anyway. A couple of months ago a terrorist group disguised a 767 as a Tri Con Flight and tried to fly it into the country from South America. They kidnaped a Tri Con captain and a Tri Con mechanic and forced them to help by threatening their families."

Cam spoke up, "We were talking about that at lunch. They were going to fly it into the Capitol building in DC. The captain got shot when they tried to overcome the terrorist."

Dee continued, "Exactly, and they did overcome the terrorist. But with the captain incapacitated there was no one to fly the 767 except a light airplane instructor who had been hijacked on a charter flight and forced to give the terrorist basic flight instruction."

Stark added, "Yeah, Captain Wells talked him through the landing."

"Right, but what you're not getting is the flight instructor was a guy from Corpus Christie, Texas. His name is Kyle Bennett."

No one spoke for a few seconds, and then Stark said, "Holy crap, the guys a hero."

Dee continued, "There were lots of heroes that day, but the two given the most credit was Kyle and a private investigator that had been hired to find him when he went missing."

Cam said, "I didn't read about that. What was the guy's name?"

"It wasn't a guy. The investigator was a girl named Madison Jones, also from Corpus."

Ed stood to shake hands with Kyle when he and Harry walked into the office. "Kyle, it's great to see you again. Congratulations on the new job."

"Thank you, sir, I couldn't be happier. The opportunity is like a dream come true."

"You'll be glad to know the investigation is almost complete, and it won't be necessary for you to testify."

"That *is* a relief. I think I've got plenty to keep me busy for the next couple of months."

"I'm sure you'll do fine, Kyle. Do you stay in contact with Madison Jones when you're in Corpus?"

"I see MJ quite often."

Ed thought, *yeah, like every day from what I hear.*

"Did you know that we've offered her a position with Tri Con?"

"Yes sir, she mentioned that."

"We were very impressed with her work, Kyle. Do you think she'll seriously consider our offer?"

"Well, I know her agency is very successful, and she enjoys her work, but I also know her business partner is getting married and moving out of state. I can tell you she gained a lot of publicity from working on the terrorist investigation and has had several lucrative offers to buy her business."

Ed smiled, "I won't keep you, Kyle. I just wanted you to know we appreciate what you did for Tri Con, and if we can be of any help while you're here, don't hesitate to call."

After walking Kyle to the door, Ed put his shoeless feet back on the desk and said, "Harry, we need to strike while the iron's hot."

"We?"

"You."

At 5:30 Kyle walked into his hotel room, dumped his books on the table, and stretched out on the bed. He examined his new Tri Con ID card and convinced himself that he wasn't dreaming. His mind churned with more numbers and facts than he would ever remember, and he knew that Phil James would not relent for the next six weeks.

He opened his cell phone and touched the contact labeled MJ. A photo of Madison Jones appeared as the phone rang.

She answered, "The ring-tone tells me this is my favorite airline pilot."

"I'm not an airline pilot yet, and after today I have my doubts."

"I don't have any doubt at all, Kyle. You'll be a great airline pilot."

"I saw Ed White and Harry Dade today. They asked about you."

"I know."

"Are you a mind reader now?"

"No, Harry called me this afternoon. He asked if I could come to Atlanta for a final debrief on the terrorist investigation."

"Did you say yes?"

"Not yet, I'm holding out for a First Class ticket and a suite at the Hyatt."

"Did you tell him that you sold the agency?"

"Of course not. If he knew I was unemployed, it would ruin all the fun."

"You know I would love it if you took the job and moved to Atlanta."

"I would only be a distraction, and you need to focus on your training."

"The only thing that distracts me is you being in Texas."

"I was hoping you'd say that. Harry wants me to come to Atlanta on Friday, but I'll have to be back in Corpus Sunday evening."

Chapter Five

Harry Dade limped into the engine overhaul shop at Tri Con's maintenance base. The foreman greeted him and led him to a roped off area with engine parts scattered over a large area. The only thing he recognized was a battered piece of cowling with Tri Con's logo painted on it. "Where's the rest of the cowling?"

"Who knows? We found this piece in the parking lot of a warehouse about a mile from the runway. The NTSB is still combing the area for more parts."

"What do you think caused it to explode?"

"Well, it didn't really explode, but it's pretty obvious what happened."

"So you told me on the phone. Lay it out for me."

"Harry, we get several of these a year, but not to this extent. It's a clear case of FOD."

"You mean foreign object damage?"

"Exactly. Usually, the engine vacuums something up off the ramp or the taxiway, and it damages the fan blades when it goes through the inlet. Normally it's just little things like nuts and bolts or rocks. Sometimes it requires an engine change to replace the blades and balance the engine, but not like this. Whatever went through this thing was big enough to knock some of the blades off and then the engine was so far out of balance the vibration caused it to shed more. Quite a few of them went through the fuselage and into the cabin."

"You do realize that this didn't happen on the ramp or the taxiway."

"Yeah, I know that. It can happen in flight too. I've seen it caused by birds and also by chunks of ice that form on the cowling and then break off and go through the engine. That's because the pilots forget to turn on the engine anti-ice when they should or turn it on after the ice forms."

"Do you think that's what happened?"

"Well, it's too warm for ice and there's no bird guts in the engine. We're analyzing all the blades we can find to see if they had defects or cracks and broke off on their own. Thank God the captain pulled the fire handle to shut off the fuel and hydraulic fluid to the engine or it could have burned big time."

"Do you have any evidence at all to indicate FOD as the cause?"

"We recovered a couple of fan blades that wound up in the cabin that have traces of blue paint on them."

"Could they have hit something after they came off to cause that?"

"Maybe, but there's nothing in the cabin painted blue."

Harry looked at the remains of the engine and rubbed his chin, "Could a surface to air missile cause this?"

"Not unless it was a dud and didn't explode."

The first week of ground school had been a brain numbing exercise for Kyle Bennett. Eight hours of class, a quick dinner, and then back to the training center for group study with his classmates. Phil James had given them the security code for access to the building after hours. Kyle and Cam Horner had found it productive to quiz each other and were beginning to understand the aircraft systems that had been taught so far. Lindbergh Walker had rented a condo in downtown Atlanta and was the only student noticeably absent from the nightly self-study sessions.

Two hours were scheduled on Friday morning for the first written exam and when Phil handed out the test, including the multiple-choice answer sheets, the tension in the room was thick. Kyle struggled with the first question, but to his relief, the next five were easier. Stark, with his fighter pilot mentality and competitive spirit, turned in his answer sheet after one hour. Phil quickly marked the wrong answers, assigned a grade, and told Stark he was free until 10:15 when the class would review the test. The other military pilots finished minutes later followed by Cam Horner. When Kyle turned in his test, Dee and Lindbergh still had their heads down in concentration. Kyle joined the others in the break room and learned that Stark had the high score so far at 94. Kyle was in the middle of the pack at 88. When Dee walked in a few minutes later, she revealed that she had passed, and that's all that mattered. When pressed she admitted to a score of 96, thus dethroning Stark, who laughed and told her to watch her six.

When the class reconvened, they found a solemn-faced Lindbergh Walker in quiet conversation with Phil.

At 11:00 am, Madison Jones stood from her first-class seat and gathered her briefcase from the overhead compartment. The trim business suit she wore gave her the appearance of a typical first-class passenger, but the shoulder length dark hair and the sky blue eyes attracted more attention than most. When she walked off the airplane and into the Jetway, Harry Dade met her with a smile. "MJ, you're looking well. I have a car and driver waiting for us on the ramp and Ed will meet us for lunch."

"Harry, I have to go to baggage claim first."

"Your bag is not at baggage claim."

"They lost my bag?"

"Of course not, it's in the car. I had Corpus put a crew tag on it, so it came off the airplane first, and the ramp guys put it in the car for us. VIPs get special service."

"You're not taking me to that barbecue place are you?"

"Not unless you prefer that to the Surf and Turf at the Hyatt."

"Okay."

Ten minutes and three blocks later, they rode the elevator to the top floor of the hotel. Ed White and several other people stood when they entered the private dining room the restaurant had reserved.

"It's so good to see you, MJ," Ed beamed. "You know Charlie Wells and Colt Adams, and I want you to meet Molly Jackson, Tri Con's Manager of In-Flight Service."

Handshakes and smiles were exchanged all around before everyone was seated. MJ thought, *I wasn't expecting to attend a grip and grin.* She was well aware of Charlie and Molly's heroics during the ditching accident. The waiter served lunch, and the conversation was all about MJ. Everyone wanted to know about her background and experience, and Ed praised her for her efforts during the terrorist investigation. She was happy when Charlie changed the subject for a brief discussion of the MD-88 engine failure and Molly updated the injured flight attendant's condition.

Harry had exchanged several text messages during the meeting and when Ed asked if he had anything to add he said, "I'm not sure. I sent Cason out with the NTSB to search the area for more engine pieces, and I've received a couple of cryptic text messages from him, but I'm not sure if it's important."

Ed asked, "Did you send him out to look for airplane parts or to spy on the NTSB?"

Molly giggled when Harry replied, "I'm offended that you would think such a thing."

Ed laughed, "What did he find?"

Before Harry could answer there was a knock at the door, and the waiter escorted a young man into the room. His appearance was that of a professional athlete, but the crew cut hair and the wary eyes indicated something else.

Ed made the introduction, "MJ, this is Cason Haley, our newest addition to Tri Con's security staff."

MJ stood to shake hands and make her manners. She had heard plenty about Cason Haley and his exploits during the recent attempted terrorist attack. The former navy seal had forged a path of mayhem through South America when he was sent to investigate and had dragged home a few live trophies as penance for his indiscretions. The trophies now resided at Gitmo in Cuba. She was surprised that he was soft spoken and well mannered.

Ed said, "Cason, please don't tell me that you have assaulted anyone working for the NTSB."

"No sir."

"That's a relief. What did you learn?"

"When we were scouting the neighborhood for wreckage I noticed several of these posters attached to phone poles and bus benches."

Ed took the paper and read it. "You've got to be kidding me."

"No sir."

"Did you show this to the NTSB?"

"No sir."

Harry glanced at the poster when Ed handed it to him, "Incredible…is this possible?"

Charlie said, "Come on guys, what's the big mystery?"

Harry held the item up for everyone to see. "This is a reward poster for a missing radio controlled airplane that was lost on the day of the accident. As you can see from the picture, it's painted a nice blue color that matches the paint on our damaged fan blades."

Charlie took the paper and looked at it, "If I find out some idiot almost destroyed one of my MD-88s with a toy airplane…I'll hang *them* from one of the phone poles."

"The photo doesn't look like a toy," Colt remarked, "That thing must have a four foot wing span, but if someone did this on purpose I don't think they would post a reward expecting to get their airplane back."

"It may not be that simple," Ed added. "We need to find out who put the poster up. It just has a phone number."

Harry asked, "You want me to call the number?"

Ed looked around the table, "We probably need more diplomacy than you normally project. We don't want to scare the guy off."

Molly said, "Don't look at me, Ed. If this guy almost killed one of my flight attendants, I'm not going to be diplomatic."

MJ picked the poster up and read it. When she looked up, all eyes were on her.

"I'm not going to use my phone to call this guy. I don't want some weirdo tracking me down with a drone."

Ed frowned, "Good thinking, you can use the house phone."

Chapter Six

Phil James began his debrief of the test, "Most of you did okay on the exam, but if you think this is going to get easier, you're sadly mistaken. We've covered a few of the simple systems with simple controls, none of which are critical to safe flight. The systems will get more complicated, and the test will become more comprehensive. It's true that 70% is a passing grade, but I promise you…that will not get you through the simulator training. Now is the time to ask questions and get answers…not when you have a handful of airplane. At this point, you could say that I am generally pleased, but definitely not satisfied. You can and will do better."

The remainder of the morning was consumed going over the questions that had been missed and the ones that had been lucky guesses. Lunch became a mini celebration of passing the first written exam, and everyone was relieved except the normally boisterous Lindbergh. Stark finally asked the question everyone wanted answered.

"Lindbergh, what did you score on the test?"

Without looking up from his plate, he answered, "I wasn't feeling well this morning. I had a crushing headache and couldn't focus."

"Can you focus well enough now to answer the question? What did you score?"

The reply was meek, "There were a hundred questions, and I missed twenty-six of them."

"You made a seventy-four?"

"I told you I had a headache."

"Well, I hope you don't fly when you have a headache."

"I can fly, Stark, and I don't really care if the water don't work in the galley, and I don't care how many band-aids are in the first aid kit. That test was a load of crap and had nothing to do with flying."

"Well, if you didn't understand a water tank with a pump and a faucet, you're not going to enjoy the electrical system either."

"Don't worry about it, Stark."

"Hey, I'm on your side, I'm just saying…"

Lindbergh took his food tray and stalked away.

"Was it something I said," Stark asked?

The waiter delivered a portable phone to the table and MJ stared at it, wondering how she had got involved in this scheme. Five airline executives and a navy seal waited patiently for her to act. *Am I about to implode my job interview? Oh well, at least I got a free lunch.*

She put the phone on speaker and punched the numbers. After three rings, a male voice answered, "This is Andy."

MJ paused and then said, "I'm calling about the airplane reward."

"Really, you found my airplane? Is it damaged?"

"I think I know where it is. How much is the reward?"

"Twenty-five dollars, but only if I get my airplane back."

"I think I can help with that. If we can meet, I'll explain it. What's your address?"

"Can't you just tell me on the phone?"

"If I did I wouldn't get my reward. When can we meet?"

"Do you know where the high school football field is?"

"The one by the airport?"

"Yeah, on College Street."

Ed was shaking his head yes.

"Okay, I'm not far from there. Can you meet me?"

"Not now, but I can be there at four o'clock."

"Will you have the money?"

"Is this a scam, 'cause I'm not paying until I get my airplane."

"That's fine, what's your name?"

"My name's Andy. I'll be there at four."

The line went dead.

Ed frowned, "MJ, I didn't think this through. Can you go out there with us at four o'clock?"

"I can, but if a crowd of people shows up, this guy will run like a rabbit."

"You're right, but I think I have a plan that will work."

You didn't think it through, but suddenly you have a plan that will work.

She asked, "Do they have good dessert here?"

At 3:30, a man dressed in sweat pants and a tee shirt walked onto the deserted football field and began a series of stretching exercises. After a short warm up, he began a slow jog around the cinder track surrounding the field.

At 3:50, Madison Jones entered the chain link gate wearing jeans and boots. She walked to the metal bleachers and sat on the second row. The ear bud in her left ear crackled, and she heard Cason Haley say, "Hey MJ, you want to come out and jog with me?"

She whispered, "Not in these boots."

"I haven't seen anybody yet, but I'll be listening when he shows up."

Another voice interrupted them, "Can you two hear me okay?"

Cason said, "Yes sir."

MJ said, "I hear you, Ed."

"Good, just play it cool, and we've got your back."

MJ thought, *I feel like an idiot sitting here watching a non-existent football game. I wonder if I could still get in my high school cheerleader uniform.* She took out her cell phone to appear to be texting or playing a game. The silence was interrupted every three to four minutes as an airliner roared a few hundred feet overhead on its landing approach. MJ heard the chain link gate squeak and turned to see a skinny teenage boy enter. *Don't come in here and get in the middle of this, kid.*

The boy looked around and spotted MJ on the bleachers. He approached as Cason stopped nearby and placed his hands on his knees as if he was out of breath.

The kid looked to be about fifteen with rust-colored hair and freckles mixed with mild acne. "Are you the lady that called about my airplane?"

"Are you Andy?"

"Yes ma'am."

"I think I know what happened to your airplane, Andy, but I need to know a couple of things to be sure. How did you lose it?"

"I accidentally let it get out of range of my transmitter and lost control. I think the batteries were weak, and it just wouldn't respond to commands."

"Where were you flying it from?"

"Right here. I was using the onboard camera to video the airplanes on final approach."

"The reward poster said you lost it last Sunday. What time did it happen?"

"It must have been about eleven o'clock. I know it was before lunch. Do you know where my plane is or not?"

"I think I do, but that must be an expensive airplane. How do you afford it?"

"It's not mine. It belongs to my dad and if he finds out it's missing my life is toast. Can you help me? Twenty-five dollars is all I've got, but I'll try to get more if you help me."

"You seem like a nice kid, Andy, and I'd like to help, but I think we're going to have to talk to some other people. I'm sorry."

Before she finished the sentence, a local cop appeared at each end of the bleachers, and when the boy turned, he bumped into Cason.

Saturday morning came far too early for Kyle Bennett. He shut off the cell phone alarm and wished that he had not agreed to the 10 a.m. study session with his classmates. MJ had been delayed for their dinner date the night before, and time management was not on the agenda for either of them. It was 2 a.m. when he returned to the cheap hotel he and his classmates had found to save money. He made it to the hotel restaurant 10 minutes late and found Cam Horner waiting for him with a pot of coffee already on the table.

"Late night, Kyle?"

"Don't ask."

"How was the date?"

"I want you to meet MJ, Cam. She's busy today with meetings, but I hope you can meet her soon."

"Is it that serious?"

"I've only known her a couple of months, but it seems a lot longer. I don't know how serious she is."

"I've only known you for a week and you were pretty quiet until yesterday when you started babbling like a mountain brook. It's serious."

"Can I have coffee, oh great philosopher?"

"Help yourself. I bought the newspaper today, but don't forget it's your day tomorrow."

"You haven't bought a paper all week. You scrounge the used ones from the lobby."

"Stark taught me that trick."

Cam took the sports section leaving Kyle with the local news. The title of an article on the second page caught his eye.

Tri Con Engine Mystery Solved

Authorities arrested a local man in connection with the engine failure of a Tri Con Jet last week. The engine exploded causing the injury of a flight attendant, who remains hospitalized in serious condition. Police reports indicate that the accident occurred when the unnamed suspect flew a radio controlled airplane into the path of the Tri Con jet as it approached Atlanta. The crew was able to land the jet with only one engine operating. Local police apprehended the man near the airport on Friday although a knowledgeable source, who wishes to remain anonymous, reports that Tri Con employee, M J Jones made the arrest possible. The investigation is ongoing, but at this point, it is not clear that foul play was involved.

Kyle read the article again. *MJ's her nickname, not her initials, and she's not a Tri Con employee...is she? Why didn't she tell me about this? Maybe she really doesn't want me involved in her life.* He folded the paper and said, "Let's head over to the training center, everyone will be waiting for us."

Harry Dade picked MJ up at the Hyatt, and when they arrived at Tri Con headquarters, she was surprised at the number of people working on Saturday. Harry explained that hundreds of Tri Con jets were in the air every minute of every day, and staff was reduced on weekends and holidays, but the operation never ceased. Walking down the hall, they met a tall, gray-haired man dressed in jeans and a plaid shirt. "Good morning, Harry. Does your wife know you're hanging out with pretty girls?"

"Probably not, this is Madison Jones."

"Oh, I've heard very good things about you, Ms. Jones. Are you enjoying your visit?"

"Yes, thank you."

"Glad to hear it. I hope to see you again."

As he continued down the hall, he looked over his shoulder, "Harry, you owe me lunch."

MJ asked, "Does he work in security?"

"Oh, I'm sorry, MJ. I thought you had met Harold. That's Harold Collins—he's the CEO of Tri Con Airlines."

"The CEO wears jeans?"

"It's Saturday, MJ. He probably just dropped by the office for a few minutes, but he's not a pretentious man. He started with Tri Con as a ticket agent and worked his way through the ranks over the years. He's not obsessed with himself."

She thought *the CEO knows who I am and Harry owes him lunch. I won't be surprised if a Unicorn shows up.*

They found Ed pacing in front of his office window, in his socks. MJ thought, *if I ever meet his wife, I'm going to ask what he has against wearing shoes.*

Harry said, "You don't look happy, Ed."

"We had a hard time finding something to charge the kid with. The DA finally agreed to reckless endangerment, but he set a low bail and the parents took him home."

"That may be the appropriate thing to do. I don't think he intended any harm…just a dumb mistake."

Ed asked, "What do you think, MJ?"

"I agree with Harry. I feel sorry for the kid, but he needs to learn a hard lesson. I hope his parents take him to the hospital and have him apologize to the flight attendant he almost killed."

"That would be a good start, but when our insurance company pays the claim for the damage to the airplane and the medical bills, they'll probably go after the parents to recover their cost."

Harry said, "MJ, you handled that situation very well. Do you have a firearm carry permit?"

"No, and I don't want one. You know my agency does forensic investigation. We don't chase bad guys."

"I understand, I was thinking more along the lines of personal protection. That could have been a different situation yesterday."

"I admit it was kind of exciting, but I don't know anything about guns."

Ed added, "As usual, I'm impressed with the way you think, MJ. You're exactly the kind of person we need to work with us on a permanent basis. Let's take a walk—I want to show you something."

A short distance down the hall, Ed opened the door to an empty office. The floor was newly carpeted, and the window offered a view of the north runway of the airport. A Tri Con jet was slowing on its landing roll. Ed said, "I think you could be very comfortable here. We have a large inventory of furniture to choose from and you can decorate the office as you wish. We'll pay to relocate you from Texas and help find you a place locally."

She was entranced with the view from the window and couldn't resist decorating the office in her mind. "Ed, you're very generous, and I hope you know how much I appreciate it, but there are personal issues and conflicts that I have to resolve in order to make a good decision. I want you to know that you and Harry are impressive professionals and it would be a privilege to be associated with you and Tri Con, a challenge I'm sure I would enjoy. But I have to consider other people, as well as myself. I also know you're shorthanded and need to fill the position, but can I have a few days to think about this."

"Of course you may. I actually have several positions to fill so there's no pressure, but you're uniquely qualified and I want you to occupy this office." He sensed a victory and added, "Harry and I want to take you to the maintenance hangar so we can check on the progress the mechanics are making on the engine that failed. On the way out, we'll stop by the warehouse and let you see the office furniture that's available to choose from. What would you think about a desk here and a credenza over…?"

Chapter Seven

Kyle knew the restaurant at the Hyatt was more expensive than he could afford, but he didn't know when he would see MJ again and he wanted the evening to be special. He resigned himself to eating sandwiches in his room the rest of the week in order to balance his budget. He could kick himself for not packing a sports jacket. The left side of the menu was very appetizing—the right side was scary. *These prices are higher than a cat's back.*

He could not take his eyes off MJ and refused to think about her going back to Texas. "Do you really have to go home tomorrow? Atlanta has a lot of tourist attractions and you could use a little vacation time."

"Oh, and of course you could take a few days off from training and show me around. I think you're falling in love with the MD-88 and I don't want to spoil your relationship."

"The airplane may not love me back. I'm not sure we're going to understand each other."

"Well, in the unlikely event that you come back to Texas, you can teach me to fly. I envy the joy I see on your face when you're flying."

"If I can't convince you to stay, maybe Ed and Harry can. I'm surprised you didn't tell me about solving the exploding engine accident."

"What are you talking about?"

"I saw your name in the paper this morning." He took the article from his pocket and gave it to her.

She read it and handed it back. "That's ridiculous. I don't know how the media comes up with their stories and I had very little to do with it. They must have an informant in the police department."

"What happened?"

She told him the story and added, "That's why I can't take a job with Tri Con. You've probably been thinking about this stupid story all day instead of focusing on your homework."

"You'd turn down a great job because of me?"

"Should we order an appetizer?"

"Don't do that, MJ."

"Don't do what?"

"I know you too well to let you change the subject, and I won't let you use me as an excuse to turn down an opportunity we both know you want."

"The Calamari might be good."

"You're impossible."

"Look, your flying career is far more important than me being a security guard. I've only been here one day and you're already distracted. You've been dreaming about this all your life."

"That's not the only thing I dream about, MJ, and surely we're intelligent enough to both have what we want."

"What else do you dream about?"

"The grilled shrimp appetizer looks good too."

They both laughed and when the meal was over, MJ signed the tab, ignoring his protest, and billed it to her room which Tri Con was paying for. They moved to a quiet corner of the lounge and ordered cocktails. Kyle continued to ask questions and she explained Tri Con's proposal, including the offer to move her household goods and her car to Atlanta.

"That reminds me, I've got to find a way to get my truck to Atlanta," Kyle said, "Maybe I'll fly home next weekend and drive it back."

"Do you think your truck would survive the trip?"

"You've got a point, but it's all I've got, and it's paid for. What kind of training program would Tri Con provide for you?"

"I understand there's a company orientation class at the ground school and then Ed talked about an FBI training course. He has an arrangement with his old pals at the agency."

"How can you turn down an opportunity like this?"

"I didn't turn it down. I told Ed I would think about it."

"Let's call him and tell him you want the job. Let's tell him you'll stay in Atlanta and start Monday."

"Let's don't."

"Why not?"

"I have an appointment on Monday to get my nails done."

"Cancel it."

"No."

"What do I have to do to convince you?"

"Ummm…tell me about those dreams you've been having."

Dee Daniels lounged in her ratty old pajamas with her nose buried deep in the MD-88 Pilot's Operating Manual. Her two bedroom Townhouse was quiet and peaceful. *What an exciting way to spend Saturday night.* When John Denver began singing *Leaving on a Jet Plane,* she picked up her cell phone and checked the caller ID. She answered, "Hey, girlfriend, I thought you were flying weekends."

"I am, but I called in sick. Dee, I need a favor."

"You want me to kill your sorry husband?"

"No, but I need a place to stay tonight. Can I come over?"

"I was just about to order a gourmet dinner—is pepperoni with extra cheese okay?"

"Whatever."

"See you when you get here."

Dee closed her book and ordered the pizza. Twenty minutes later the doorbell rang and she opened the door to her best friend, Cindy Lane.

"Oh Cindy, not again."

Her friend's flight attendant uniform was wrinkled and torn and her lower lip was cut and swollen. Drops of blood stained her white blouse and fresh bruises appeared on both arms.

"Cindy, you have got to get away from this."

"I know. I've left for good this time. I hate him."

"Let's get you cleaned up, sweetie. We'll get you into some PJs so you can relax."

Cindy sat down on the couch and began to sob. "I've wasted two years of my life with this loser and all I've got to show for it is a busted lip and a variety of bruises."

"What set him off this time?"

"I was getting ready to go to work and he was mad that I didn't fix his dinner."

"You need to report him, Cindy, and have him locked up. Let me call the cops."

"Don't do that."

"Well, you need to do something."

"I did. I threw a wine bottle at him."

"Did you hit him?"

"No, but it felt good anyway. I'm getting a divorce and I'm never going back."

"Now you're talking girl. You can stay here as long as you want."

"I hate to ask you, Dee, but maybe just a couple of nights until I figure out what to do. I'm thinking about transferring to a different crew base so I can make a fresh start."

When the doorbell rang, Cindy cringed into a defensive posture with a look of dismay on her face."

"It's just the pizza, Cindy, relax."

"I'm sorry. Thank God he doesn't know where I am. I'm never having another relationship with a man."

Dee quietly left the townhouse on Sunday morning with Cindy still sleeping in the spare bedroom. She arrived at the training center to find most of her classmates, including Lindbergh, already arguing about the aircraft electrical system. Since it wasn't an official training day, everyone wore jeans except Lindbergh who probably didn't own a pair of jeans. At least he had lost the coat and tie. Somebody had brought a box of donuts and she snared one before they all disappeared. "Where's Kyle?"

Cam answered, "His girlfriend's still in town. We gave him an excused absence, but he has to buy coffee for everyone tomorrow."

"Does he know that?"

"No, but since you're the last to arrive, you get to tell him."

"I think he'll take that deal, but it doesn't seem fair that he gets a day off to socialize while we do group study. I say we quit at noon and go over to my place and burn some burgers. If everybody chips in five bucks, we can feast."

Everyone thought it was a splendid plan. Dee added, "There's a community pool so bring your trunks if you want to swim."

Stark said, "Swim trunks? Oh, it's a formal gathering?"

Dee answered, "Don't make me send you to your corner for time out. Somebody explain to me what a generator relay does..."

At noon, they gathered their books and piled into the two available vehicles. Lindbergh took three passengers in his rental car and Dee took the other two. After a quick stop at the hotel to trade books for swim trunks, they proceeded to the grocery store for supplies. A short argument ensued over what kind of beer to buy, and then they were on their way and in a playful mood. Dee had warned

Cindy the night before that she was inviting the class over and welcomed her to join in if she felt up to it.

They filled a cooler with ice for the beer and Stark took charge of preparing the burgers. "Chop those onions, Lindbergh, and don't drip tears on them."

"Wash your hands, Stark, and don't overcook my burger."

Cam reported that he had the grill fired up on the back deck, "The sooner you two stop harassing each other, the sooner we can eat."

"Out of my kitchen, Horner, I can't create with all this chattering. Go watch TV with the Air Force geeks."

After forming the ground beef into perfect patties, Stark carried the tray out to the deck. He found Dee talking to another woman. Cindy had found jeans and a tee shirt in Dee's closet that fit relatively well and she had resolved not to spoil the party.

Stark tried not to stare and was disappointed when he saw the wedding ring. *Now that is one attractive lady. Even with a swollen lip she's beautiful. Try not to say anything stupid.*

"Stark, this is my friend, Cindy. She likes her burgers medium rare."

"Medium rare it shall be, Cindy. Did you fall off a horse?" *Crap! Why did you say that, idiot? Real smooth.*

He tried to balance the tray with one hand so he could shake hands with the other. One of the beef patties slid off onto the deck with a resounding plop. Lindbergh was walking out the door and put his hands on his hips. "That's your burger you just fumbled. Give me the tray before you embarrass us further. Ladies, we only let him out on weekends and special occasions."

Attempting a recovery, Stark said, "Button your fat lip, Lindbergh, or we'll put you back in your cage." *Oh crap! That was brilliant. Please just shut up.*

Lindbergh added, "As I was saying…"

Dee intervened, "If you juveniles could just start the burgers, maybe we won't starve to death."

Chapter Eight

Stark retreated to the grill but continued to steal glances at Cindy as he listened to the burgers sizzle. Cindy grinned at Dee and whispered, "He's a little awkward, but he's also really cute. Have you asked him out yet?"

"Girlfriend, after a week of ground school, my brain's fried like those hamburger patties. That's the last thing on my mind, and it's not me he's sneaking looks at."

"Well, he's sure not looking at me with my split lip and bruises."

"Don't be so sure."

"Where's he from?"

"He's a Navy fighter pilot from somewhere in Florida I think."

"He won't last long once he starts flying the line. Some flight attendant will have him walking down the aisle in no time."

"God help him."

Cindy laughed for the first time in two days.

When the meal was finished, there was not a crumb in sight and everyone agreed that Stark was the Burger King. Cindy declined the invitation to swim, but she and Dee found a poolside table with an umbrella and watched the water polo contest. Dee explained that everything was a competition with pilots and they would argue for the next week over who had won. When Cam shamed Dee into joining the competition, Stark grabbed two beers from the cooler and walked to the chair she had vacated.

"Cindy, will you allow me to redeem myself by revising my opening remarks?"

"If one of those beers is for me I will."

"Great, let's hydrate."

"Do you have a first name, Mr. Stark?"

"Gary…do you have a last name Miss Cindy?"

"Lane."

"Cindy Lane…that sounds like a street." *Oh Crap! Just walk away, idiot!*

He was relieved when she laughed. "I'm sorry, Cindy. I can't seem to put together a coherent sentence today."

"That's what ground school does to you. You'll recover eventually."

He finally composed himself and within ten minutes he knew she was a flight attendant, she was married but getting a divorce and her bruises were not really the result of an accident.

"I'm so sorry, Cindy, no woman deserves that, especially an attractive lady like you."

"I'll be fine as long as I can make myself presentable for my next trip. Long sleeves and heavy lipstick will probably do the trick. My only problem now is all my things are still at home and if I ask Dee to take me there, he'll know where I'm staying."

"I'll take you and help you load everything."

"It's not your problem Gary Stark. I'll find a way to handle it on my own."

"Nonsense, we'll take Lindbergh's car and do it now. Once you have the things you need, you can relax and rest much easier."

"You don't want to get involved in this. Lately, he's not been very stable and he has a temper."

"What's your point?"

She laughed, "I tell you what—you can take me over there and if he's not home, we'll get my things and I'll be forever grateful."

He put his hand to his chin as if in deep thought, "Let me think…a beautiful woman indebted to me. Yeah, okay."

Stark explained the situation to Lindbergh and asked for the keys.

"How many beers have you had, Stark? I'll drive and you can entertain us with your inane remarks."

The three of them arrived at the condo complex and Cindy determined that her husband's car was not in the parking lot. She walked to the front door and unlocked it, "You guys just wait while I pack my things and then you can help me load up."

Suitcases and boxes began accumulating and Lindbergh took the first batch out to the car. He didn't notice the small SUV that drove into the parking lot or the large man who got out and walked down the sidewalk toward Cindy's open door. When he had the items loaded, he turned in time to see the man enter the condo. *Oh great! Here we go.*

He jogged across the parking lot and walked in the door in time to see Stark trying to get up from the floor. Cindy was yelling at the man and he slapped her, causing her to fall on top of Stark. Lindbergh yelled, "Hey Bozo!"

When the man turned, he saw Lindbergh in mid air performing some sort of spin move. The last thing he remembered was a weird oriental scream before Lindbergh's foot caught him in the jaw and he went down for the count.

"Can't you two stay out of trouble for five minutes? Let's get this stuff loaded and go have a beer."

Stark helped Cindy up. "What in God's name was that, Lindbergh?"

"I took some personal defense classes in college. I'm not big enough to fight like a man."

"Dude, you gotta teach me that."

"Later, let's go before Bozo wakes up and we have to hurt him again. The cops are probably on the way."

"He took me by surprise and I had an armload of boxes."

"You gonna tell that to the cops or are we leaving?"

"We're going."

It took Tommy Lane a few minutes to realize where he was and what happened to him. His anger was white hot and it only increased when he discovered the huge wet spot in the crotch of his pants. *You're dead Cindy. You and your boyfriend. I knew you were fooling around. I'll find you and you'll both suffer a slow agonizing death, and I'm going to enjoy every second of it.*

He cleaned himself up and iced his jaw and considered calling the cops. *No, I'll just handle this myself.* He booted up the computer on his desk and entered Cindy's password for her Tri Con employee scheduling page. He wrote down her scheduled flights for the remainder of the month and then called up her email contacts. They were all female friends or relatives. He read her inbox and history and then checked the sent messages. The pain in his head was increasing and he decided to wait until he was thinking straight before trying to find her. He knew it was just a matter of time.

The training center cafeteria was packed at 7:30 on Monday morning. Everybody wanted coffee before classes convened at 8:00. Stark sought out Dee and asked how Cindy was doing.

"Much better than you—that's quite a shiner you got there tough guy."

"Don't give me grief, Dee—the guy took me by surprise. You should have seen Lindbergh flying around like a helicopter. He's a better wingman than I thought."

"Cindy asked me to thank you. She wanted to tell you herself, but we didn't have your cell number."

"Give me your phone and I'll put my number in your contacts. We should all have each other's numbers."

"We need a cover story for your black eye. We're all on probation for the first year and domestic disturbances and fist fights would not be smiled upon."

"I know. Lindbergh says that he will swear we were practicing Karate and had an accident. He's covering for me."

"You know, flight attendants are pretty good psychologist and I think Lindbergh has never had a lot of close friends. I think he's really enjoying being accepted as one of the boys."

"Well, I've changed my opinion of him, he saved my bacon."

"Yeah, me too. He just needs to relax and stop trying to impress everybody. That was a really sweet thing you two did for Cindy."

Kyle spotted them and sat down at the table, "You okay, buddy? Cam told me what happened. Sorry I wasn't there to help."

"No problem, did you get the cover story?"

"I got it. Did Lindbergh really knock a guy out?"

"I wouldn't believe it if I hadn't been there."

"Sweet!"

Madison Jones woke up at five a.m. with nowhere to go and nothing to do. By six, she was bored out of her mind and pacing her kitchen. She couldn't remember the last time she had a day without an agenda. After graduating college, she had immediately gone to work for an insurance company in Dallas as a claims investigator and remained there until the day she moved back to Corpus Christie and opened her own agency. Selling the business had been a financial windfall, but now that she had fulfilled her obligation to help the new owners transition, the inflated bank account didn't make her feel successful. Being task oriented and proficient at multi-tasking, she was miserable with no task before her and no problems to solve. *Everyone I know is on their way to work and here I sit twiddling my thumbs. Maybe I should actually make an appointment to get my nails done. Maybe I should have my head examined.*

Her relationship with Kyle was confusing and sometimes frustrating. She had experienced her share of dating but had never had the time or desire for a long term commitment. The two months she had known Kyle certainly didn't qualify as long term, but for the first time in her life she was not considering an exit plan. On the contrary, she found herself looking far into the future. She continued wandering from room to room as if being in motion would relieve the boredom. *I'm twenty-seven years old and having delusional daydreams. Kyle is fully committed to his career. I'm his go-to diversion when he's not thinking about airplanes. Get over it!*

She picked up her cell phone to call the nail salon and realized they wouldn't be open for another three hours. She almost dropped the phone when it vibrated with an incoming text. Kyle's photo filled the screen and she clicked open the message to read. "Are you bored yet? An exciting airline career awaits you in Atlanta, Georgia. When you wake up, call Tri Con and graciously accept their offer. I miss you, MJ, and I'm not trying to pressure you—however, I will come to Corpus and drag you over here in my ragged pickup truck if necessary. I'd put a smiley face here if I knew how. Seriously, please think about it. Gotta go to class—enjoy sleeping late and call or text when you can."

Why can't I tell when he's serious and when he's not?

With nothing better to do, she booted her laptop to check email. When it stopped scrolling messages, the most recent was from Harry Dade. *Good grief, what time does he start work?*

> Good morning, MJ (or afternoon as the case may be). In hopes that we will get a positive response from you, I'm attaching several forms that we will

need to process your employment.
When you're ready, you can fax or
email them back and it will expedite
matters on our end. Also, you will find
the contact information for the moving
company that will pack and store your
household goods until you're settled
here. They will arrange to have your
vehicle transported also. Please call
anytime if you have questions. I've also
left an open-ended ticket at the counter
in Corpus for your return trip to
Atlanta. We look forward to hearing
from you.

She read the attachments and thought, *Harry, you're way too sure of yourself.*

Chapter Nine

Tommy Lane overslept on Monday morning. He arrived at work without a shave or shower and the left side of his face was a solid blue bruise with yellow and green hues interspersed. Tommy worked the sales floor at a big box electronics store and when he walked in, the manager confronted him immediately. "Tommy you're late again. What happened to your face?"

He tried to speak without moving his jaw any more than necessary and mumbled, "I'm surry. I tok a full yeserday an th pan pill I tok mad me overslup."

"You can't serve customers looking like a bum and smelling like booze. Have you been drinking?"

"I hud a foo las nigh ater I full."

"Look, you've only been here six months and you've already used two weeks sick leave. You can't work in your condition and I can't give you more time off. I'm going to have to let you go, Tommy."

"Guv me ah bak, I jus had a accdent."

"I'm sorry, but we've had customer complaints about you also. It's just not going to work out. I'll mail your paycheck to you. Good luck."

The unbruised side of Tommy's face turned red and he grabbed the front of the manager's shirt, lifting him to his toes and walking him backward. "Yo thin I guv a rip abo thi sory jobe? I shou kic yo as to nex wee…" The guard working the security position at the store exit grabbed Tommy from behind and shoved him toward the door. "Get out now or I'll have the cops haul you out."

Tommy glared back at the manager and continued to point his finger and spew mixed syllables as he was escorted out.

Tommy had just been fired for the third time in two years and it occurred to him that he might not have Cindy's salary to fall back on this time. He drove home, took two Tylenol and went back to bed

Phil James had been teaching pilots a long time and he was largely unimpressed with Stark's cover story. However, he was very pleased with the way the entire class backed the fiction with eyewitness accounts. *This bunch might possess better crew skills than I thought. I can't wait to hear the real story. If I didn't know better, I'd think they were being coached by the master, Colt Adams.* He launched into the lecture of the electrical system and didn't give it another thought. He noticed that Lindbergh was much more attentive and asking better questions. *I hope I don't have to spoon feed this brown-nosing little Wus for the entire six weeks.*

The day could not end soon enough for Kyle. At five o'clock his brain was saturated and the aircraft electrical system was more of a mystery than when the day began. He was further frustrated by the fact that MJ had ignored the numerous messages he had texted during the day. To add insult to injury, the maid had not cleaned his room and the only towels available were the ones wadded on the bathroom floor.

He was about to call house cleaning when his cell rang with MJ's ringtone. He answered, "Hey, I thought your phone died."

"I'm sorry—it's been a hectic day."

"Must have been a riot at the nail salon."

"I didn't make it to the nail salon, some other things came up."

"Nothing bad I hope."

"That remains to be seen."

"Anything I can help with?"

"Maybe, did you fill out health insurance forms for Tri Con?"

"Yeah, I just took the standard coverage. Why?"

"I was thinking about adding the dental option."

"Are you serious? Did you…"

"Yes, but you have to promise me…"

"When will you be here?"

"Kyle, I…"

"Where will you be staying?"

"Listen…"

"Can I meet you at the airport?"

There was silence in response.

"Are you there, MJ?"

"Can I speak now?"

"You better not be kidding."

"I'm not kidding, but…"

"I want you to meet all my classmates."

Silence again.

"MJ?"

"Kyle, do you know what standby means."

"Of course."

"Then shut up and let me talk."

"Can I ask you something first?"

"No."

"I just want to…"

"Shut up."

"Okay."

"I'm trying to tell you that I'm not coming to Atlanta unless you promise that you won't let it interfere with your training. We'll both be very busy and we have to set some boundaries or I'm not going to do it."

Silence

"You can talk now."

"Thank you. When will you be here?"

"I'm not sure. Do you remember my friend, Susan Burrow?"

"The DEA agent?"

"Right, she invited me to stay overnight in New Orleans on my way to Atlanta. She's still trying to talk me into taking a job with the government."

"Don't even think about it, MJ."

"I'm not, but I want to visit anyway. The movers are coming to pack tomorrow so I'll probably be in Atlanta Thursday or Friday."

"Can I meet you at the airport?"

"I'm driving my car."

"I thought they were going to transport it to Atlanta."

"I told Harry I was going to drive my car, but they could transport my old pickup truck and he agreed."

"What pickup…oh baby, you're going to send my truck?"

"Yes, if you want me to."

"Do they have damage insurance?"

"Get serious. How would you know if they damaged that thing?"

"If you're going to bad mouth my truck, I'm hanging up. Where will you be staying?"

"Nowhere near that dump you live in. Tri Con maintains furnished Townhouses for visiting executives and I get to stay there until I find a place."

"I'll take you to dinner Thursday night and we can explore Atlanta this weekend."

"Kyle, you're not listening to me. No dinner and no exploring."

"Have you ever been stalked?"

"I'm going to explain this one more…"

After a long nap and a couple of scotch and sodas, Tommy's rage had subsided to the point where he began to function more normally. He blamed all his problems on Cindy and he intended to enjoy some payback. He had been selling computers and Smart Phones for the last six months and it occurred to him that he didn't have to look for Cindy. He opened his cell phone and touched the app labeled 'Find a Phone.' Entering the password resulted in a map with two circles on it. One was his cell phone and the other was Cindy's. Zooming the map to its lowest scale revealed Cindy's phone located at a Townhome community a few miles away. *There you are, darling!*

He noted the name of the street and then found his list of Cindy's contacts. *I might have known you'd run to your friend's house. You two deserve each other.* He wrote down Dee's address and smiled as his plan came together. Opening a drawer in the desk, he shuffled through several file folders until he found one labeled insurance. Cindy bought life insurance through Tri Con's employee benefits program and premiums were deducted from her paycheck automatically. He had already emptied their joint savings and checking accounts, a grand total of $6300, and stashed the cash safely away, but the $250,000 life insurance would solve his cash flow requirements for the foreseeable future. He was happy to see that the policy paid double for accidental death. Tommy Lane was listed as the sole beneficiary.

After a long day of ground school and then a cram session with her classmates, Dee arrived home at 8:30. Cindy had prepared a light dinner for them and an hour later they relaxed with a glass of wine. "Cindy, I believe you've been cleaning house. My place usually never looks this good."

"Gotta earn my keep and what else do I have to do."

"I want the recipe for your pasta sauce. That was incredible and I hope you stay for a long time. I could get used to this."

"Evidently I'm not very good long term company. After a month or so, you'd probably start knocking me around and beating me up."

"Stop that, Cindy. It's not your fault you married an idiot...at least not totally your fault."

"I'm too tired to analyze that comment, but thank you I think."

"Stick with me, kid, everything's going to work out fine. I hate to spoil a good party, but I'm wiped out. I'll be quiet when I leave in the morning."

"I'm going to bed too. I love the peace and quiet in your neighborhood."

At three a.m., Tommy checked Cindy's phone location and found it still nestled in the townhome complex. He stuffed the few things he needed into a backpack and drove to the address listed for Dee Daniels. The neighborhood was quiet and only a few homes had lights showing in the windows. An online sales brochure had illustrated the interior layout of the Townhomes and all featured two bedrooms located on the back side of each home. After scouting the area, he parked three blocks away and hiked back.

The streets were dimly lit with street lights located only at intersections, and it was pitch black at the rear of the building. He crouched for a few moments and listened for any activity. His dark clothing and the hat pulled low over his eyes made him almost invisible. He carefully opened the backpack and removed the towels that cushioned the two large wine bottles. When he opened the bottles, the odor of high octane gasoline polluted the air. He stuffed rags into the necks of the bottles and waited for the gasoline to soak the cloth. He knew the bedroom on his right was the smaller of the two and assumed Cindy would be sleeping there.

The flame from the cigarette lighter easily ignited the rag protruding from the first bottle. When it was burning strong, he hurled it at the window. The glass pane broke easily and a satisfying *whoosh* came from inside the room. He felt exposed in the glow of flames from the window and hurriedly ignited the second bottle and threw it into the other bedroom. He could feel the heat now on his face and the acrid odor somehow gave him a feeling of great satisfaction. Three minutes later he was driving away with a smile on his face. *I hope your boyfriend is in there with you, darling.*

Twelve minutes later, the first fire truck arrived to find the interior of the Townhome fully involved, with flames through the roof and smoke billowing from the windows. The only people the firemen encountered were neighbors wandering around asking questions and getting in the way. It would take twenty minutes to knock the flames down enough to enter the residence.

Chapter Ten

Phil James walked into the classroom on Tuesday morning with an aircraft manual in one hand and coffee in the other. The first thing he noticed was the empty seat at the second table. He made small talk and told a couple of jokes to kill a few minutes in order to give his tardy student an opportunity to arrive. At ten after eight, he gave up and began the lecture. *If she shows up with a black eye, I'm going to have to find out what's going on with this bunch.*

At eight thirty, his curiosity got the best of him and he asked, "Does anybody know where Dee is?"

Lindbergh offered, "Traffic was really bad this morning. She's probably stuck on the freeway."

Cam added, "We'll share our notes with her, Phil, to get her caught up."

"Horner, you can't even read your own notes. That's a noble gesture, but the FAA requires attendance for the total number of approved hours for the course."

Stark asked, "What can we do to help, Phil? We'll all stay late to make up the time."

"Assuming she shows up sober, with a good excuse, we'll see what happens. For now, don't say anything outside the…"

The door opened and Dee Daniels hurried in looking frustrated and embarrassed. "I'm sorry, Phil, and I apologize to everyone."

"Dee, I realize you're the senior pilot in the class, but don't push your luck."

"I'm so sorry."

"The fact that you're not wearing makeup or jewelry indicates you did the best you could. Have a seat."

"Thank you. I called the training office, did you get the message?"

"Yes, they said you had a late date last night and required a little extra sleep this morning…completely understandable."

Everyone enjoyed a good laugh to relieve the tension. Dee wasn't amused but accepted her punishment.

"Have a seat and try to stay awake. We need to move along."

When the class took their first break and gathered at the coffee machine, Stark made an astonishing announcement. "I've discovered that there's a restroom located next to every break area in the training center and behind every coffee machine there's a urinal."

Lindbergh said, "You're a sick man with a misguided imagination. Dee why were you late?"

"You won't believe what happened. The house next door burned to the ground in the middle of the night. The fire department evacuated the houses on either side and I didn't get back into my place until 7:30."

"Was anybody hurt?"

"No, the house was empty. I actually lived in that house until a few months ago. A water pipe busted in the upstairs bathroom and I was on a three-day trip. When I got home, the ceiling had collapsed and the entire first floor was flooded. The leasing company offered me the place next door and the insurance company replaced my damaged things. Thank goodness there was no one in there. It was an inferno."

Stark asked, "Is Cindy okay?"

"I'm sure Cindy's fast asleep. We were up half the night and the neighborhood stinks to high heaven."

Kyle asked, "Does Tri Con lease Townhomes in that development?"

"I don't think they actually lease them, but they have an agreement with the owners to use them sometimes in exchange for free travel privileges."

"I think you're going to have a new neighbor this week."

Tommy was livid as he watched the local news. Somehow he had firebombed an empty house and although the home was a total loss, no one was injured. He didn't understand how that happened, but he was more determined than ever. *You got lucky this time, Cindy, but not for long.*

He was slightly alarmed when the fire chief was interviewed and reported that the fire appeared to be intentional, but he was confident he had covered his tracks well. *I guess I can't try that again for awhile, but that won't stop me.*

He went back to the computer and pulled up Cindy's flight schedule again. *Let's see what we can do to make your next flight exciting. Tri Con Flight 1412 from Atlanta to Miami departing at 7:45 on Friday morning. Don't count on seeing Miami, darling.* He began making a list of things he would need.

Cindy wanted to smash the alarm clock when it began ringing at five a.m. on Friday morning. Instead, she turned it off and tossed it into the open suitcase beside the bed. Wobbling into the bathroom, she reached into the shower and turned on the hot water. While she waited for it to heat up, she looked in the mirror and planned the attack on her wounds with lipstick and makeup. She also decided that living with Dee was not good for her figure. *I must have gained five*

pounds this week sitting on my butt and eating Dee's groceries. A run on the beach in Miami should help that.

Her morning routine was well practiced and a few minutes later she walked into the kitchen, dressed in her flight attendant uniform, to find coffee brewed and bowls of cereal ready to consume. Dee yawned and said, "Well don't you look pretty all dressed up and ready to fly."

"I don't know about pretty, but I'm definitely ready to get out of town."

"You look great, and it'll do you good to get away from your troubles for a few days. Finish your cereal and I'll fix coffee for us to have on the way to the airport."

Traffic was busy at the terminal, but Dee stopped at the main entrance and waited for Cindy to get her suitcase from the back seat. "Enjoy your trip, girlfriend. Call me when you get in on Sunday and I'll pick you up."

"I'll never be able to thank you enough, Dee, but I'm gonna try."

"You can vacuum again next week and we'll be even."

"I hope you do well on your test today."

"Thanks, so do I."

Cindy pulled her suitcase into the terminal and stopped at the ATM machine before going to flight ops. After inserting her card, she requested $100 dollars from the checking account and waited for the machine to do its magic. It seemed to take longer than normal and then a message appeared. "Unable to complete transaction. Insufficient funds."

Tommy, I'm going to kill you.

She repeated the process and requested a withdrawal from savings only to read the same message.

God forgive me for hating someone so much. Why did I put his name on accounts he's never contributed a dime to. I hope Lindbergh broke his neck.

Opening her wallet, she counted twenty-three dollars and change. With no time to waste, she hurried to flight operations to make her sign in time. She found the other two flight attendants she would be working with and together they made their way to the gate to prepare the airplane for boarding. Her mood improved when she found that she would be working the tourist cabin of the MD-88 with Lee Heath. Lee was the consummate professional, but everyone loved her personality and sense of humor. *God knows I could use a laugh.*

After stowing her bag, she began counting the snack trays in the galley and checking the beverage supplies. When the crew call chime sounded, she answered the phone. The forward flight attendant said, "Peeps are on the way. Did you complete the cabin security check?"

Glancing forward at the 130 empty tourist seats, she said, "Yeah, we're ready."

Hanging up the phone, she started forward, looking under the seats and in the overhead storage bins for anything unusual, but then she saw passengers entering the cabin and knew it was too late. *I'm off my game today. I'm sure Lee checked anyway.*

Walking forward in the cabin, she glanced under seats and into open bin doors, but she wasn't even halfway when a portly gentleman called out, "Oh, Miss. Excuse me Miss, are you the stewardess?"

God, don't do this to me today. You know I'm not well. Please send me passengers with functioning brains.

She smiled, "Can I help you, sir?"

"Is this the flight to Miami?"

"I believe it is."

"Is this seat 32B?"

She pointed to the placard above the seat, "I believe it is."

He pointed to his large bag, "Where should I put this?"

Lead me not into temptation... "I believe it will fit in the overhead bin, sir."

"Can I get a Bloody Mary?"

There'll be a beverage service once we're airborne, sir."

Swimming upstream in the crowded cabin was no longer an option and she retreated to the rear galley to allow the chaos to sort itself out. Lee had finished cutting lemons into wedges for the beverage service and smiled, "You have that homicidal look in your eye. Did someone yank your chain?"

"No, that's just my normal pre-flight tendency."

"I like your attitude, girl, we'll have fun today. Did you hear about the pilot who was so dumb he thought asphalt was a hip disorder?"

Cindy laughed, "I think I flew with him last week."

"Was he wearing black pants and a white shirt?"

"Yes."

"That's him."

They swapped jokes until the passengers were seated and then walked through the cabin closing overhead bins and answering questions. Cindy was glad to be back at work and looked forward to putting distance between her and Tommy. It felt good when the airplane accelerated down the runway and rotated into flight. Lee continued her monolog of funny stories and soon Cindy's side ached from laughing.

Madison Jones arrived at Tri Con headquarters a few minutes before eight on Friday morning. Harry Dade was already at his desk and shuffling papers. "Well, good morning, MJ. I wasn't expecting you until later in the day. You must be exhausted after the long drive."

"Actually I had time yesterday afternoon to get settled and enjoyed a good night's sleep. I woke up thinking about the imported Brazilian coffee you brew every morning and couldn't resist the temptation."

"I warned you it's addictive, but I'm happy to see you. Let's get you a cup and then we'll find a couple of guys to help you arrange your office. Harry led the way to the executive conference room where they filled their cups and enjoyed the aroma of the fresh brew. The pleasantries were interrupted when he answered his cell phone and asked questions.

"What time?"

"Did you email the audio file?"

"What's the flight number and the ETA?"

"Okay, we'll take it from here."

He punched off the call and said, "Sorry, MJ, we need to get back to the office, we just received a bomb threat on one of our flights."

Back at his desk, Harry opened the email from the reservations supervisor and clicked on the audio file. The pleasant voice of a female agent came through the speaker.

"Good morning, Tri Con Airlines, how can I help you?"

"There's a bomb on Flight Fourteen Twelve to Miami, and this is not a joke," the masculine voice announced before hanging up.

Harry frowned, "Well, that was short and sweet."

MJ asked, "What happens next?"

Harry looked at the email again and wrote down the phone number the res' agent had obtained from caller ID. "Let's see if we can identify the caller."

"Shouldn't we warn the flight?"

"The dispatcher in flight control has already taken care of that. It's up to the captain to handle it now."

Chapter Eleven

Cindy was stunned when the captain called to brief the flight attendants during the climb after takeoff. The dispatcher had informed him of the bomb threat and his decision was to return for landing in Atlanta immediately. Cindy was afraid to admit that she had not completed the security sweep of the cabin, but guilt weighed heavily on her now and she knew if a bomb were eventually found, it would be her fault. She felt the airplane level off and begin to slow and then the captain made his announcement.

"Ladies and gentlemen, this is the captain. We've been informed of a security threat against our flight this morning and, unfortunately, it will be necessary to return to Atlanta for additional security screening. There is no immediate danger that I'm aware of—however, we take every precaution to ensure your safety. We'll expedite matters as much as possible and we anticipate landing in approximately fifteen minutes. There's no reason to be overly concerned at this point and your flight attendants will have further instructions for you once we have landed. I regret that we will be delayed, but I sincerely appreciate your patience and cooperation. Thank you."

The cockpit call chime sounded immediately and when the captain had all three flight attendants on the phone, he said, "Make a sweep through the cabin and look for anything unusual or anyone that acts suspicious. I'm going to put us on the ground right away and it'll be a short taxi to the remote pad. You can plan on the passengers deplaning through the rear stairs unless I tell you different."

The knot in Cindy's gut tightened as she walked through the cabin. Every passenger looked suspicious.

Harry answered his phone and after a brief conversation he punched it off and pushed his chair back from the desk. "The captain's bringing the flight back to Atlanta, MJ. This will be a good opportunity for you to see the security procedures. Let's take a ride."

Ignoring the speed limit signs on the airport's access road, Harry passed several tugs pulling baggage carts and talked to ground control on a handheld radio to receive clearance to cross taxiways. Approaching a remote area of the field, MJ could see fire trucks and numerous airport police cars lining the taxiway. A group of Tri Con ramp workers huddled around a train of empty baggage carts and several buses idled nearby.

Harry parked the car in the grass beside the taxiway and monitored the radio. "They're cleared to land so it won't be long."

A minute later the radio crackled, "Ground, Tri Con Fourteen Twelve is with you, off Nine Left."

"Tri Con Fourteen Twelve, you're cleared to the remote site."

In the distance, a Tri Con MD-88 appeared with yet another fire truck trailing it on the taxiway. MJ saw the policemen get out of their cars and spread out on either side of the taxiway. The firemen pulled fire fighting hoods over their heads and manned the nozzles on top of the trucks. Harry handed MJ a set of ear plugs and said, "You should always keep several of these handy."

A ramp worker jogged out onto the taxiway with a set of wands and directed the captain to the designated stopping point between the fire trucks. The scream of the jet engines, even at idle, made MJ glad she had the ear plugs. A ramp rat ran out and placed chocks beneath the tires of the main landing gear and the engines began to wind down. *I think my eardrums are bleeding.*

Harry changed frequencies on the radio and they heard, "Captain, this is the fire chief. Everything okay in there."

"Morning, Chief. Nothing unusual to report, but be aware of the hazmat in the rear cargo hold. Something packed in dry ice."

"Okay, thanks for the heads up. You sending the people out the rear stairs?"

"Yes sir, as soon as somebody opens them."

A ramp rat opened an access panel at the rear of the fuselage and the rear stairs dropped. Passengers began streaming out of the airplane with their carryon luggage. They were directed toward the waiting buses where two bomb-sniffing dogs and their handlers walked along the line inspecting people and bags. Two TSA agents used wands to screen each passenger before allowing them on the bus.

The ramp workers opened the cargo doors and began unloading bags and lining them up on the taxiway. The handlers allowed the dogs to sniff each bag as they moved down the line. Harry explained, "The passengers will be taken off the buses in groups of about ten and they'll each be required to identify their luggage. When every bag has been matched to a passenger, the ramp guys will load them up and take them to the terminal. Any unclaimed bag will be turned over to the bomb squad. If everything goes well, the passengers will be screened again and, along with their luggage, they'll be on their way to Miami."

"Does this happen often?"

"Fortunately, no. But it's expensive when it does. It usually turns out to be some whako who's graduated from calling in false alarms to the fire department to calling in bomb threats on airplanes. Occasionally we find a jealous husband or wife or someone else that just wants to disrupt the trip for a particular passenger. Some sort of personal revenge motive. The threat is usually not very credible due to the extensive screening process, but we can't take a chance."

"It looks like everyone's off the plane."

"I think so—let's go talk to the crew."

The two pilots were loading their bags and flight kits into the back of a maintenance van for the ride to the terminal. Harry greeted them, "Captain, I'm Harry Dade from corporate security."

"Yeah Harry, I remember you from the security classes you taught. I'm innocent, but the copilot's a little suspicious."

Harry smiled, "You think he'll talk, or will torture be required?"

The copilot frowned, "I confess…the captain did it."

MJ thought, *are all airline people insane?*

The three flight attendants came down the stairs and the pilots helped them load their bags. Harry asked, "Did anybody notice anything out of the ordinary…any passengers acting unusual?"

Lee said, "Passengers acting weird is the new normal. One guy asked me to have dinner with him in Miami, but when I asked if I could bring my husband and two kids he suddenly remembered a prior commitment."

Harry laughed, "That doesn't sound unusual—you probably get that offer often. Do you have a husband and two kids?"

"Of course not, but he didn't know that."

Everyone agreed the flight had been routine and Harry and MJ returned to the car as the airplane was towed away to be more closely searched. MJ asked, "What happens now?"

"The crew and passengers will reunite at the terminal and go to Miami. Meanwhile, we'll see if we can trace the call."

"Did you notice the makeup one of the flight attendants used to cover the bruises on her face?"

"I sure did. I'm gonna let you pull her personnel file and review it. That is if you want to start work today instead of Monday."

"Can we have barbecue for lunch?"

"MJ, we're going to be a great team."

Phil James had spoken the truth when he said the tests would become more difficult. Lindbergh viewed the aircraft electrical system as a maze of abstract diagrams highlighted by mysterious acronyms he couldn't translate. *There are one hundred questions and I have two hours. That's a little over a minute to answer each question.*

He took a wild guess at the first three answers, because he had no clue. He felt better about number four and five and kept moving. Beads of sweat formed on his forehead and he knew he had totally misjudged the depth of knowledge that Tri Con required of its pilots. He was barely halfway through the test when he realized an hour had passed. A few minutes later, his classmates began turning in their test and soon he was alone with twenty questions left to answer. He was in trouble and he sensed that Phil knew it too.

Sitting at the podium, Phil flipped through his instructor's outline and prepared to lecture on the hydraulic system. When Lindbergh finally turned his test in, Phil began marking the answer sheet with a red pen. He stopped when he had marked twenty-eight wrong answers out of the first ninety questions. He quickly read through the last ten and said, "Let's talk about a few of these, Lindbergh. I think you may have misunderstood the question on some of these."

After discussing a few of the questions and answers, Phil wrote seventy-two on the answer sheet and said, "Make sure you read the questions carefully."

Lindbergh had just been given a huge break and he knew it. "Phil, I know I've got to work harder and I will. For what it's worth, everybody in the class thinks you're a great instructor and it's not your fault that I'm behind the power curve."

"Here's the problem, Lindbergh. When the lights go out in the cockpit on a dark rainy night with ice on the wings, if you don't understand the electrical and pneumatic systems, you're going to die and you'll take a lot of innocent people with you. I hope that gives you some perspective on what we're trying to do here. I want your test scores at ninety percent and I want them there next week. I'll work as hard as you will, but that's where we're going."

"I understand."

"You've got four weeks to get ready for the oral exam, and if you don't know this airplane inside and out, the FAA inspector will shoot you down in flames and he won't think twice about it. I can't recommend you for the test if I don't think you'll succeed. Don't waste a minute between now and then."

"I know and I'll…I promise to…you know…thank you."

"You're welcome. Go take your break so we can get started again."

Stark was waiting in the hallway when Lindbergh came out of the classroom. "What did you do?"

"I passed…barely."

"You idiot. I'm not going to let you screw this up. You're going to operate on two hours sleep every night until you get your scores up. You get your butt here at eight tomorrow morning and plan on staying all weekend. No excuses!"

"I don't want to ruin your weekend, Stark, but I need all the help I can get."

"Shut up. We're starting early and staying late and you're going to recite chapter and verse until I say stop. Get used to it, I own you, Lindbergh."

"Yes sir, Captain Bligh."

"Shut up."

Chapter Twelve

When Phil dismissed the class at five o'clock, Kyle immediately checked his cell phone for messages and found none. *Where is she?* He had helped MJ get settled in the townhouse the night before and realized it was only a block from Dee's place. She sent him home early to study for his test and promised to stay in touch. His disappointment bordered on anger that she had not at least left a text. *Is she trying to tell me something?*

His mood improved considerably when he walked out the door of the classroom and found MJ waiting in the hall. She asked, "Did you pass the test or are you unemployed?"

"I scored a ninety-two, so I get to stay another week."

"In that case we should have dinner, I'm starving."

From down the hall, someone called out, "Kyle, we're not going to hold the elevator all night. Either leave that woman alone or invite her to dinner."

He took MJ's hand and led her to the elevator. "Everyone, this is MJ."

After an awkward moment, Dee said, "Nice to meet you, MJ, I'm Dee Daniels and the rest of these guys are not worth knowing. Just ignore them."

Stark said, "Don't listen to her, MJ, her previous life as a flight attendant has jaded her view of the human condition. We're trying to rehabilitate her. Have dinner with us and maybe you can help the poor woman."

Kyle made the introductions all around as the elevator descended. Cam Horner had discovered an "all you can eat" country buffet a few blocks from the training center and the price fit everyone's limited budget. Dee and MJ visited the salad bar while everyone else piled fried chicken and mashed potatoes on their plates. When everyone was seated, Cam declared, "Man this is good. I don't think this chicken's been dead very long."

MJ giggled and Kyle said, "Just humor him, he's primitive but harmless for the most part."

Stark asked, "Dee, did Cindy go back to work today?"

"She's doing a three day. She'll be back Sunday morning, which reminds me, are we going to cook out this weekend?"

Everyone agreed that it was a splendid idea.

Kyle asked, "Can I bring a date?"

"No, but I've discovered that MJ and I are neighbors and she's going to attend to help me referee."

Tommy Lane was still nursing his wounds, but he was happy that he had disrupted Cindy's flight. After making the call from an untraceable pre-paid cell phone, he returned home and logged on to a flight following website to track the flight on his computer. He laughed as he watched the flight return to Atlanta and enjoyed a beer to celebrate. *That was sweet, and I'm just getting started.*

He fell asleep in his recliner while waiting to see if the flight would take off again and woke up after noon with an empty beer can on his lap. He located Cindy's phone on Miami Beach and stared at the icon with hatred. *When I get through with you, Tri Con will be sorry they ever hired you, and your stupid friends will be sorry they ever met you.*

He popped another can of beer and went to the mailbox to see if his final paycheck had arrived. The paycheck wasn't there, but he didn't care, he still had plenty of cash after emptying Cindy's accounts. Shuffling through the junk mail, he noticed an official looking envelope and read the return address. *Why am I getting a letter from a lawyer?*

He was duly informed that Cindy had filed for divorce and he had one week to vacate the condo and turn over the family SUV. As he read the proposed terms, his anger boiled over and he threw the half-empty beer can across the room. The spinning can spewed foam on the wall and the carpet. He paced the room and kicked an end table, knocking a lamp to the floor. He kicked the lamp and sparks spewed when the bulb broke. *You're not going to be around to get a divorce.*

The doorbell rang and he ignored it, going to the refrigerator for another beer instead. Someone began pounding on the door and his anger boiled again. He jerked the door open, ready to attack whatever idiot wanted to sell him something. He found two cops staring at him and then glancing at the beer in his hand. "Are you Tom Lane?"

"Yeah, so what?"

The cop held out an envelope. "This is a restraining order. You've been served."

He took the envelope. "What are you talking about?"

"You are to stay away from your wife. No contact of any sort. Do you understand?"

"What if she contacts me?"

"She won't."

The cops turned and walked away.

Slamming the door, he threw another beer against the wall.

He finally calmed down and realized that at least he had caused trouble for her and it wasn't over yet. He opened the laptop and typed in, 'Recent news for Tri Con Airlines.' He smiled when he saw two local TV stations had posted brief articles about the morning's bomb scare. The headline for a previous story also caught his attention. "Remote Controlled Airplane Causes Tri Con Jet's Engine to Explode."

He read several articles about the near fatal incident and then did a Google search for remote controlled airplanes. *Oh yeah! Cindy, meet my little friend.*

He searched the net again and found several local hobby clubs that offered lessons for flying remote controlled airplanes. A few minutes later he was signed up for his first lesson on Saturday.

After the bomb threat on the first flight, the remainder of Cindy's three day trip had been routine. The layover in Miami had lifted her spirits and the second night in Jackson, Mississippi had been short but restful. Working with Lee, and her ever-present sense of humor, had been just what she needed to get her mind off her problems, but it was time to return to the real world and deal with it. She had a few dollars left in her wallet and a credit card that was within a few hundred dollars of being maxed out. As the airplane taxied to the gate in Atlanta, she did the mental math. Payday was approaching, but she was in debt up to her eyeballs with payments due on the condo and the SUV, both of which were in her name but not her possession. *I must be the stupidest woman who ever lived. How could I let a fool like Tommy Lane do this to me? I'm broke and owe more money than I can ever pay and I'm mooching off my best friend. Dee must think I'm the biggest loser in history.*

Dee sat in the classroom on Sunday morning and listened to Stark and Cam try to explain to Lindbergh the various ways the landing gear could be extended, with or without hydraulic pressure. Across the room, another loud debate raged on about the function of the hydraulic aux pump. She barely heard the ding of her cell phone alerting her to a text message.

"Dee, your idiot BFF just landed. If you're busy, I'll take a taxi."

"No, I'll pick you up at baggage claim in twenty minutes."

"No hurry, just look for the homeless woman in the flight attendant costume."

Dee put the phone away and interrupted Stark, "Cindy just landed. I'm going to pick her up."

"Why don't you let me do that? Maybe you can get through Lindbergh's thick skull and explain what makes the wheels go up and down."

"Last time I left you alone with my best friend you got into a fight and came back with a black eye."

"I'll be a perfect gentleman, Dee, and I'll deliver her back here safely and unmolested."

"You promise?"

"Absolutely."

"Don't wreck my car."

Cindy stood on the sidewalk at baggage claim as traffic crawled by fighting for a place to stop long enough to load people and bags. When she saw Dee's car in the jam, she hurried toward it and was surprised to see Stark pop out to take her bag. "What have you done with my girlfriend, Gary?"

"Wow, you look great in uniform."

"What have you done with my girlfriend, Gary?"

"She's trying to save Lindbergh from a hydraulic nightmare. I offered to drive the taxi."

"I'm too tired to argue, let's go."

He held the door for her and then rushed around to hop in the driver's seat. "Did you have a good trip?"

"Define a good trip."

"Hey, I'm just a rookie. You'll have to educate me."

"Talk to me a year from now and we can debate the good and bad."

"Are you asking me for a date?"

"I'm married."

"What happened to the wedding ring?"

"Behave yourself, Rookie."

"We're cooking out again this afternoon, but we're grilling steaks. You up for meat and potatoes?"

"I'm starving."

"I'll grill you the best steak you've ever had."

"Oh goody, a man who cooks. Do you dust and vacuum too?"

"Normally I only perform survival skills involving food and shelter, but for you I would take on extra duties."

"Just get me away from this stinking airport and all these people."

"My pleasure, Miss Lane."

"Mrs. Lane."

"You really know how to hurt a guy."

"You ain't seen nothing yet."

They both laughed.

Chapter Thirteen

MJ insisted on providing the salad and dessert for the cookout. She refused to ride in Kyle's ragged truck, and they walked the short distance to Dee's Townhouse. Kyle carried two huge covered bowls of salad, and she stuffed three bottles of salad dressing in his pockets. MJ carried two pies she had baked.

Dee greeted them, and after storing their culinary contributions in the refrigerator, she and MJ hugged as if they had known each other for years. They followed the sound of laughter and the aroma of cooking meat, and walked out to the deck. When MJ saw Cindy talking to Stark, she thought, *well hello again. I know you.*

Dee made the introduction and Cindy said, "Don't you work in corporate security?"

"I'm a newbie, I just started on Friday."

"I saw you with Harry Dade after our bomb scare."

"That was me, although I had no clue what was going on."

"Me either, I'm just glad nothing exploded. Does anybody know who made the threat?"

"I don't think so, but I'm just watching and learning at this point."

"Well, whoever it was sure screwed our day up. I hope you catch them."

Stark interrupted, "How do you like your steak, MJ?"

"Medium rare would be great, thank you."

"No problem…Cindy, you want to give me a hand here?"

"You definitely need supervision."

Dee said, "I'll nuke the potatoes if you'll help, MJ."

Back in the kitchen, MJ said, "Your friend seems really nice."

"She is, but Cindy's had a rough time lately. She's getting a divorce from her jerk of a husband and I couldn't be happier about it."

"I'm sorry to hear that."

"Don't be…it's a good thing, believe me. I'm sure you noticed her battle scars. She should have had him thrown in jail."

"Sounds like a messy situation."

"He won't go away easy. The guy's a leach and he's accustomed to her supporting him. Now she's broke and owes more money than she can pay back in the next ten years. There's no chance he's going to get a job and help out."

"Do you think she's in danger?"

"Frankly, I wouldn't be surprised at anything he does. I think he's mental."

Monday morning dawned wet and windy, but it didn't hinder MJ. She arrived at corporate security at six thirty, planning to begin organizing her new office before the work day officially began at eight. A little solitude in her new environment would increase her comfort level and keep her ahead of the game. She was anxious to investigate Cindy Lane's husband and determine if he might be responsible for the bomb scare, but she was also trying to resolve her own feelings of guilt. To her dismay, she discovered she was jealous of Kyle's relationship with his classmates. Listening to their conversation and watching them interact made her realize that he was not as much of a loner as she thought. The class had become close friends in a short period of time, and they obviously had things in common that she could not begin to understand. The things they talked about and the lingo they used may as well have been a foreign language. MJ felt a little insecure about competing with that.

Kyle had a way of making her feel special, and she was always the center of his attention, unless an airplane flew over. She was accustomed to that distraction and found it amusing until yesterday. During the afternoon cookout and swim party, every time an airplane flew over, eight faces turned to the sky and regarded the event worth their unspoken evaluation. Did they think it was going to fall from the sky? Were they critiquing the performance? Was it a cult ritual of some sort? She knew it was childish of her, but they shared something with Kyle that she could not.

She pushed those thoughts to the back of her mind as she exited the elevator and entered the lobby of the security offices. Any hope of acclimating herself alone was dashed when she heard laughter coming from the conference room. *How on earth could anything be that funny at six thirty in the morning?*

She could not reach her office without passing the conference room, and she found Harry Dade, Cason Haley, and CEO Harold Collins, still chuckling. The three of them greeted her with smiles and Harold Collins said, "Good morning, Miss Jones, Harry tells me you are officially one of us now. How do you take your coffee?"

He filled a cup from the urn as he asked the question.

Okay...the CEO is serving me coffee...I'm sure I'll wake up any minute now and reality will prevail.

Taking the cup, she said, "Thank you very much. It smells wonderful."

"You're most welcome. The airline operates on coffee and jet fuel, and I'm not sure which is the most consumed."

Harry said, "Did I tell you about the flight attendant who asked the captain how he liked his coffee?"

Collins said, "No, but this should be good."

"He told her he liked his coffee the same way he liked his women."

Cason asked, "What did she say?"

"She told him, 'Sorry, we don't have stupid coffee.'"

MJ intended to smile, but found herself laughing along with them instead. She was tempted to share a blond joke, but thought better of it.

Collins refilled his coffee mug and said, "I suppose I should go find a decent tie to wear and make myself presentable. The

Honorable Henry Walker is visiting from Washington today and we need his support for a few things."

"Who is he," Cason asked?

"He's the chairman of the Senate Select Committee on Aviation. Miss Jones, I'm happy you're here. Maybe you can add some class to this bunch."

Collins strolled away and Harry asked, "How was your weekend, MJ?"

"It was interesting. I ran into our bruised flight attendant from the bomb threat flight."

"Do tell."

She related what she had learned about Cindy and her divorce.

"That is interesting indeed. Let's set up a meeting with Molly Jackson and review Ms. Lane's personnel file. Meanwhile, Cason can run a background check on the wife beater. Better yet, he can teach you how to do it."

Cason said, "No problem, MJ, I'll help you set up your office computer and get you logged into the system. I'll walk you through the process."

Molly Jackson worked through the mountain of Monday morning paperwork on her desk and wished she were flying the line. Her secretary buzzed to announce, "Molly, Ms. Jones from security is here for the eleven o'clock appointment."

Molly greeted her at the door, "Hey, MJ, I hear you've graduated from toy airplanes to bomb threats."

"I have no idea what I'm doing, but don't tell Harry."

"Welcome to the club. My advice is to act busy and look pretty. It's always worked for me."

"I'll remember that."

"So, you're interested in Cindy Lane?"

"Actually, I'm more interested in her soon to be ex-husband."

"It wouldn't be the first time an irate spouse called in a bomb threat."

"So I hear."

"I don't know Cindy, but I've looked at her file and it's clean. She seems to be an excellent employee."

"I get the same impression, but her husband is another matter. He appears to be a small time loser. Several misdemeanors and run-ins with the locals. Never held a job for more than a few months."

"Sounds like what we call a Tri Con scholarship. Some guy latches on to a flight attendant and takes advantage of all the airline benefits while she puts him through college or he just enjoys a life of leisure."

"At least she's dumping him. What's her family background?"

Molly leafed through the file. "Looks like she's an only child...the only relatives listed are her mother and an elderly grandfather. She's a local girl...went to high school and college right here in Atlanta. Her maiden name is Morgan...the same as both relatives."

"I won't take up any more of your time, Molly, but I appreciate the background information."

"I'm glad you dropped by. I needed a break from paperwork and I always like to know if one of my flight attendants appears on someone's radar. Come by anytime, MJ, you don't need an appointment. In fact let's have lunch later this week. I'll fill you in on all the gossip."

"I'd like that very much. See you soon."

Cindy received the good news at 11:30 on Monday morning. Her lawyer called to inform her that Tommy had vacated the Condominium and left the SUV in the parking lot. She planned to put the Condo on the market as soon as possible. There would be very little profit if any, but at least she wouldn't be burdened with the payments each month. If the home didn't sell soon, she would probably have to sell the SUV also. She dreaded every payday and the nightmare of trying to stretch her income to cover the payments. Both credit cards were nearing their limit and making minimum payments was causing the interest to eat her finances like a cancer. She remembered that today was the end of the month and her paycheck would be directly deposited into her checking account. Time to pay the bills and hope to have enough left to feed herself for two more weeks. *I've got to pick up some extra trips, or I'm going to starve to death.*

Using her smart phone, she logged on to the Tri Con Credit Union website to record her new checking account balance after the paycheck deposit. She scrolled to the bottom line and saw a balance of thirty-eight dollars and change. *What the...*

Scrolling back up, she saw the paycheck deposit followed a few minutes later by a withdrawal of the same amount. *Tommy!*

The last day of the month created two exciting events for the pilot class. The first cause of celebration was payday. The meager compensation awarded a new hire pilot was nothing to write home about, but the first airline paycheck was exciting anyway. Being gainfully employed and receiving a paycheck enabled the second event. Phil led the class to a complex of business establishments, located two blocks from the training center, one of which was an approved vendor for Tri Con pilot uniforms. As the tailor made his sales pitch, he explained that they could shop freely and their credit was good due to the fact that he accepted easy payroll deduction payments from Tri Con.

When he felt he had made his case, he asked, "Who would like to be measured first?"

Everyone looked at Dee. The seniority culture had been established.

The tailor sized her up and selected a jacket from the rack. She slipped it on and stood in front of the mirror. The three gold stripes on the sleeves glowed like neon. The tailor tugged here and there and had her lift her arms. He made chalk marks on the sleeves and wrote notes on a clipboard. Next he selected a first officer hat with the gold Tri Con symbol on the front and had her try it on. He walked around her a couple of times, appraising his work, and then hung the jacket and hat with a tag labeled D. Daniels. Next he selected a pair of pants and sent her off to the dressing room.

The shopping spree began and an hour later everybody had a bag stuffed with white shirts with epaulets and shoulder bars with three gold stripes, gold first officer wings to be pinned to the shirts and the jackets, new black uniform shoes, and the hat. The tailor promised to complete the alterations on the jackets and pants within the week. In addition to the uniforms, everyone had selected a black leather flight kit. The brain bag would be used to carry their aircraft manuals and charts and would sit beside them in the cockpit for years to come. The tailor promised to have their names engraved in gold on the bags when they picked up their uniforms. With wide grins on their faces, they went to lunch.

Dee announced, "The credit union is only a block from here and I need to visit the ATM."

Stark asked, "Can we set up direct deposit for our paychecks?"

"It's the smart thing to do. You're almost always going to be out of town on payday."

"I'm going with you to open a checking account and get an ATM card."

The entire class decided to do the same thing.

Dee led the parade and when they approached the entrance to the credit union, she saw Cindy getting in her SUV. Her eyes were red and puffy, and her posture was slumped with defeat and dejection. She attempted a smile when she saw them, but it was a wasted effort.

Dee recognized the look and waved the others through the door. When Stark hesitated, she nudged him away and faced Cindy, "What did he do this time?"

Cindy looked down and almost whispered, "He emptied the checking account again after my paycheck was deposited. I just withdrew my thirty-eight dollars and closed the account."

"Good girl. How did you get the SUV?"

"My lawyer talked the judge into making him move out and give me the car back."

"You're not going back there alone, Cindy. I want you to stay with me."

Cindy's eyes misted and her lip trembled, "I don't know what to do. I'm just stupid."

"That's true, but I love you like a sister."

Cindy almost smiled, "Thank you for that candid observation."

"You're not stupid, sweetie, but you've got to make this idiot go away, and you're staying at my place until you do."

"I've got thirty-eight dollars and a half a tank of gas, can you afford me?"

"I'll claim you as a dependent on my tax return."

"I'm going to see if I can borrow some money from my Mom, but I think I need to get a second job until I can sell the house."

"We'll worry about that later. Go home and relax. I'll be there after class and we'll cook something decadent and fattening."

"I don't deserve you, Dee."

"Go home and fix your face."

Chapter Fourteen

Cindy dabbed at her eyes with the back of her hand as she drove back to Dee's. She felt like crawling in a hole and never coming out. She sat in the driveway with her head on the steering wheel and hated herself. When her cell phone trilled, she wondered if it would be possible to receive more bad news. Digging the phone out of her purse, she answered and expected the worse.

"Hey Cindy, Kim in crew scheduling. I've got a deal for you."

"Really?"

"You have a request in for extra flying, and I've got a Houston turn around leaving in about an hour. You want it?"

"Sure, I can do that."

"Great, you've got it...Flight 906 departs at 15:10 and you'll be back about eleven tonight."

"I'm on my way."

After a quick change into uniform and a comb through her hair, she was back in the car and speeding to the airport as she calculated the extra pay. Three blocks later, a short whoop of a siren drew her attention to the rear view mirror and flashing blue lights. She pulled to the curb and glanced at her watch. Forty-five minutes 'till departure.

The cop approached her window with pad and pen in hand. "Ma'am it's a local custom to actually come to a stop at stop signs."

"I'm sorry. I just got called out for a trip, and I'm trying to get there on time."

"I'll need your driver's permit, please."

Taking the license, he walked back to his squad car and crawled into the driver's seat.

Forty minutes till pushback. Come on man, what's taking so long?

Five minutes later the cop walked back to the window. "Ma'am, would you step out of the car, please?"

"Are you serious?"

"Please step out."

A second patrol car parked in front of her and a female officer got out. "Ma'am, please step to the rear of the car and lean forward to place your hands on the vehicle."

Thirty minutes till departure. This is crazy.

The female cop did a quick frisk and asked, "Do you mind if we have a look inside the car?"

"I'm trying to get to work, and I'm running late."

"We'll try to be quick."

"Please hurry. I know I ran the stop sign and I'm sorry, but my flight leaves in thirty minutes."

The other cop opened the passenger door and began rummaging around inside. Cindy watched the second hand on her watch as it crawled around the dial. *Please hurry!*

The cop finally walked back to the squad car and placed two zip lock bags on the hood. "Ma'am, we're placing you under arrest for possession of a controlled substance, crack cocaine to be exact. The female cop opened the back door of the squad car. "Please have a seat. Watch your head."

Those words finally broke Cindy Lane. She simply ceased to function and the cops poured her into the caged back seat as she mumbled words and sobbed uncontrollably

MJ mumbled to herself as she tried to tame the new desktop computer and force it to perform simple tasks. *Why don't they all*

work the same? Harry walked in and asked, "MJ, are you talking to yourself?"

"I tried, but I discovered it requires a password. It wasn't important anyway."

He smiled, "You're sense of humor is refreshing. I just got a call from one of my buddies at the local PD. Cindy Lane keeps turning up in unexpected places."

"Where did she appear this time?"

"In the city lockup—pending a first appearance in court tomorrow."

"Let me guess—another domestic dispute and she clocked her husband."

"No, they stopped her for a traffic violation and realized there was a lookout for her tag number. Someone reported the vehicle was being used in drug trafficking."

"They can't arrest her for an anonymous accusation."

"No, but she gave them permission to search the car, and they found two bags of crack under the passenger seat. A quantity large enough to charge her with distributing. I doubt if it has anything to do with the bomb threat, but I just thought I'd let you know."

He waved as he went out the door. MJ picked up the phone and punched numbers, then waited for an answer.

"Good afternoon, In-Flight Service, Janie speaking."

"Janie, this is Madison Jones, is Molly available?"

"Let me see, please hold."

Molly answered, "MJ, I was just about to call you. Did you hear about Cindy Lane?"

"How did you know?"

"The flight attendant network is much more efficient than the internet. Very little goes un-reported, whether it's true or not. Not to mention the fact that my secretary's husband is a city detective."

"What will happen to her?"

"Well, I guess that depends on you. She's suspended as of now, and we'll see what happens when you investigate the situation.

There's no tolerance for drugs in the airline business, so it doesn't look good."

"Has she had a random drug test lately?"

"I've still got her file right here. The Pee Police nailed her last week and she passed with flying colors."

"I don't suppose that proves anything, but it's a start. We'll want to know if any other employees are involved."

"I've gotta run, MJ, but let me know what you find and if I can help."

Cindy processed into the detention center like a Zombie. She stared straight ahead, with vacant eyes, as she was strip searched and then given a gray jumpsuit and a pair of slippers. She continued to check her watch until it was taken from her an hour after her flight's scheduled departure time. She would describe the experience later as an emotional decompression followed by an emergency descent to the bottom of her soul. She bypassed denial and anger and dove straight into the dark pit of acceptance. She wasn't capable of feeling sorry for herself, and at least the bottom of the pit was a destination…maybe a final destination.

Eventually, she was escorted to a cell and nudged inside. She stood there in silence, holding a bare pillow and a folded blanket in her arms. She was aware of movement to her right, but she didn't care. Someone said, "Hey girl, don't be just stand there. You blocking my view."

Cindy ignored the words and stared at the wall.

"Don't be giving me no silent treatment, girl. I been in here by myself too long."

The woman who got up from the bunk was three inches taller than Cindy and of considerable girth. Survival instincts roused Cindy's awareness and she backed up against the bars. Her cell mate was older, probably near fifty, and looked like she had been through several wars and had the scars and tattoos to prove it.

She approached Cindy, staring into her eyes like a wary animal. After a moment, her gaze softened and she took the pillow and blanket from Cindy's arms. "Don't you be worrying 'bout nothing, girlfriend. Nobody gone mess with you."

The woman spread the blanket on the empty bunk and fluffed the pillow. "You get comfortable and tell Kitty 'bout yo self. Why they put a pretty thing like you in here?"

Cindy sat down and let the tears flow. Kitty sat beside her and put a long arm around her shoulders. "You cry all you want to, child. Plenty of time for that and it be good for you. Then you tell me yo story."

Everyone laughed at Stark as he wandered around the classroom wearing his new first officer's hat. Kyle said, "Your head looks better, but I don't think it's going to make you any smarter."

The evening study session was winding down and yawns were contagious. Dee's cell phone began to vibrate and rattle on the table. She answered the call and the frown on her face indicated that it was not good news. Gathering her books, she said, "I gotta go."

"What's wrong, Dee?" Cam asked.

Everyone looked at her with concern, and she hesitated before answering.

"Cindy's been arrested."

Stark stood up, "Are you serious?"

"I don't know the details, but her mother said they found drugs in her car. She hates drugs, and people who use them, so her slimy husband has somehow set her up."

The entire class was on their feet, and Stark said, "Let's go get her out."

"Unless you're planning a jailbreak, that's not going to happen. Her Mom says she has a bond hearing in the morning. Even then, we don't have money to bail her out."

Stark said, "I'm a member of the credit union. I can borrow money."

A chorus of voices agreed to chip in.

Dee asked, "Does anybody know a lawyer?"

Lindbergh said, "Yeah, I do. This is wrong in so many ways. I should have kicked that Bozo's head more than once. Everybody hold your water, I got this."

He punched buttons on his cell phone and walked into the hallway. As he walked out the door, they heard him say, "Hey Dad, you still in town?"

Five minutes later he came back to explain, "My old man's in town on business and he knows lots of lawyers. He's going to call me back."

The discussion for the next fifteen minutes involved justice, redemption, revenge, and anger management. Stark was fined several times by the kangaroo court for unnecessary profanity. The conversation came to an abrupt halt when Lindbergh's phone rang and he listened with only brief comments.

Putting the phone away, he said, "Dee, you can pick Cindy up in about thirty minutes. My Dad happened to be having dinner with a good attorney. When you go down there, don't ask any questions and don't answer any either."

Stark said, "Let's go!"

Dee answered, "I'm going alone. She's going to be depressed, embarrassed, and probably mad enough to be spitting bullets. I don't want her to try explaining things to you simple minded idiots. Let me do this. Lindbergh, I don't know what you did, but I think I love you."

He smiled, "Don't get emotional and start acting like a girl, First Officer Daniels. That goes for you too, Stark."

Stark threw a wad of paper at him, "Shut up!"

Chapter Fifteen

MJ began her Tuesday where she ended her Monday, trying to coax the new computer into submission. At eight-thirty, she was about to surrender and ask Cason Haley for help when an unexpected guest arrived at her office door. Molly Jackson entered, and without preamble, she announced, "MJ, I need help and Harold Collins suggested I throw myself at your mercy."

"As long as it doesn't require this electronic boob tube, I'm all in."

"You may be sorry. I'm under the gun here, and it's unfair to involve someone who just arrived on the property, but I'm desperate."

"How can I help?"

"Let me bring you up to speed. Mr. Collins called me to his office first thing this morning where he introduced me to Senator Henry Walker and Cindy Lane. It seems that the senator thinks Cindy is being treated unfairly and falsely accused. How he got involved is a mystery to me, but that's where we're at. The State Assistant Attorney General interviewed Cindy at the jail last night, and not only deemed her innocent of all charges and set her free, but at her request he also freed her cellmate who was locked up for braining her cheating husband with an iron skillet."

"You're going to have to slow down and let me digest this slowly, Molly. This new computer has scrambled my brain like I've been bashed with a skillet. Who is Senator Walker?"

"I should have explained—he's the head of the Senate Select Committee on Aviation in Washington. His influence on regulations and appropriations is such that we try to keep him smiling."

"I'm beginning to get the picture."

"Let me color it for you as it appears to me. He was in town last night to speak at a fundraiser for the Governor's re-election, when he somehow got a case of heartburn about Cindy Lane. The State of Georgia, the City of Atlanta, and Tri Con Airlines need an airport expansion, and both the local prosecutor and the sitting judge need his endorsement for re-election. At some point after dessert and before his speech, Cindy and her cellmate walk. No more heartburn.

"My appearance was required at the impromptu meeting this morning so Collins and the senator could assure me that they have 'every confidence' I will do the right thing about Cindy's suspension. At that point, Cindy and I were dismissed."

"Where is she now?"

"In your lobby reading a magazine."

"Somehow I think Mr. Collins will have more to say about this."

"You can bet on it. When the senator leaves, he's going to tell me to put her back on the payroll, but if he sees her in uniform before we know she's clean, she and I both will be looking for a job. That's where you come in."

"I'll have to get some guidance from Harry, but I suggest we explain to her that she will need a new security clearance because of the arrest. That way you can hide her somewhere and we can delay the clearance as long as we need to before you decide to let her fly. Meanwhile, if Harry approves, we can do some investigating."

"That's brilliant, MJ. I knew there was a reason I liked you. By the way, the prosecutor ordered the cops to bring Cindy's husband in for questioning about the drugs. I don't know if he's doing his duty or covering his butt, but he might be interested in your thoughts about the bomb scare."

"I knew there was a reason I liked you, Molly. Shall we bring Cindy in for a chat? I think Walmart has a sale on skillets."

"I may have a coupon."

Cindy was exhausted after two insane days of drama. Her house and car were returned, Tommy had robbed her bank account again, she had been arrested and jailed, causing her to no-show a trip, and then by some miracle set free. Now, practically penniless, she was fighting to keep her job at Tri Con. She had suffered the heartbreak of having to call her mother from jail, and she was determined not to burden her further with her personal problems.

Dee skipped the after class study session and hurried home to check on her friend. The aroma of baked chicken greeted her and Cindy handed her a glass of wine. "After the last few days, I'm surprised you're not drinking something stronger than wine."

"I've found that I don't need alcohol to make my head spin. It seems to occur naturally."

"What happened today?"

"I don't know where to begin."

"Do you still have a job?"

"No, but I'm back on the payroll."

"Now my head's spinning."

"Molly took me off suspension, but I can't fly until I get a new security clearance. She gave me a temporary desk job in her office until that happens."

"Wow! You must have done some fast talking to get that deal."

"Not me. The senator did the talking. He explained to Mr. Collins and Molly that I was being set up, and after some subtle threats, they agreed to look into it."

"You better be careful, Molly can have a short fuse."

"I think she's okay. She marched me down to security and we had a long discussion with that new girl. I spilled my guts and I think they feel sorry for me."

"You mean Kyle's girlfriend, MJ."

"Don't ever underestimate, MJ. That girl's a lot smarter than she wants anybody to know. She pointed out how stupid I am without making me feel stupid. I learned a lot about ending relationships."

"How so?"

"She explained to me that since Tommy and I have the same cell phone account, he's probably stalking me by using the 'Find a Phone App.'"

"That's scary."

"Tell me about it. I'm changing the account tomorrow. She advised me to open new bank accounts, although it's a little late for that. She also asked me if he had the password for my Tri Con employee sign in and access to my schedule. Of course, I no longer have a schedule, but we changed my password anyway. She advised me to change the locks on the house and have the car re-keyed. I'm telling you, she's really smart. I would never have thought of those things. Guess who the beneficiary of my life insurance was?"

"Cindy, please tell me you changed that."

"I logged in on MJ's computer and changed it immediately to my mother. I think MJ believes me and I like her. Molly even seemed sympathetic. I may actually survive all this somehow."

"If there's any justice in this world, you will survive and thrive while Tommy slowly sinks into a cesspool. He's due for a little payback."

Cindy flinched and turned a little pale when the doorbell rang. "Are you expecting anyone?"

"Don't panic, Cindy, I'll see who it is."

Dee quietly approached the door and looked through the peep hole. She didn't recognize the large woman peering back. She cracked the door but left the security chain in place. "Can I help you?"

"I got somthin for Miss Cindy."

"Do I know you?"

"My name Kitty. Miss Cindy my fren."

"Wait just a moment, please."

Closing the door, Dee asked, "Do you know someone named Kitty?"

Cindy rushed over to peek out, and then opened the door, "Girl, how did you find me?"

"You tol me you stay with yo girlfriend in this neighborhood. Saw yo car in the driveway."

"Come in and give me a hug."

Dee watched in awe as the two hugged. *I'm losing my mind.*

"I made you a present fo getting me out the jail."

"What is it?"

"Kitty's best apple pie."

"Wonderful. Stay for dinner, and we'll have pie for dessert."

"Caint stay, my ride's waiting on me and we got to be somewhere."

"Can you come back another time?"

"Maybe, but can I use yo cell phone fore I go?"

"Sure you can."

Kitty took the phone and walked to the door for privacy to make the call. After a few minutes, she returned the phone and said her goodbye. "I owe you, girl, and you needs anything jus let Kitty know."

Cindy walked her to the door and watched as she walked down the driveway, where two men leaned on an older car. One slid behind the wheel while the other opened the door to help Kitty inside. Dee joined her as the car rumbled out of sight. "Do I even want to hear this story?"

"Don't pre-judge people, Dee. She's one of the nicest women I've ever met."

"If you say so. Can I have some of that pie?"

The Econostay Lodge, five miles south of the airport, had been the focus of interest for several people during the day. The extended stay facility featured reasonable rates for weekly or monthly guests. When MJ explained the 'Find a Phone' function to Cindy, she secretly used the App to locate Tommy's phone and noted the location. She and Molly later passed that information to the detective at the local PD, who had originally told his wife, Molly's secretary, that Cindy had been arrested. MJ also related her suspicion that Tommy might be behind the bomb threat. The detective did a quick check and found that Tommy had paid a month's rent in advance. In light of his busy case load, Tommy could wait a day or two.

MJ wasn't the only one who understood the value of Find a Phone. Kitty used the App frequently to track her philandering spouse, although he had no idea. Cindy's phone was very similar to her own, and it only took a few seconds to locate Tommy's phone at the Econostay.

Chapter Sixteen

Three days passed before an inquiry from the prosecutor caused Tommy Lane to bubble to the top of the local detective's priority list. Accompanied by a patrol officer, the detective knocked on Tommy's door with no response. The 'Do Not Disturb' sign did not deter him and the patrolman's uniform was enough to convince the maid to open the door. The room featured an unmade bed, towels on the floor, and an abundance of empty beer cans, but no Tommy. The maid said the room had been unoccupied for several days. She agreed to call the detective if Tommy showed up.

MJ had been patiently waiting for the detective to get in touch. "Ms. Jones, it looks like Tommy Lane is temporarily unavailable."

"Temporary as in out to lunch?"

"He hasn't been around for several days according to the housekeeper."

"Do you think he skipped town?"

"No, his stuff is still there. His wallet, watch, and cell phone are on the nightstand and his laptop is on the desk. The computer is still logged in to the internet."

"Of course, you would need a warrant to legally search the laptop."

"That's correct, but an illegal search revealed some interesting website visits. As luck would have it, I happened to have a thumb drive with me at the time."

"I've found the gray areas of the legal system to be most interesting and sometimes very productive."

"Gray is my favorite color."

"Detective, are you available for lunch?"

"Are you buying?"

"I believe the benevolence of a grateful Tri Con might be in play."

"Even better. Are you familiar with the barbecue joint called *The Flying Pig*?"

"You mean the place commonly known as *The Tri Con Stew*?"

"How about eleven-thirty?"

"I'll bring the wet wipes."

Harry and MJ bought the detective's lunch and came back to the office with the thumb drive. Along with Cason Haley, they gathered at MJ's computer. She scrolled the mouse and said, "This guy is more ambitious than I thought."

Harry observed, "I didn't know there was this much drone technology on the internet. Cason, how much do you know about drones?"

"I know they saved my butt more than once in Afghanistan. I also know some of them cost millions of dollars."

MJ kept scrolling, "Looks like he discovered the cheaper versions. He's been researching radio controlled airplanes."

Cason added, "The military uses something like that too, but only for spying and intelligence. They use miniature versions that fly around undetected taking video and infrared images for reconnaissance."

MJ said, "I don't think he wants to recon his wife."

"He's also researching plastic explosives. How does that factor in," Harry asked?

Cason thought about it, "What if he loaded the model airplane with plastic and flew it into something."

Harry asked, "Would it explode?"

"Probably not by itself, but add a detonator and an impact switch and you've got major fireworks. The military has a model called the *Switchblade*. It launches from a tube and then the wings and propeller extend like a switchblade knife. It's a Kamikaze model. They just fly it into whatever they want to blow up."

"He wouldn't go to all this trouble to harass his wife. There's more to it."

MJ said, "Revenge can be a strong motivator."

Cason frowned, "Let's not forget what a model airplane did to the MD-88 engine and one of our flight attendants."

Harry said, "I tried to kill that publicity, but was unsuccessful. We need to find this psycho."

Cason asked, "You want me to have a look around his room and see what else I can find?"

"Not officially."

"Sweet."

Tommy Lane slowly became aware that he wasn't dead. Reality crept into his sub-conscious like a dissipating fog. At first he wasn't sure if the deafening roar was real or imagined. He was further confused by the fact that he could not see. *Am I blind?*

A screeching noise interrupted the roar, and he thought he heard a bell ringing briefly. He realized that he was lying down and being jolted around against something hard and cold. His head bounced like a dribbling basketball. *This is not a dream. I've gone insane!*

He tried to sit up and was relieved to find that his hands worked. When he raised his bouncing head from the hard surface, his thought process almost cleared. He leaned back against a hard surface and cushioned his head with his hands. The roaring noise was unbearable. He had a million questions and no answers. He couldn't cope and he didn't want to. He was happy to slip back into oblivion, and as he did, a random memory passed through his mind. Someone knocking on the door. Something about maid service. A big woman saying, "Mista Lane, me and my boys here gone fix you up."

The disappearance of Tommy Lane did not cause distress for anyone involved. Cindy became more relaxed and content with each passing day, and after two weeks she found herself smiling more than she had in years. The desk job proved to be more enjoyable than she could have imagined, and her co-workers were impressed with her work ethic and attitude. Molly invited herself to MJ's office to discuss the situation.

"Have you found anything in Cindy's background that seems suspicious?"

"Not at all. In fact, I think her only lapse of judgment was when she married the loser."

"I agree. Everybody in the office really likes her and she does an excellent job with everything I throw at her. Any word on her husband?"

"Nothing. He just vanished, and the local PD won't open a case without a missing person report, which Cindy declines to file."

"What do you think happened?"

"His wallet and cell phone have been laying on the night table in his room for over two weeks. The cops think he's dead, but if he is, I'd feel much better if we had a body. I think he's a psycho and capable of anything. We need to find him either way."

"What should we do about Cindy?"

"As far as I can see, there's no reason she can't return to flying status."

"That's good to know, but I may keep her in the office another couple of weeks. I could use the extra help, and maybe the husband thing will resolve itself soon."

Phil James was cautiously optimistic about his ground school students. Lindbergh was the weak link in the chain, but his scores had improved to the mid-eighties and he had undergone an attitude adjustment. Phil stood at the podium and used a tissue to clean his glasses before beginning his final pep talk.

"I was pleased with the review yesterday. It's been a pleasure working with you and I want you to know how much I appreciate your attention and hard work. You'll have the remainder of the morning to complete the final written exam, so take your time and think through the problems. This afternoon, a representative from flight training will be here to brief you on the simulator program and give you your training schedule for next week.

"The only thing on the agenda tomorrow is the FAA oral exams. The inspector will be with you for about two and a half hours and is free to ask anything he feels appropriate. Four of you will have morning time slots and everybody else will be here in the afternoon. I'll have the schedule and which inspector you'll be with later today.

"If anyone has questions, now would be the time to ask."

Lindbergh raised his hand.

"Lindbergh, will you please stop raising your hand like a third grader and just speak up."

"Sorry, Phil. How many questions on the final exam?"

"Normally a hundred and fifty, but there's always one student who's a pain in the butt, and he gets two hundred."

There was an awkward moment before Phil began laughing and everyone joined in, including Lindbergh. "Do I get extra time since my test is longer?"

Phil smiled, "No, I want you out of here as soon as possible."

When everyone had their test, the room fell silent and the only sound for the next two hours was the scratching of pencil on paper and an occasional cough. Phil sat at the podium and played solitaire on his cell phone while trying to stay awake. His game was interrupted by an email from the local FAA office with the oral exam schedule for the next day.

As usual, Stark finished first and turned in his exam, and as usual, Lindbergh was last. Phil sighed with relief when he graded the test and Lindbergh scored an eighty-eight. "How many did you guess at?"

"All of them, but they were educated guesses."

"Your oral is scheduled at one o'clock tomorrow afternoon. The inspector's name is Garrett, and he must be a new guy. I don't know him."

Lindbergh turned red in the face. "You've got to be kidding."

"Why would I kid about an oral exam?"

"This is not fair, Phil. Charles Garrett works in the Pittsburg District Office of the FAA. He's one of my Dad's friends and he's given me every check ride I've ever taken. I'm not going to take a free pass on this oral. I want a local examiner like everybody else. If I can't pass the oral on my own, then I don't deserve the job."

"I don't have any control over the FAA, Lindbergh. They control us."

"My Dad thinks he controls everything, but not this time."

Kyle could not sleep. He tossed and turned and numbers ran through his head like a movie reel. At dinner with MJ, she had told him, "You remind me of a long-tailed cat in a room full of rocking chairs. Relax, you'll do fine."

Relaxing wasn't going to happen. He arrived at the training center for his nine a.m. exam with red eyes and a touch of nausea.

Cam Horner, who would be taking his oral with a different inspector, asked, "You want coffee?"

"No, I might throw up."

"Me too…just thought I'd ask."

Kyle paced around the classroom while Cam sat at the table and used flip cards to quiz himself. At ten after nine a guy walked in with coffee in one hand and a briefcase in the other. He wore a suit and tie with an FAA ID badge on a lanyard around his neck. "Which one of you is Bennett?"

Kyle stopped pacing, "I'm Kyle Bennett."

The guy set the briefcase down and extended his hand, "I'm Pete Stewart. Let's use the room across the hall—it has a better view. Are you ready?"

"Yes sir."

"Let's go. Bring your brain bag with you."

When they were seated Stewart said, "I need to see your pilot's license, medical certificate, and radio operator's permit."

While Stewart did the paperwork, he asked, "Aren't you the guy who landed the 767 a few months ago?"

"It landed itself, but I was there."

"I know the captain who got shot. He thinks you're the greatest thing since grits."

"He's much braver than I am. I hope he's back in the cockpit soon."

"Me too. Let's see if we can get you in the cockpit with him."

Stewart opened the pilot's operating manual and said, "There are five pages of system limitations that you should have memorized. Let's start with that. What's the max gross takeoff weight of the airplane?"

Kyle recited a number.

"What's the max zero fuel weight of the airplane?"

"Kyle recited again."

The questions kept coming and after completing the five pages, the inspector picked up an emergency checklist, "For every emergency procedure there are certain initial action items that you must complete from memory. What are the initial action items for an engine fire?"

Kyle recited.

"What are the initial action items for an explosive decompression?"

Kyle recited.

When all the emergency checklist procedures had been analyzed, they moved on.

"Tell me every item that is operated by the left hydraulic system and what you would do if that system lost pressure."

The questions continued at a steady pace for the next two hours. Finally, Stewart closed his book. "You did good, Kyle. My only suggestion is that you review the electrical power sources for the auto flight system. Your weather minimums for approach will be affected by certain power losses. They'll cover that for you in the simulator. Let's do some paperwork and get out of here."

Kyle felt like he had been through a meat grinder. He felt beat up and depleted. He was exhausted, but he realized his appetite had returned. He hauled his brain bag into the deserted hallway and found several rooms with *Test in Progress* signs on the doors. He checked his watch and headed for the cafeteria hoping to share his good news with someone. While waiting in the order line, he spotted Stark and Dee at a table. He waved, and Stark raised a thumb in the air in the form of a question. When Kyle returned the thumbs up, Stark stood and performed a simulated golf clap. Kyle chuckled and gathered his burger and fries.

Both Dee and Stark had afternoon orals and they asked questions at the same time. Kyle frowned, "Sorry guys, I'm not answering any more questions for at least two days. My fountain of knowledge is empty."

Dee said, "Don't make us beat it out of you."

"It wasn't so bad. The guy covered everything, but it was the same stuff Phil has been preaching for weeks. The first thing you will get is limitations and initial emergency action items."

Dee asked, "Who was the FAA guy?"

"Pete Stewart. He's all business, but a nice guy."

Stark said, "That's who I've got too at one o'clock. Tell me some of the questions."

"Well, there will be several hundred...where do you want me to start? You won't have a problem, Stark. Your scores are better than mine."

"Easy for you to say."

Dee asked, "Did you hear about Lindbergh?"

"What did he do now?"

"He refused to take the oral because he didn't like the inspector he was scheduled with."

"Has he lost his ever loving mind?"

"Possibly."

Stark waved at Phil James when he saw him looking around the cafeteria. Phil walked over and said, "So far, so good. Everybody passed this morning. Dee, your oral is still at one o'clock, but you're now with a different inspector."

"Don't tell me they found a woman inspector to be politically correct."

"No, it's some new guy named Garrett. He was supposed to be with Lindbergh, but things got shuffled around. Don't worry about it—I'm sure you'll do fine."

"Phil, we're all getting together at my place tonight to debrief. We'd love to have you join us. Bring your wife too."

"Sorry Dee, we can't make it tonight, but I appreciate the invite."

Chapter Seventeen

By six o'clock the party was going strong and the mood was one of great relief. The burden had been lifted and the celebration was on. Cindy and MJ served as hostess and prepared the appetizers. Cam asked, "Where's Lindbergh?"

Dee answered, "His oral was scheduled at three o'clock so he should be done by now."

"Why did he ask for a different inspector?"

"Who knows? This is Lindbergh we're talking about. I ended up with the guy he was supposed to be with and he seemed nice enough to me. I was in there less than two hours and we talked about politics and social issues for at least an hour. Once we finished the limitations and initial action items, the guy seemed lost."

"You got lucky, Dee. My guy went through every system in detail and he didn't stop until he found something I didn't know. I think the man designed and built the airplane and he didn't just want facts and figures—he wanted to know what I would do if this happened or that happened. I was scrambling, believe me."

"To be honest, I feel a little cheated. This Garrett guy was a Santa Claus, and I don't think he knew much about the airplane."

At seven o'clock Stark was about to go back to the training center and look for Lindbergh when he finally walked in the door. The room fell silent and everybody stared at him until he spoke. "Why is everybody looking at me?"

Stark put his hands on his hips and glared, "What did you do, Lindbergh?"

"I took my oral and passed of course. Was there any doubt?"

Stark grabbed him in a bear hug.

Lindbergh said, "Get a grip, you Navy puke. Don't try to molest me just because I'm the best-looking man in the room."

"Why are you so late?"

"The guy was impressed and wanted me to explain things to fill in the gaps in his knowledge."

"You lie like a rug. You almost flunked, didn't you?"

"Of course not. I was magnificent."

"We'll see how magnificent you are next week. They paired us up as simulator partners, and you better not screw up."

"Worry about yourself, Stark, I'm gonna ace the check ride."

"You're just lucky to be paired up with a Navy pilot. Watch and learn my boy."

As usual, the eight pilots began the good-natured harassing of each other and insults and laughter filled the room. MJ and Cindy found themselves excluded and chatted together on the couch.

Cindy said, "You and Kyle make a great couple. Are you two thinking about a permanent relationship?"

"Kyle's not thinking about anything but his airplane."

"I know it seems that way, MJ, but I don't think that's true. I've been around pilots a long time, and sometimes it seems like they're full of themselves, but that's usually not the case. This bunch insults each other mercilessly, but it just drives them to outdo one another. They would go to war together and fight for each other. You have to remember that they see the world from the windshield of an airplane, and they have much broader horizons than we do. The more distant the horizon is, the more it makes them want to see what's beyond it. They don't always see what's right in front of them, but eventually they will."

"That's an interesting point of view, Cindy, and I appreciate it."

"Yeah well, look who's talking. My life's not exactly an endorsement for my opinions."

"Have you heard anything from your husband?"

"No, and I hope I never do. We're due in court for a divorce hearing on Monday, but nobody even knows where he is."

"Was he served with the notice of the hearing before he disappeared?"

"Yes, along with a restraining order and an eviction notice."

✈

MJ was waiting for Harry when he arrived on Monday morning. "I may have found a way to get Tommy Lane back on the radar."

"What are you thinking?"

"He's due in court this morning for the divorce proceedings. If he doesn't show up he will be in contempt, and we might be able to influence the judge to issue a warrant for his arrest. That would open a case against him even if Cindy doesn't file a missing person report."

"I think Ed plays golf with the prosecutor—let's have him call and clue him in. Maybe he can have a word with the judge. What time is the hearing scheduled?"

"Nine a.m."

✈

At eleven a.m. Ed briefed MJ and Harry. "MJ, your idea paid off. A warrant was issued and the local PD put Tommy Lane's name in the national data system. There's good news and there's bad news."

Harry said, "What's the good news?"

"The good news is he was arrested in San Diego, California four days after he disappeared from here. He was found in a boxcar of a freight train when it arrived at its destination. Here's the crazy thing—the boxcar was locked from the outside. He was battered and dehydrated when railroad security detained him for being a stowaway and turned him over to the San Diego cops."

"What's the bad news?"

"After about a week in custody, the railroad declined to press charges. Since there were no warrants for him, they let him go."

MJ thought out loud, "Why would he go to California, and why would he leave his wallet and cell phone here?"

Harry answered, "Maybe he wanted everyone to think he was dead."

Ed added, "Or someone loaded him up and shipped him out. Since the boxcar was locked from the outside, I tend to think the latter. If this were just about a suspected bomb threat, I'd say forget it, but the information on his laptop troubles me."

Harry said, "I'm almost sure he made the bomb threat. Cason checked the web history on his laptop and the cell phone. Lane tracked the flight as it returned to land and then again when it departed the second time for Miami."

Ed paced the room in his socks, "Do I want to know how Cason accomplished that?"

"Probably not."

"Okay, stay on this and see what turns up. Try to find out who he associates with and who would exile him to California."

MJ asked, "Do we have a contact for railroad security in San Diego?"

Ed answered, "No, but that might be a good place to start. I'll give you a number for someone I know in Homeland Security. They can probably tell you who to talk to."

When Cindy left the courtroom, her lawyer explained that there was very little they could do until and unless Tommy showed up. He also reminded her that his fee was due. After writing the check, her account was once again almost depleted. She had sold various household items to keep the cash flow going, but now her back was to the wall again. She was still mooching off Dee and had lost track of what she owed her. Her lawyer advised her that bankruptcy was an option she should consider. He explained that his fee for bankruptcy was very reasonable.

The thought of not paying her debts was repugnant so she drove the SUV to the local dealer and had it appraised. The price the dealer offered would pay off the remaining loan, and leave her with a few hundred dollars extra to help pay the next condo payment. She signed the papers and waited for the check to be processed. When her cell phone rang, it only reminded her that the phone bill was due also. She glanced at the screen and thought *this is not a good time, Stark.* She answered anyway.

"What do you want, Gary?"

"Would you promise not to hang up if I told you?"

"No."

"I want to take you to lunch."

"I thought you were in the simulator today."

"My report time is later this afternoon and I borrowed Lindbergh's car to do some errands. Let me pick you up for lunch."

She knew she should say no, but what came out was, "Can you pick me up at the Ford dealer?"

"Absolutely."

Thirty minutes later, with the check in her purse, she found Stark patiently waiting. He opened the door for her and asked what she would like for lunch.

"Where do rich airline pilots have lunch?"

"Taco Bell, but we can go anywhere you like."

"It's too nice to be inside. Let's do the drive through and have a picnic in the park."

"My thoughts exactly—we are so compatible."

"You're full of it, Gary."

"Be nice. Are you having your car serviced?"

"Not exactly. Let's eat—I need to be back to the office at one."

The park was practically deserted and they chose a picnic table in a shady spot. Sitting across from each other, with tacos and soft drinks between, Gary asked, "Is your divorce final now?"

"My divorce hasn't even started."

"Why not?"

"You have taco sauce on your shirt."

"Sorry...I'm a slob."

"I can see that. Please try not to drip food on your uniform shirt when you eat in the cockpit."

"Flight attendants serve food in the cockpit?"

"Only if the pilots are nice. You should probably bring a lunch from home."

"You're mean, but I still like you. Are you going to let me take you out when the divorce is done?"

"I don't go out with slobs."

"I'm serious, Cindy. I think you're beautiful and you're smart and fun to be with. I want to be friends and I want to take you out."

"We are friends, Gary. I wouldn't be having lunch with you otherwise, but you know my life is a complete disaster right now. If I were a normal person, I would go out with you, but I'm not. You shouldn't be thinking about dating anyway. You need to concentrate on training."

"I'll be finished with training next week."

"And you'll have lots of people to date too. You should ask Dee out."

"No way!"

"Why not?"

"I think Dee's great, but I wouldn't date a pilot."

"Why not?"

"Because they have a reputation of being self-centered egotistical jerks."

"You know...I think you're right...I'll have to remember that and take your advice."

"Of course, there are exceptions."

"You're right again...some of them are exceptionally egotistical."

They both laughed and he asked, "When can I take you out?"

"You're displaying a total lack of judgment, Gary. I'm an emotional wreck and a financial disaster. I wouldn't wish me on my worst enemy."

"You're being ridiculous. You just need a fresh start."

"Take me to work, and go study for your simulator session."

"Can I call you tonight?"

"Only if you promise not to talk about airplanes and simulators."

MJ didn't recognize the caller ID when she answered her desk phone. A male voice said, "Ms. Jones, Homeland Security tells me you need information on a stowaway."

"Yes, thank you. We're interested in this guy for an unrelated matter. Can you give me some details?"

"Not much to tell. The yard workers found him when they unloaded a box car here in San Diego. We detained him and then gave him to the cops. Pretty routine."

"Does that happen often?"

"It's not unusual. It's just a way to get free transportation. As a matter of fact, we apprehended another stowaway that same night in an adjacent car. They didn't seem to know each other even though they both boarded in Atlanta."

"How do you know where they boarded?"

"Because they were both in freight cars with dedicated, high-value loads from Lockheed Aircraft in Atlanta. The boxcars were loaded in Atlanta and then locked and sealed. They were not unlocked until they reached San Diego. They probably didn't realize the cars were going to be locked for four days because neither of them brought food or water. They were in pretty bad shape when we found them."

"That's quite a coincidence."

"Yeah, I thought so too, but we just turn them over to the cops and the lawyers. They're normally pretty harmless and it usually costs more to prosecute them than it's worth."

"What can you tell me about the second guy?"

"Older guy, probably in his fifties. Claimed he'd been kidnaped and locked in the freight car."

"Do you think that's what happened?"

"Who knows? These bums come up with all kinds of sob stories. Sorry, I don't know more to tell you. I can send you the incident reports if you like."

"Yeah, let me give you an email address."

A few minutes later the email arrived and MJ discussed them with Harry and Cason.

Harry asked, "Who is James McElroy?"

"Another stowaway on the same freight train." The name had been stuck in her mind since reading the report. *Why does that name sound familiar?*

Cason asked, "Does he have a record?"

"Yeah, neither of them had ID on them, but when they ran their fingerprints, they came up in the system. Lane had an assault charge and McElroy was busted for drugs a couple of times. Nothing to brag about."

Harry rubbed his chin, "I don't see how this helps us much, but stay on it and let us know if we can help."

MJ went back to her desk and read the reports again. *James McElroy...where have I heard that name?*

Chapter Eighteen

Tommy Lane stepped off the Greyhound bus in downtown Atlanta. He didn't have any baggage. It had been a nightmare of paperwork trying to get his bank to transfer funds to him in San Diego since he had no driver's license or other form of ID. He couldn't fly without ID and four days on the bus had not improved his disposition. He was convinced that somehow Cindy had orchestrated his train ride and he planned to deal with her once and for all. *You might just take some of your pilot friends with you, darling.* He took a taxi to the Econostay Lodge and found a single night clerk at the front desk.

"My name is Tommy Lane and I left some personal items here a couple of weeks ago. I want them back."

The young man put his paperback novel down and said, "Let me check, Mr. Lane."

He disappeared into a back room and left Tommy drumming his fingers on the counter. The clerk quickly located the box with Tommy's name on it and then took his cell phone out of his pocket. "Hey, the guy you asked about is here to pick up his stuff."

"Lane?"

"Yes."

"Stall him. I'll have somebody there in a few minutes."

The clerk walked back to the front desk. "I found some things that might be yours, Mr. Lane. Can I see some ID, please?"

Tommy exploded, "You little idiot, my ID is with my things. Get it right now or I'm gonna start taking you apart. Look in the wallet and you'll see the driver's license with my picture on it. If anything is missing I'm gonna take you apart anyway. Show me where my things are."

No further encouragement was necessary, and Tommy followed the clerk into the storage room. He ripped the box open and found his wallet and credit cards along with the cell phone and laptop. Another box contained the clothes he'd left.

The clerk no longer had thoughts of stalling Tommy. He just wanted him gone, but that wasn't going to happen. Tommy said, "I want a room for the week."

"Yes sir, Mr. Lane. Let me get you a registration form."

Tommy scrawled his name and gave the clerk a credit card. "Where can I get something to eat?"

"There's not much available this time of night, but I can order you a pizza if you like."

"Make it quick, I want to go to bed."

Tommy took his boxes and left. The night clerk breathed a sigh of relief and picked up his paperback. He had only read a couple of pages when two men approached the counter. "Where's he at?"

"Room 212. He's expecting a pizza."

One of the guys dropped fifty bucks on the counter, "Have a nice evening."

MJ received the good news at mid-morning the next day when the local detective called. "MJ, the long lost Mr. Lane has returned."

"Wonderful, have you arranged accommodations for him?"

"Not yet. He checked back into the Econostay last night, but he's out and about this morning. The maid gave us a heads up and she's going to let us know when he comes back to the room. He'll be dealing with the judge by the end of the day, and I assume he'll have a few days in the cooler to get his mind right about court appearances."

"Outstanding, Ed may want to let him explain the contents of his hard drive to the FBI and the ATF. I appreciate the help."

"No need to thank me. On the other hand, if you come across more of those Tri Con meal vouchers, let me know."

"I'm sure we can find some of those. Will you call me when you have him in custody?"

"Count on it."

Tommy Lane's morning wasn't going well. The now familiar roar and rattle of the freight train was something he had hoped to never experience again. He tried to make himself comfortable between two large wooden crates, but his butt was already bruised from bouncing on the hard floor. The smell of creosote from the wooden railroad ties made him want to puke. He was starving and would kill for a glass of water, but he had been here before and knew he would survive. The only comfort he found was in his hate for Cindy and her pilot friends, as well as Tri Con in general. *If you think you can run me out of town and get rid of me, I'm happy to let you believe that, but I know how to play the game now. Next time you won't see me coming.*

He bounced again and stood to rub his backside. Leaning on one of the crates to maintain his balance, he could see a shipping label. In the dim light from a crack in the door, he squinted to read the destination. Bangor, Maine.

Cindy stood in front of the mirror and put the final touches on her morning makeup. She contemplated how she had come to love hating Tommy and the joy of not seeing him for weeks. *I may be*

broke and I may soon be homeless, but the satisfaction of openly hating you is almost worth it.

Dee had convinced her to continue staying with her while she sold the furniture and appliances in her Condo. Hopefully, the Condo itself would sell soon and relieve her financial burden. She was determined to avoid bankruptcy if at all possible, but that eventuality was rapidly approaching. She planned to quietly leave without waking Dee, but the smell of coffee made that unnecessary. She found her friend at the kitchen table with her nose in a training manual.

"Dee, you should be sleeping in…you need your rest."

"I tried, but if I don't get my V1 cuts under control, I'll be looking for a job. I'm having nightmares."

"What's a V1 cut?"

"It's when an engine fails on the runway after you're already committed to takeoff"

"If you're still on the ground, why don't you just stop?"

"Not enough runway to stop. You have to continue the takeoff on one engine."

"Did you crash the simulator?"

"No, so far I've got it off the ground every time, but that's not good enough. You have to maintain the runway heading, keep a steady climb rate, run the emergency checklist, and talk to the tower also."

"Don't worry—they won't fire you until you pay off the pilot uniforms and other supplies they're deducting from your paycheck."

"Wow—that makes me feel better. You're in a good mood this morning, are you and Molly still getting along?"

"Molly's great to work for and she wants me to stay in the office, but I told her I'd like to go back to the line for a few weeks until I decide. I'm back on flying status next week. Despite all my problems, I haven't actually been this happy in a long time."

Cindy's cell phone rang and she began digging in her purse to find it. "If that's Stark I'm going to change my number."

Dee laughed and went back to her manual as Cindy answered the call, but when she looked up a minute later, Cindy was pale and had a look of horror on her face. When she ended the call, she sat down at the table and knew that happiness was an illusion and an emotion she would not enjoy again in the foreseeable future.

Kyle Bennett sat in the right seat of the simulator and marveled at how realistic it was. In position for takeoff, the 10,000 foot runway appeared in bright sunshine and he could see the Tri Con hangar at the end, almost two miles away. After the first couple of days, he no longer thought of it as a simulation. His mindset was that he was flying an airplane and he operated as such. It had taken both he and Cam some time to get used to the speed at which things happened and the exactness that the instructor required, but they were more comfortable with each passing hour. Cam sat in the left seat and acted as captain for Kyle's training session. At the end of two hours, they would swap seats and roles.

From behind them, the instructor asked, "Are you two ready?"

They both gave a thumbs up and the instructor continued, "Okay, Tri Con 123 maintain runway heading, climb and maintain one zero thousand, cleared for takeoff.

Cam triggered his radio mic and repeated the clearance. Turning to Kyle, he said, "The checklist is complete and you're cleared to go."

Kyle pressed the top of the rudder pedals to release the parking brake and advanced the throttles a few inches. The airplane began to roll and when he saw both engines spool up evenly, he pushed the throttles up more and said, "Auto throttles."

Cam pushed the auto throttle button and checked to see that the system set takeoff power on both engines. "Power's set...eighty knots, looking good."

Kyle focused on keeping the nose wheel locked on the centerline of the runway as the speed increased. At 120 knots, Cam announced, "V1."

Suddenly, the nose of the airplane swerved left and Kyle pushed the right rudder pedal almost to the floor to keep the airplane in the center of the runway.

Cam said, "Left engine fail."

Kyle continued to focus out the windshield and work the rudder, "Roger."

Cam watched the airspeed and announced, "Rotate."

Kyle gently lifted the nose of the airplane and Cam said, "V2."

Coaxing the airplane off the ground, Kyle trimmed the rudder and said, "Positive rate, gear up."

Cam moved the gear handle up and as the wheels retracted, the instructor's voice came through the radio, "Tri Con 123, contact departure."

Kyle said, "Declare an emergency and tell him we lost an engine."

"Tower, Tri Con 123, has an engine failure and we're declaring an emergency."

"Roger, Tri Con 123, what's your intentions?"

"We'd like to return to land."

"Roger that, contact departure and they'll vector you back for landing."

Cam switched frequencies, "Departure, Tri Con 123, climbing to ten with an emergency."

"Tri Con 123, maintain runway heading and let me know when you're ready to turn, you can level at three if able."

"Climbing to three thousand, we'll let you know."

Kyle concentrated on maintaining heading and climbing, "Flaps up, and after takeoff checklist, then read the engine failure emergency checklist."

Cam busied himself with reading and accomplishing the checklist items. The engine failure also resulted in losing a generator, a hydraulic pump, and a pneumatic source. After completing the checklist and cleaning up the system problems, they requested a turn back to the airport. Cam continued working the radio, talking to ATC, notifying the company dispatcher of the problem, and notifying the flight attendants. The instructor changed his voice to a high falsetto to portray the flight attendant. Lastly, Cam made a PA announcement to the passengers, informing them of the situation.

At that point, the instructor announced, "Okay, I'm freezing the simulator. You can both relax. Nice job guys. Kyle, you handled everything well, but you're working really hard. Don't forget you've got an autopilot available. Remember the briefing—if I don't want you to use the autopilot, I'll fail it."

Cam said, "I like your flight attendant voice."

"Thanks, a little humor relieves the boredom. Keep your hands away from the controls and I'll reset us at the end of the runway for takeoff again. I'm going to set you up for a check ride scenario. This time we'll do a night takeoff with visibility of 300 feet in fog and icing conditions. Your only outside visual cues will be centerline lights and a couple of runway edge lights. Keep that nose nailed to the centerline when the engine fails, and when you clean up the systems, make sure you open the pneumatic cross feed valves to deice both wings. Plan on taking this one all the way to landing."

Kyle thought *300 feet visibility at over 100 knots? That's not much more than the length of the airplane.* He looked at Cam and said, "Well, okay then."

Chapter Nineteen

Harold Collins sat at his desk wrestling with the problem of how to improve customer service. The competing airlines flew the same aircraft and similar schedules, so his employees were the only real difference. Hiring new employees with a passion for customer service was a real challenge. He had recently walked through the terminal unannounced and was not entirely happy with his observations. His thoughts were interrupted when his secretary stuck her head in the door.

"The Vice President of Public Relations is on line three. Are you here?"

"Yeah, I'll take it."

He pushed the button and said, "Is the golf course closed today?"

"Actually I'm playing with some of our TV advertisers this afternoon. You want to play?"

"No thank you but have a good time."

"I will...the reason I called is to see if you have time for a little public relations duty."

"Will I have to take a turn in the dunking tank?"

"No, nothing like that. Evidently one of Tri Con's long time advocates in the business community has had the audacity to die and we probably should be represented at the service. Could you make time to appear on our behalf?"

"When?"

"Saturday morning at eleven."

"Who is the deceased?"

"A gentleman named Alexander Morgan."

"Never heard of him."

"Me either, he was ninety-four years old and evidently hasn't been active in a long time, but I understand he was well respected and an advocate for Tri Con in his day. It might behoove us to pay our respects."

"Okay, I can move some things around and take a couple hours to attend."

"You're a good man. I'll have the details sent over to you."

A short while later the secretary delivered the memo and directions to a church in a small town south of the airport. Collins instructed her to keep his schedule open from ten until two in the afternoon on Saturday.

On Saturday morning, Collins dressed appropriately for the somber event and drove himself through the rural countryside to attend the service. Funerals were always awkward for him. He found it difficult to express himself in a way that he thought would be meaningful to a grieving family, especially if he didn't know the person well. He arrived in the small community a few minutes before eleven and found the Baptist Church on the outskirts of town. The red brick structure was not especially large, but the white steeple and the stained glass windows made it an impressive house of worship. He could see what he assumed was a fellowship hall attached and beyond that the church cemetery with an awning erected at an open gravesite. The parking lot was full, but he was directed to an open field beyond the church where he drove across the grass and parked between an old pickup truck and a Lincoln limousine.

As he walked back to the church, he encountered men and women in business suits like himself, but just as many in work clothes or overalls. Many of them carried covered dishes to the fellowship hall. Mr. Morgan must have been a man of diverse acquaintance. When Collins entered the vestibule, he was given a program and directed to one of the few remaining seats on the back row. The people in the church were indeed a diverse group, come to pay their respects, but he could see that there was only one row of seats reserved at the front for family. He had barely sat down when the organist began to play and everyone stood once again. A moment later the family was escorted in.

The usher led two women down the aisle. The older lady appeared to be in her fifties and did not look familiar, but he immediately recognized the younger woman with her. Cindy Lane wept openly as she held her mother's hand.

When the two of them were seated, the usher looked back and signaled to someone at the rear of the church. Collins was surprised to see eight Tri Con pilots in uniform march down the aisle in step and take seats just behind the two ladies. He unconsciously inspected the uniforms and found them neat and properly worn. In fact, they looked brand new. Then he recognized Kyle Bennett and Lindbergh Walker and began to understand. *Why is my new hire pilot class attending a funeral?*

Opening the program the usher had given him, he read about Mr. Alexander Morgan. The gentleman was predeceased by his wife and survived by his only daughter, Mrs. Miriam Morgan Latimer, and his only grandchild, Mrs. Cynthia Latimer Lane. After a number of musical selections, the preacher chronicled Mr. Morgan's life. He had been a veteran, a farmer, a businessman, and a lifelong Christian. He related stories that made people laugh and stories that brought tears, but it was obvious that Mr. Morgan was loved by everyone who knew him. The service concluded with a beautiful solo and then the announcement that interment would be in the church cemetery and everyone was invited to the fellowship hall afterward.

He was surprised once again when the eight pilots stood to serve as pallbearers. The two ladies followed them as they escorted the casket through the aisle and then the church was emptied from the front pews first. He saw the tall redhead stand up in the third row and also recognized Madison Jones as she and Molly walked toward him.

Molly waved as they passed and when he walked out she was waiting for him.

"Mr. Collins, you caught me taking unauthorized time off."

"Miss Jackson, I'm sure you and I both have more comp time on the books than either of us will live long enough to take."

"That's quite possible. Did you know Mr. Morgan?"

"No, I'm only here to represent the company. Did you know him?"

"Only that he was Cindy's grandfather. As you know she's been working in the office for me and we've become quite close. I wanted to be here to support her."

"I see, did you arrange for the pilots to be on the agenda."

"No, that was Cindy's request. Dee Daniels is a former flight attendant and one of the pilots. She's Cindy's best friend."

"Please tell me that Senator Walker is not somehow involved."

She smiled, "I hope not, but I'm glad he intervened on Cindy's behalf. She's actually quite special and I would hate to lose her as an employee."

They continued to chat as they walked to the cemetery and stood together for the graveside service. The preacher spoke once again, quoting several scriptures and elaborating on how he felt they applied to Mr. Morgan's life. There was a final hymn that everyone joined to sing and then a closing prayer. The preacher walked to the family and shook their hand and offered words of comfort before leading them back to the fellowship hall.

Collins was conflicted about whether he should go to the hall. It might be intrusive if he did or it might be rude if he didn't. Molly seemed to read his thoughts, "Cindy will be so glad you came, Mr. Collins, she will want to thank you I'm sure."

He and Molly joined the long line of people and when they entered the hall, the family was at the door and greeting everyone individually. Molly received a hug from each of them and he received a handshake. Mrs. Latimer said, "It means a lot to us that you would take the time to come Mr. Collins. The flowers from Tri Con are beautiful. Thank you so much."

He felt welcome and was now glad he had come. Cindy thanked him also and Mrs. Latimer said, "Mr. Collins, I know you must have a busy schedule, but I hope you can join us for lunch. We would love to have you and the church ladies will talk bad about anyone who doesn't eat their food."

"Well, I certainly don't want to add anyone to the long list of people who talk bad about me. Are you sure I won't be intruding?"

"Of course not, and I only hear good things about you. In fact, I would very much appreciate the opportunity to talk to you in private after lunch if you have time."

"In that case, I happily accept your kind invitation, Mrs. Latimer, and I'll try to restrain my enthusiasm for good food to a socially acceptable level."

He and Molly joined the family in the line at the buffet and then moved to one of the long tables. He was seated between Molly and a gentleman in bib overalls who introduced himself as Billy Ray and said he was glad to meet him. As he looked around the room, he recognized several members of various boards of directors and also many corporate officers of Atlanta companies. All things being equal, he preferred lunching with Billy Ray, who explained that the *Farmer's Almanac* forecast an early planting season and good spring crops.

The food was excellent and everyone except the pilots seemed to relax and enjoy the fellowship. Collins didn't think it was the food that they were having a problem digesting, but rather the fact that they were lunching with the CEO of Tri Con. It didn't diminish Billy Ray's appetite at all. He insisted that Mr. Collins try his wife's home made cake and when it met with his approval a bag suddenly appeared with a large foil-wrapped slice inside to take with him for later. It occurred to him that this was exactly the type of caring human relationship that he dreamed of for his employees and customers. He would like to hire everyone in the room, with the exception of those who had arrived in limos, and appoint Billy Ray as head of customer relations. No corporate advertising budget could ever be large enough to create the basic warm respect that the people here felt for each other. He noted that Molly fit right in and had excused herself to help the ladies with cleaning chores.

At last everyone was sufficiently stuffed and he followed Mrs. Latimer to one of the large plastic cans to dispose of their paper plates and plastic utensils. "Mr. Collins, I don't want to impose on your time but I would like to briefly discuss some things in private."

Collins had assumed earlier that this must have something to do with Cindy's arrest and said, "I'm at your disposal ma'am."

"Thank you, I won't take long."

They walked down a corridor and entered one of the children's Sunday school rooms. Mrs. Latimer offered him a seat under a picture of *Mary and Child* and said, "I have some concerns about Cindy and how her grandfather's death may affect her at Tri Con."

"I understand Mrs. Latimer and don't worry—Cindy can take as much time off as is necessary to recover from her loss."

"Actually, Miss Jackson has already told her that and we appreciate it, but that's not what concerns me."

"In that case, how can I be of help?"

"There are some things that Cindy doesn't know about her grandfather and I wasn't fully aware of myself until recently. I would appreciate it if our conversation could be kept confidential until I have time to explain it to her."

"Of course, you have my word."

"Thank you. My Dad became infatuated with aviation in general and Tri Con in particular at a very early age. It was not his area of expertise, but he could see from early on the great potential for airlines. He became friends with some of Tri Con's founders, long before the mergers and explosive growth of the sixties and seventies.

He invested in the airline when it needed financing the most, back in the forties. He had many other business interest as you can tell from some of the people attending the funeral today. But Tri Con was always the thing that excited him the most, and he continued to invest until about ten years ago when he felt the company lost its identity and began to look like many other mediocre corporations. However, he did not divest his holdings and maintained his position, hoping for a change in direction by Tri Con management.

"I was not aware of any of this until he confided in me recently, when his health began to deteriorate, and I have not burdened Cindy with the details. Before he passed, he formed what is known as the Morgan Family Trust, and all his holdings now exist in that entity with Cindy and myself as Trustees.

"Cindy loves her work at Tri Con and her grandfather was so happy that she was enjoying a position that allowed her to interact with and serve other people. He could charm a snake and I think that talent has rubbed off on Cindy. The conflict that concerns me is that Cindy is just a basic employee but she now owns a block of Tri Con stock. I'm not sure how that affects her relationship with other employees and management."

"I appreciate your concern Mrs. Latimer, but I don't think it's a factor at all. Tri Con maintains an employee stock purchase plan as well as a company stock option in our 401K plan and in fact most of our employees are shareholders."

"Well, I think you've answered one of my questions. I wondered if you were here today because you knew of Mr. Morgan's holdings in the company and obviously you didn't. That makes me appreciate your presence even more."

"To be honest, I didn't know that Cindy was related, but I was informed that Mr. Morgan was a long time supporter and thought Tri Con should pay our respects."

"That in itself separates you from the other businessmen who are here. They're here on business—believe me. Before we go on Mr. Collins, I should tell you that the Morgan Family Trust controls over a hundred million dollars in assets and a considerable portion of that is in shares of Tri Con Airlines stock. I'm sorry if I misled you earlier."

Collins looked up at the picture of Mary and Jesus and then broke out laughing, "I'm sorry, I wasn't aware of that. You must think I'm a total idiot, and you're probably right. As for your concerns about Cindy, I assure you she can continue her career and advance only as her merit allows. Although I should warn you that Molly Jackson thinks she's special and is grooming her for a management position. Her secret is safe with me—however; if she decides to fire me I'll go quietly."

Latimer laughed too, "I hope you don't think I intentionally set you up. I'm glad you didn't know. Now that you do, I would like to meet with you sometime soon and discuss some of my father's concerns about Tri Con's future."

"I don't think this is the place to discuss business Mrs. Latimer, but I'll be happy to make time for you at your convenience."

"Thank you, and please call me Miriam."

"Thank you, Miriam, and please call me Harold."

"There's one other thing, Harold. I was in shock when my father disclosed his holdings to me, and I'm still trying to process it. I haven't told Cindy any of this and I don't want her to have to deal with it while she's grieving. If it could be our secret for now, I'd sincerely appreciate it."

"As I said, Miriam, the secret is safe with me and I look forward to meeting with you when you feel it's appropriate. Once again, you have my sincere condolence for your father's passing. I only wish I could have known him."

She dabbed her eyes and said, "Thank you."

Collins walked out to his car with a bag of cake in his hand and a song in his heart. He was of the profound belief that it might be possible to have your cake and eat it too.

Chapter Twenty

The tears would not stop for Cindy. Molly tried to console her, "Cindy, you should take at least a week off and spend some time with your mother. She's going to need your help and support."

"I know, and I appreciate it. She's the only family I have left."

"My mom is the only family I have too. Take care of each other. Tri Con will survive without you for now."

"I was useless enough before, and now I feel totally lame."

"You're not useless, and you'll come back stronger than ever. Call me and let me know what you need."

Cindy awoke on Monday morning to the smell of frying bacon. The bed she had slept in as a teenager seemed much smaller now, but the aroma of her mom's cooking brought back memories. She couldn't control the tears. *If I could only go back and start over*

again, I'd do things so much differently. My granddad deserved so much more from me.

She padded barefoot to the kitchen and gave her mom an extended hug. "Are you going to fatten me up while I'm here?"

"You're going to need your strength. We have to write thank you notes and get them in the mail."

"That could take all day. I've never seen so many cards and flowers."

"Get the toast out of the oven."

"Who were all those people at the funeral? I didn't know half of them."

"Me either. I guess we'll find out when we write the thank you notes."

At mid-morning, they were still opening sympathy cards and responding. Cindy opened a pink envelope with her name on it and found an unsigned card with the words, "Thinking of you as always." A hundred dollar bill fluttered to the floor when she pulled the card out. She recognized the almost unreadable scrawl. *Stark, you idiot! You don't have money to waste.*

She remembered the pilots were taking their simulator check rides today. *I should have called to wish him luck.*

Cindy's mom continued to stuff envelopes and said, "I'm going to need your help settling your grandfather's affairs. There are some things we need to discuss."

"Mom, I'm just not ready for that yet. I can't bear the thought of going through his personal belongings and deciding what to do with them. It breaks my heart to think of selling his things to pay off debts."

"I don't think that will be necessary."

"There are some things I'd like to have as keepsakes if possible, but I don't feel up to making decisions right now. Can it wait?"

"I suppose it can, but there will be a lot to deal with and I need you to be clear headed when we do."

"I won't let you down, mom, but I need some time."

Kyle Bennett set his brain bag down in the briefing room and plopped down in the chair. His shirt had perspiration rings in the armpits and his knees were a little shaky. A minute later, the FAA inspector followed him into the room. "Congratulations, Mr. Bennett, I thought you did very well. I made some notes during the ride and I want to debrief a few minor things, but I'm happy to sign you off."

Kyle exhaled and slumped lower in the chair. "Thank you. I think I could have done better on the first missed approach."

"That's one of my notes. I think you just got in a bit of a hurry. You have to react quickly, but just be methodical. A missed approach is not an emergency. In fact, it's a normal procedure unless wind shear is involved. The three important actions are power, flaps, gear, but there's no panic. Think of it more as power…flaps…gear. Take a couple of breaths between each item and be smooth. I'm sure your instructor mentioned 'approach climb performance' and the fact that the airplane will climb with full flaps and gear down. Your missed approach was safe enough, but I just wanted to remind you what the airplane is capable of."

"I appreciate that."

"Just a couple more things and we'll get out of here—they're probably going to need this briefing room."

Ten minutes later, Kyle walked out and realized for the first time in weeks, he could relax. He stood at the second-floor railing and looked down at the row of simulators below. Two of them were closed up and in motion with red flashing lights warning people to stay away. Long hydraulic pistons extended and retracted to move the cockpits up and down and left and right as thick electrical cables swayed beneath the machine. He wondered what maneuver was being performed.

Stark came out of one of the briefing rooms behind him. With a grin on his face, he asked, "Are you done?"

"I am."

"Are you awesome?"

"From the grin on your face I'd say we both are."

"Thank God that's over with. I think a celebration is in order."

Down below, one of the simulators pitched forward abruptly and then leveled out.

Kyle asked, "Who's in there?"

"Lindbergh...looks like he's doing his stall series. Dee's in the other box. Everybody else is finished."

"I can't wait to fly a real airplane. Phil James says it's easier than the simulator."

"I just hope it doesn't have as many emergencies as the simulator."

Kyle laughed, "I promised MJ I'd take her to lunch if I finished in time—you want to go with us?"

"I think I'll hang around to give Lindbergh and Dee a hard time. Tell MJ to call me if she gets tired of hanging out with you."

Kyle chuckled, "No chance, buddy. You'll have to find your own girls."

With that thought in mind, Stark dug his cell phone out of his bag as Kyle walked away. His call was answered on the third ring with a soft, "Hello."

"Hello yourself, beautiful lady. Can I take you out tonight?"

"You must be calling for Cindy. She just stepped out of the room for a minute."

"Oh...I'm sorry, Mrs. Latimer. You sound just like your daughter."

"Yes, but you don't sound like her husband."

"No ma'am, I'm just a friend."

"Indeed…here comes Cindy. Hold on."

He could hear muffled voices and then, "Stark, have you lost your mind? Did you just ask my mother out…Really?"

"I'm…she sounds…I mean…"

"Just shut up. Did you pass your check ride?"

"I…uh…yes."

"I guess miracles still happen. Now that you're an airline pilot, maybe you can date women closer to your age."

"Cindy, I…"

"I can't talk right now, Stark. I think my mother almost fainted, and I have to try to explain her only daughter's scandalous behavior. Call me tomorrow."

MJ looked up from her desk and saw Kyle standing in the office door with his brain bag in his hand. "You look like a pony that's been rode hard and put away wet. Is it over?"

"It's all over…I've been deemed airworthy."

She walked over and hugged him. "I'm so proud of you. I told you it wouldn't be a problem. Does this mean I get to see you in that cool uniform again?"

"I start my IOE on Thursday."

"What's an IOE?"

"Initial Operating Experience. I get to fly my first trip with a line check captain to see if I know what I'm doing."

"I want a picture of you in your uniform."

"I think my appetite is back. Can I take you to lunch?"

"Does ten pounds of flour make a big biscuit? Let's go."

Walking through the employee parking lot, she said, "Let's go to the sub shop for sandwiches, and don't even think about putting me in that ragged truck."

"You can drive us in your car—I'll sit in the back seat like a celebrity."

"No, you drive and I'll sit in the front seat like your girlfriend."

They chose a table at the restaurant and Kyle attacked the sandwich with abandon. MJ asked, "Has anybody heard from Cindy?"

"I don't know. I think the funeral hit her pretty hard."

"It was a really nice service, and I like their church. We should go there again."

"Would you like to get married there?"

She unconsciously squeezed her sandwich and mayonnaise dripped on the table. "I...uh...Look, I know it's been a big day for you...passing your check ride, and me letting you drive my car, but don't get carried away."

"If you say so, but it is a very nice church. If we were married, would you let me drive your car again?"

"I want a chocolate chip cookie to take back to the office."

"Call in sick and take the afternoon off."

"You need to get a grip, First Officer Bennett."

"You need to lighten your grip. You're squeezing the innards out of your sandwich."

"Did you see how many people were at the funeral?"

"I know. Everybody from the CEO of the airline to Cindy's cell mate at the city lockup."

"Who are you talking about?"

"You didn't meet Cindy's cell mate?"

"No, did you?"

"She was the heavyset woman sitting right behind you and Molly. Cindy introduced her to me after the service and she seemed nice enough for an inmate. Her name is Kitty something or other. One of those Mac names...McDonald...McSmith...McJones..."

MJ stopped chewing and swallowed. "McElroy."

"What?"

She took out her cell phone and scrolled through emails. She opened an attachment and said, "There it is. Her name is on the records the detective sent me about Cindy's release. Catherine McElroy." Pushing her chair back, "I knew I had seen that name somewhere. I need to get back to the office."

"What about the wedding?"

"Not necessary, I'll let you drive."

She was on the phone, dialling the local detective, as soon as they were in the car.

"What do you know about Catherine McElroy?"

"You mean Kitty Mac? She's a local character who runs a brewery."

"She works for a brewery?"

"Not exactly, she is the brewery. She runs a neighborhood bar and lounge and makes her own illegal beer and whiskey."

"I thought she was in jail for assaulting her husband."

"She was. We don't hassle her about the brew as long as nobody complains. It's good stuff and the price is right. She doesn't tolerate trouble in her bar, and the judge has instructed us not to interfere with the citizens rights to peaceful assembly. Her husband, James, is another story. We bust him on a regular basis for dealing drugs. Don't tell me one of them has applied for a job at Tri Con."

She laughed, "No, nothing like that. I'm just grasping at straws on the Lane thing. I'll let you know if I find anything."

"Yeah, you do that. I don't want to get blindsided by anything you and Harry stir up."

"Never happen—we're in cahoots pardner."

"We better be if it involves the local culture."

"Talk to you soon."

She punched the phone off and turned to Kyle, "You didn't hear any of that."

"You're not going to bust Cindy's friend are you?"

"No, but I'm going to bust her scumbag husband if I can. You didn't hear that either."

"Is it true that husbands and wives can't be forced to testify against each other?"

"Can you even spell matrimony?"

"Sure, h-i-t-c-h-e-d."

"That's what I thought. I pronounce you and your airplane hitched. Get me back to the office."

"Does that mean we can talk about it later?"

"Maybe."

MJ looked up Kitty's release records again and found an address and phone number. When the call was answered, she said, "Ms. McElroy, my name is Madison Jones with Tri Con Airlines..."

"I'm on the no-call list. Don't be calling trying to sell me nothing."

"No, wait—I'm a friend of Cindy Lane."

"You know Miss Cindy? She in trouble?"

"No, but I'm trying to help her with a problem."

"You a poleese woman?"

"No, I'm not...just a friend."

"What 'bout Miss Cindy?"

"She's trying to divorce her sorry husband, but he's disappeared and won't come to court. The judge issued a warrant to arrest him, but he's run off. We're trying to locate him and get him into court so the judge can slap him around and grant the divorce. He showed up in town a few days ago but then he took off again before the cops could arrest him. I understand you had a similar problem and your husband disappeared too."

"What's yo name?"

"Madison Jones."

"You who they call MJ?"

"Yes ma'am."

"Miss Cindy tole me 'bout you. Give me yo phone number."

When she had the number, the line went dead.

MJ stared at the phone, *that wasn't much help. Why would anybody get married and go through this kind of crap...on the other hand...would I marry Kyle if he were serious...was he serious?*

For the next twenty minutes, MJ's thoughts bounced between Kyle, moonshine whiskey, remote controlled airplanes and Kitty McElroy...mostly Kyle. When the cell phone buzzed, she looked at the caller ID. *Cindy.*

"MJ, did you talk to Kitty."

"I hope you don't mind, Cindy. I didn't want to disturb you with what you have on your plate right now."

"It's okay...what did she tell you?"

"Nothing, she's protecting you."

"She seems to enjoy doing that, even though I keep telling her she doesn't owe me."

"Well, she would probably still be in jail if you hadn't sprung her."

"I don't know about that, but she just called and told me a wild tale that's hard to believe. I don't know what to do about it."

"Can I help?"

"You have to promise me that you won't do anything to get Kitty in trouble."

"My only interest is preventing Tommy Lane from doing anything to harm you or Tri Con. I can't prove it yet, but I'm convinced he called in the bomb threat on your flight and I suspect he has plans to do more. I think Kitty knows where he might be."

"She does, but you have to believe me when I tell you I knew nothing about this."

"What can you tell me?"

"It's a long story, and I'm still not sure I believe it."

"I've got all day, take your time."

Chapter Twenty One

Harry laughed, "She actually had him shipped to San Diego, along with her own husband?"

MJ wasn't amused, "Evidently her bouncers at the lounge are fiercely loyal and do whatever she asks."

Harry couldn't control his mirth and continued to laugh, "I'm sorry, MJ, but I think it's hilarious. She could have at least given him a bottle of the moonshine to make the trip easier. Cason's going to love this story."

"Obviously they knew if he came back he would go to the hotel to retrieve his things and they shipped him out again."

"I love it."

"I'm glad you're entertained, but we need to get him back."

"What do you have in mind?"

"I don't want to involve Kitty if we don't have to, and I don't want to steal the local cop's thunder. I'd like to keep him as a resource for future use if possible."

"I assume you have some sort of devious plan to accomplish that."

"I've got an idea that might work."

"What's the worst thing that could happen? Go with it."

The pilot class graduation party went on late into the night and MJ laughed at the grown-ups acting like children. None of the pilots were married and Dee invited several flight attendant friends to join the fun. Predictably, the pilots recounted every moment of their simulator check ride and were miffed that the ladies were not impressed. They were full of confidence and convinced that they had effectively conquered the airline business. The flight attendants smiled in amusement and ate the free food.

MJ made a graceful exit at midnight and arrived at the office the next morning envying the flight crews who had the day off. At ten a.m. Harry walked into her office and sat down. "Tommy Lane is in custody in Bangor, Maine."

"Imagine that!"

"The prosecutor called Ed a few minutes ago to inform him."

"Will they send him back here to face the judge?"

"Yeah, the railroad doesn't want to fool with him. Our detective friend is going to Bangor tomorrow to pick him up."

"Will he fly Tri Con?"

"Of course…round trip."

"We're selling tickets and making money."

"I'll put you in for a bonus. How did you do it?"

"I called my contact at railroad security and gave him Lane's itinerary."

"How did you know he would arrive last night?"

"I had a tracking number."

"Even I don't believe that. Tell the truth."

"It is true. Kitty's bouncers locked him in the boxcar with a crate of her illegal booze bound for a club in Bangor. Cindy talked her into giving us the tracking number for the hooch."

"So this time the cops were expecting him and knew he had an arrest warrant in Georgia."

"Amazing how that works."

"Good job…he should be back here by tomorrow night and they'll keep him in custody until a bail hearing can be scheduled. Meanwhile, we'll feed the prosecutor the evidence on Tommy's computer and have him charged with terrorist threats."

"More problems for Cindy. I hope she can deal with it."

Cindy loved her mother dearly, but she could not live with her. Explaining her marital problems had been difficult and embarrassing. "I know you never liked Tommy and I should have listened to you. You were right, as usual."

"Any man who would hit a woman is not worthy of a wife, Cindy."

"Mom, please don't lecture me. I made stupid decisions and ignorant mistakes, but I'm painfully aware of each of them. Please don't remind me."

"I'm sorry, Honey. I just want you to stay away from that slime ball and make yourself happy."

"I'm starting over, Mom, and this time I'll be smarter."

"I know you will, dear. By the way, we really need to discuss your grandfather's affairs."

"I know, and I promise I'll help you with that, but can it wait until next week? I have my own affairs that need my attention and then I'll take the time off and give you all the help you need."

"It might do you good to get back to a normal life, but we have to make decisions and I can't do it alone. It's important."

"I didn't want to worry you with this, but they found Tommy and he's been arrested for not appearing in court. I need to meet with my lawyer and get this over with. I'll be at Dee's and you can call me anytime. I'm less than an hour away if you need me."

"If you can get your divorce, it'll be worth it. Let me know how I can help."

"Can I use grandpa's car?"

"Of course you can, but it's about fifteen years old. We'll have to see what kind of shape it's in."

Tommy Lane was happy to be back in town—even though he had been returned in handcuffs and locked up overnight. Clean shaven, appearing harmless and innocent, he sat with his lawyer at the defense table. The court clerk read the charge of 'failure to appear' and the judge gave the go-ahead signal to the young assistant prosecutor, who had been assigned the routine task of keeping Tommy locked up.

"Your honor, Mr. Lane willfully disregarded his court appearance and has intentionally obstructed and delayed his divorce proceedings at every opportunity. In addition, he has violated a restraining order and we anticipate additional charges of making terrorists threats. We ask that the court remand the defendant to custody until a new hearing date can be scheduled."

The judge yawned and gestured to the defense lawyer. "Your honor, we apologize for the misunderstanding. My client has been out of town and simply confused the date of the hearing. I assure you that we are more than happy to go forward with the divorce case and intend to show that it is my client who has, in fact, been threatened and indeed assaulted. Once again, you have our sincere apology for the misunderstanding."

The judge folded his hands and looked over his glasses. "Is that to say that your client pleads guilty to the charge, based on ignorance of the law?"

"Your honor, we are at the mercy of the court as to the failure to appear. It won't happen again."

Turning to the assistant prosecutor, the judge asked, "Are you telling me there are additional charges?"

"Yes, your honor, we anticipate several more serious charges."

"You may proceed."

Looking confused, the young lawyer shuffled papers and hesitated.

The judge glared, "We have a full docket, are you prepared to proceed or not."

"Your honor, we believe the defendant is a danger to the public and should remain in custody."

"How wonderful of you to share that opinion with the court. Perhaps we could discuss our beliefs in a religious setting at some future date. Show me some facts and a warrant or rest your case."

"Your honor, we...uh...rest."

"Thank you. Mr. Lane I find you guilty as charged and fine you two hundred dollars for wasting my time. In addition to that, I find you in contempt of court and fine you three hundred dollars. Your total fine is five hundred dollars. You may pay the fine or remain in jail until the hearing date. What say you?"

"Thank you, your honor, I'll pay the fine."

"See the clerk, and if you fail to appear again, I'll make sure the divorce is the least of your problems. The clerk will call the next case."

Ed called a meeting and broke the bad news. "This is a major screw-up on the city's part, but at least we know where he is now. MJ, I want you and Harry to keep building the case against Lane. Gather as much evidence as you can. I'm going to make some phone calls and have him put on the fed's watch list. Cason, I want you to make sure he doesn't cause problems until we can nail him legally. Keep tabs on him and don't let him get freight trained to Siberia."

MJ was livid. She dialed Cindy's number. "The prosecutor dropped the ball. He sent a boy to do a man's job, and the judge released Tommy. I'm so sorry."

Cindy couldn't restrain her anger and expressed it verbally, including several choice expletives. MJ let her vent and then said, "I take responsibility, and I'm so sorry it happened. It's my fault."

"It's not your fault, MJ. The legal system hates me as much as everybody else. My only hope is Kitty."

"If Kitty ships him out again, you may never get the divorce. Please don't do that. You can stay with me until the hearing and I'll see that he doesn't bother you."

"Thanks, but I'm back at Dee's and we'll be fine. I'm going to ask Molly to put me back on flying status so I can get out of town. I don't even want to be in the same city with him."

Cason Haley was happy to get out of the office. Doing a little recon on Tommy Lane was his idea of fun. He started by contacting one of his ex-seal team members who now ran a private security firm. "Shade, I need a favor."

"Do you always have to call me Shade?"

"I didn't know you had another name. You were the only guy in Iraq that could find shade in the desert. Shade was your call sign and that's good enough for me."

"What do you need, Casey?"

"You got time to do a credit card hack on a guy I'm tracking?"

"I can do it or I can walk you through how to do it."

"Teach me later—right now I just need to know what he's up to."

"Give me his name and email address and I'll send his records to you in a few minutes."

When the email arrived, the subject line read, "Yesterday is the only easy day." Cason smiled and opened the attachment to find the last three months of Tommy's credit card charges. The two transactions made earlier in the day caught his attention. The first was for a rental car and the second was a motel. *Thirty-nine bucks at the Skyline Motel...living large are we?*

After changing to jeans and a pull over shirt, Cason drove to the motel west of the airport. The establishment featured two floors, and all the rooms had exterior entrances facing east toward the runways. He backed his truck into a spot that provided a good view of the parking lot and looked for rental cars. He noticed a small white compact, with a rental sticker on the back window, parked in front of a first-floor room. When he walked into the motel office, the desk clerk looked up but didn't speak. Cason said, "My buddy, Tommy Lane, checked in a little while ago and reserved a room for me next to his. Thirty-nine bucks, right?"

"That's the airline employee discount rate."

"Yeah, that's what he said. Sign me up."

The clerk looked at his computer screen. "You want 107 or 109?"

"Nine is my lucky number."

After retrieving a bag from the back seat of his truck, Cason walked through the parking lot and noticed the small white rental car was parked outside room 108. The curtains to the room were closed. As he passed the car, he dropped his room key. When he bent to pick it up, he attached a magnetic tracking device to the frame of the car. Opening the door to room 109, he ignored the musty smell and set his bag on the bed. *Must be my lucky day...there's a connecting door to Tommy's room.* Placing his ear to the door, he could hear the TV in the other room. He opened his bag and removed a GPS unit and activated it. The rental car outside the room was displayed with a flashing symbol. *James Bond would be proud of me.*

Next he removed a small recording device. After testing the recorder, he used a suction cup to attach the sensitive mic to the connecting door. Pushing the earbud into his ear, he could clearly hear the TV game show next door. He stretched out on the bed and crossed his feet. *Let's get to know each other, Mr. Lane.* A few minutes later, he heard a cell phone ringtone.

Tommy had retrieved his belongings from the Econostay without incident, and then drove to the Skyline. After his trip to Bangor, and the night in jail, he fell asleep watching TV and was irritated when the phone woke him. He recognized his lawyer's number.

"Tommy, we have a new hearing date set for next Friday. You have got to show up this time. I think we can close this thing out with a good result, but you've got to cooperate with me."

"I'm not paying any alimony, and I'm not paying any of her bills. I want the car and half of everything else."

"According to the information you've provided, there's nothing to divide. We can contest anything she asks from you, but otherwise I advise you to just walk away."

"She's the one who wants the divorce. She should have to pay."

"Tommy, she doesn't have anything. I'm happy to ask for the moon and stars and I'm happy to keep billing you for my fees, but once again I suggest you just get out and move on."

"Let me think about it."

"Great, call me when you decide."

Tommy opened his briefcase and found the life insurance policy. He caressed it like a long lost treasure. *We're not divorced yet, darling, and I'm still next of kin.* He opened his laptop and clicked on a website he had saved earlier. A photo of a large radio controlled airplane appeared and he clicked on *find a dealer near you.* He picked up his cell phone and dialed.

"Hobby Shop, Monica speaking."

"Monica I'm interested in your radio controlled aircraft inventory."

"We have quite a few in stock or we can order whatever you need."

"I'm thinking about a Vulcan RCX-40."

"Sure, we sell those and we can help with the assembly also."

"Do you have that available in the store?"

"Yes sir, we do. As a matter of fact, that's one of the models that we demonstrate every weekend at the RC Aero club meet."

"Where's the club location?"

"I can email you a map with the club info if you'd like."

"That would be great."

Tommy gave her the email address and ended the call.

Cason had only heard one side of each conversation, but the other half was easy enough to guess. He opened his own laptop and typed RCX-40 into the search box.

Chapter Twenty Two

Kyle had enjoyed his days off since the simulator check, but the thought of actually flying the airplane filled his every waking moment. His biggest fear was doing something really stupid the first time out. He checked his uniform several times a day to see that it wasn't wrinkled or stained and he emptied and repacked his brain bag several times. *God, please don't send me out with a captain that's a jerk. Not now...please.*

His prayer for mercy was interrupted by the cell phone.

The male voice asked, "Is this First Officer Bennett?"

Oh man...I really like the sound of that. "Yes, it is."

"This is Carl Smail in Tri Con crew scheduling. I wanted to confirm that you're aware of your IOE trip tomorrow morning and see if you have any questions."

"Thank you, sir. I probably have more questions than you have time to answer."

"We're here 24/7 so don't ever hesitate to call. Have you got the local and toll-free numbers?"

"Yes sir."

"Call me Carl. If you've got a computer handy, I'll walk you through the process of signing into the scheduling system on the internet. That will probably answer some of your questions."

Twenty minutes later Kyle said, "Thank you so much for your help, Carl. I think I'm catching on."

"No problem. I'm working day shift so I'll be here when you check in tomorrow. Make sure you stop by and say hello. You're flying with Robbie Jenner and he's one of the best check captains. A nice guy."

"I'm glad to hear that, I need all the help I can get."

"Do you know where to park and how to get to flight ops?"

"Phil James gave us a tour. The security code is the same as the training center, right?"

"It is, but they change it about once a month, so check your bulletins. I look forward to working with you, Kyle. See you tomorrow."

Kyle stared at the computer screen and the trip rotation he had been assigned to fly...a three day trip with twelve landings and overnight layovers in Baltimore and Knoxville. He dug the manuals out of his brain bag and studied the runway layout and approaches for each of the airports. He felt overwhelmed. The phone rang again.

"Is this Kyle Bennett?"

"Yes."

"Kyle, my name's Robbie Jenner. We'll be flying together tomorrow. I just wanted to introduce myself and see if you have any questions."

"Thank you, sir. I'm not sure I know enough to ask a question."

"Call me Robbie, and I know the feeling. Would it be possible for us to meet about an hour early tomorrow so we won't have to rush?"

"I would appreciate that."

"Great, I'll see you in flight ops about eight o'clock and I'll show you the check in procedure and then we can get started."

"I'll be there."

"For planning purposes, I'll fly the first leg and let you get acclimated, and then you can do as much of the flying as you want after that. The more landings you do, the better. Enjoy your evening and I'll see you then."

Kyle was up at 5 a.m. and standing in flight operations at 7:15. The uniform made him feel extremely conspicuous and uncomfortable. Pilots and flight attendants rushed about checking in for their trips and chattering like monkeys. *How am I supposed to find my captain?* A large cork bulletin board dominated one wall, and rather than stand in the middle of the room looking like a lost child, he joined a group of pilots at the board. Advertisements outnumbered bulletins by a large ratio and everything was for sale…autos, boats, real estate, airplanes, lawn mowers, and on and on. *This is better than E-Bay.*

He began checking out the real estate and was surprised when someone beside him said, "You're the only guy I see wearing a shiny new uniform. You must be Kyle."

The man appeared to be in his mid-forties and almost as tall as Kyle.

"Captain Jenner?"

"Guilty, but just call me Robbie. Did you find any bargains on the board?"

"Nothing I can afford."

"Let's find a computer station and I'll show you how to sign in. You have to be checked in at least an hour before departure time."

After logging on with his employee number and password, Robbie taught him how to access the flight plan, weather, and preliminary weight and balance for the first leg of the trip. They printed hard copies and moved to a table where Robbie taught him how to use a highlighter to mark the key data they would need later.

"Grab your flight operations manual and we'll highlight some sections I want you to be aware of. Sometimes the real world is a little different than the training environment."

It seemed like only minutes later, Robbie said, "Looks like our ride is arriving. The TV monitor on the wall says our airplane is on the ground and will be at Gate A-24 in about ten minutes. You ready to fly?"

The concourse was packed with passengers scurrying around like rats in a maze. Walking beside Robbie, and pulling his suitcase and flight kit behind him, Kyle thought everyone was looking at him. *This uniform is gaudy. I feel like an imposter.*

Gate A-24 was crowded with passengers, sitting and standing. The screen above the podium announced the destination as Houston and the departure time. Robbie began a conversation with the gate agent and Kyle looked for a place to hide. *I wonder if these people know I'm a rookie.* The gate area featured large windows, providing a view of the ramp and a bustle of activity. A sleek Tri Con MD-88 came into view and began a slow turn into the gate. The swept wings, the T-shaped tail, and the powerful twin engines at the rear of the fuselage fascinated Kyle. He looked upon it as an art lover would view *The Mona Lisa,* but Da Vinci could never compete with Boeing in his mind.

Trying to look inconspicuous, he stood against the wall as passengers streamed out into the concourse. A flight attendant came out, holding hands with a small boy, and Kyle watched as she delivered the unaccompanied minor to his mother. As she returned to the entrance door, she smiled and said, "Are you taking us to Houston?"

"I think so."

"Great," she held her hand out, "I'm Alma."

"Nice to meet you, Alma, I'm Kyle."

She disappeared down the boarding tunnel as the copilot came out. As he rushed by, he said, "No squawks. Have a good one."

"Thanks, you too."

Robbie appeared and said, "Let's aviate. We'll stow our bags in the cockpit and then I'll go out with you for the walk around."

The barrage of information began and Kyle knew he couldn't process it all, but he tried. The barrage continued when they returned to the cockpit. Robbie emphasized being methodical and forming good habit patterns. He offered numerous tips for setting priorities and being efficient. As they began reading the checklist, they were interrupted by the mechanic who came in to fill out the maintenance log and insisted on telling a joke before he left. They were halfway through the checklist when Alma interrupted to tell them the cabin was hot. Robbie took the opportunity to complete the flight attendant briefing while she was there. After discussing the weather, flight time, and security update, she turned to Kyle. "Are you one of the new pilots?"

"I'm afraid so. This is my first flight."

With a mischievous grin, she said, "Don't worry—we'll take care of you."

She took their beverage order and left. Robbie said, "You'll get used to the interruptions. Just make sure you complete the entire checklist."

Kyle was still trying to catch up when the gate agent came in with the final paperwork. "You've got a full boat, gentlemen. Come back to see us soon."

Forty-five minutes had passed in the blink of an eye, and Kyle knew he would have to get much faster than that. Robbie taxied the airplane away from the gate as Kyle manned the radio and talked to ground control. He realized it had been over two months since he had flown a real airplane. *Hope I can remember how to do this.*

The cockpit was laid out exactly like the simulator, and everything looked the same, but somehow it was different. The sound was not the same. The background hum of electronics and the hiss of air conditioning were a constant. The steady stream of radio chatter between ATC and other airplanes had not been present in the simulator either, and was a distraction. There was also a unique smell to the cockpit. Old leather and years of spilled coffee came to mind, but 150 humans confined to an aluminum tube probably contributed to the olfactory senses also.

When they were established on the taxiway, and had completed the taxi checklist, Robbie said, "I've changed my mind about flying the first leg. I want you to take us to Houston."

Kyle was surprised. *Did he do that on purpose, just to see how I would react? I've contrived unexpected situations for my students many times to see how they would handle it.*

"Thanks, Robbie. I appreciate it." *Did I pass the test?*

"There are ten airplanes ahead of us for takeoff, and you can figure about two minutes for each one, so you've got plenty of time to look over the departure procedure and be ready."

Robbie switched his mic to the PA system and began his welcome announcement to the passengers. "Ladies and gentlemen, my name is Robbie Jenner, and I'm your captain this morning. On behalf of First Officer Bennett and myself..."

Kyle listened to the spiel, and it occurred to him that he was much more nervous about talking on the PA than flying the airplane. He had been practicing his PA announcements in private but had his doubts if he would ever be comfortable with public speaking. Stark had suggested that he imagine a beautiful redhead, sitting in seat 34B, and speak to her directly. He would never admit that he had included that technique in his practice and it seemed to help.

He reviewed the departure procedure and saw that it was fairly simple...basically runway heading to ten thousand feet and expect radar vectors on course. Switching to map mode, he saw the flight path depicted properly on the instrument panel. The airplanes ahead of them continued to take off at one and a half to two-minute intervals and his heart beat a little faster as each one roared past.

Robbie said, "When we're number three in line, you can make the PA announcement for the flight attendants to prepare the cabin for takeoff. That gives them about five minutes to do their thing, and strap in."

"Okay." *How will I ever remember all the little things that are not in the book?*

His mind raced ahead to the takeoff and departure procedures and he remembered the mistakes he had made in the simulator. *I've got this...I mean, I do have this don't I?*

He glanced up to see only three airplanes ahead of them and Robbie said, "Go ahead and set them down, Kyle."

He was nervous about talking on the PA, but he had practiced so many times it should be easy. His hand was almost steady as he reached for the mic trigger. His voice was a little squeaky, but audible, "Ladies and gentlemen, we'll be taking off shortly and..."

Robbie frantically waved and pointed to the radio. Kyle panicked and stopped talking in mid-sentence. Robbie said, "You didn't switch your transmitter. You're talking to the tower."

A voice came from the speaker, "Very nice, gentlemen. Thanks for sharing that, but we'll let you know when it's time."

Kyle turned red in the face and slumped in his seat. Robbie shook his head and reached down to switch the transmitter to PA. "Try again."

Kyle took a deep breath and tried to compose himself. He waited a long moment and then triggered the mic again, "Ladies..." His finger slipped off the trigger. "Ladies..." The lump in his throat made him cough. Robbie held his hand up and then triggered his own mic.

"Flight attendants please prepare the cabin."

Kyle wanted to open the window and make a fast exit. "I'm sorry, Robbie."

"Don't dwell on it, we're next."

The cabin intercom dinged and Alma asked, "Ladies... Are you guys okay up there?"

Kyle carefully switched his mic to interphone and answered, "We're good."

"If you say so...the cabin is ready for takeoff."

"Thank you."

He switched back to the tower and immediately heard, "Ladies and gentlemen, Tri Con 806 is now cleared into position and hold, Runway Nine-Left."

How did they know I was the dimwit that made a PA to the tower?

With a red face, he managed to squeak out, "Tri Con 806, position and hold."

Robbie chuckled, "Before takeoff checklist."

Kyle fumbled for the checklist and read the last few items and checked them as Robbie taxied onto the runway and lined up on the centerline. "You've got the airplane."

Kyle looked up at the two miles of concrete in front of him and watched the previous airplane lift off.

"Kyle, we're moving, you gotta hold the brakes."

"I got it, thanks." *Focus, you idiot.*

"Tri Con 806, Runway Nine-Left, wind zero-seven-zero at eight, fly runway heading, cleared for takeoff."

Robbie read the clearance back as he reached up and flipped on the landing lights. The lights signaled to everyone on the airport that they were rolling. "Take us to Texas, Kyle."

The throttles moved easily in his hand and the acceleration was much different than the simulator. "Auto throttles, please."

Robbie punched the auto throttles on and verified the takeoff setting, "Power's set, eighty knots and looking good."

The airplane drifted slightly left of centerline and Kyle corrected with rudder.

Robbie called, "V1," and almost immediately, "Rotate."

Kyle's palms were a little sweaty as he slowly applied back pressure to the elevator. The nose lifted as the main wheels continued to rumble on the concrete. Robbie called, "V2," as they reached a safe flying speed, and like magic, the airplane made Kyle's dream come true. He was flying a jet airliner full of passengers and it was just like he always thought it would be, except better. He glanced at the vertical speed indicator and said, "Positive rate, gear up."

Robbie reached over and raised the gear handle as the tower said, "Tri Con 806, contact departure."

Habit patterns learned in the simulator made the next few minutes routine as Kyle called for flaps up, slats retract, and the after takeoff checklist, and Robbie covered the radio calls. After a few heading changes, that Kyle accomplished without incident, they were climbing west and talking to Atlanta Center.

Passing 14,000 feet, and cleared to 23,000, Robbie asked, "You want the autopilot?"

"Can I hand fly it a little longer?"

"Sure, but I'm turning the seat belt sign off. Don't spill anybody's Martini."

Bright sun, blue sky, old leather, and spilled coffee—Kyle tried to hide his smile. *Thank you, God.*

Chapter Twenty Three

Ed paced back and forth in his socks while MJ and Harry studied the computer screen on his desk. In MJ's mind, the image of the RCX-40 radio controlled airplane morphed into Tommy Lane with a loaded gun. The impressive six foot wingspan seemed to reach out to surround her in a choke hold. Harry took his glasses off and cleaned them with a tissue. "The payload capacity of this thing could carry enough explosive to obliterate a house."

"Or an airplane," Ed added.

Harry asked, "What's the plan?"

"We can't be solely responsible for investigating and preventing a potential attack. I'm calling the cavalry in. The FBI will be assigning the case to an agent as soon as they have one available. Meanwhile, they've asked the local police to keep Lane under surveillance."

"What about Cason?"

"He can't stay on Lane twenty-four hours a day and I can't spare him for that anyway. When the locals show up, bring him back to the office and he can check in with them once or twice a day."

"He may not be happy about that."

"I'm not happy about it either, but it's all we can do for now."

MJ looked back at the computer screen and sensed the little airplane smiling and mocking her. *Where is Kyle flying today?* It would not be the last time she asked herself that question. She had unknowingly been initiated into the club of pilot's wives and girlfriends all over the world who asked that question every time something bad happened.

Cindy was emotionally drained from grieving her grandfather's passing and dealing with her failed marriage and impending bankruptcy. She was indebted to Molly for finally assigning her a trip, and she put her mother off once again, promising to help sort her grandfather's affairs as soon as she returned. The next three days would be her healing time. Long duty days and short layovers would occupy her mentally and physically. Her bruises and abrasions had completely healed and she sensed her emotional wounds might finally also mend. The only thing she couldn't be optimistic about was financial freedom, but she planned to attack that problem with hard work and frugality.

Standing in the entrance door of the Boeing 767, she greeted two hundred passengers with a broad smile and the sunny disposition of a caring human being. She found humor in the dumb questions they asked and answered in a way that made them feel more intelligent than they deserved. She felt competent and professional and attributed her renewal to Molly's constant encouragement. *Is it possible that I could actually be normal after all?*

She happily went about her preflight duties and when she walked through the first-class cabin, just prior to takeoff, a nice looking man in a business suit beckoned her over. She accepted the business card he offered as he smiled and said, "I'm so glad that Tri Con employs more attractive flight attendants than other airlines. I would love to show you around Los Angeles sometime."

She put on her sweet innocent smile and added just a touch of twang to her southern accent. "Well, aren't you the sweetest thing. Thank you so much for that nice comment and we're so happy to have you aboard today. Make sure you're buckled up for takeoff now."

She retreated to the forward jump seat and allowed him to enjoy watching her walk away. *I'm getting my groove back, Tommy Lane, and you can rot in Hades.*

She took her seat as the takeoff roll began. Her partner sitting beside her said, "Making new friends are we?"

Cindy handed her the business card, "Just doing my job. I'm sure he'll be your friend too."

Her seatmate tore the card in half, "No thanks. Been there, done that."

They both giggled as the airplane climbed, and Cindy's spirit soared along with it.

Despite his miscues with the PA, Kyle's spirit was high as a kite. He tried, with little success, to wipe the grin from his face. Robbie continued to lambaste him with tips and techniques that were much more practical than the training program. "Training is all about learning the systems and knowing what to do when things go wrong. Flying the line is about making sure things go right."

When they were cleared for descent, Robbie said, "You did a nice job with the takeoff and climb. The airplane responds very well with power and you have a nice touch on the controls. You'll have to work a little harder with the reduced power and lower speeds for approach and landing. You're welcome to make an auto landing on this first one if you'd like to watch the autopilot demonstrate the attitudes and power settings."

Is this another test?

"If it's okay with you, I'd like to hand fly it, but maybe use the auto throttles for speed control."

"Let's plan it that way. I'll turn on the seat belt light at 18,000 feet and we'll do the descent checklist. After that, you can kick the autopilot off anytime you want and have at it."

It occurred to Kyle that this was much easier than the simulator. He had been in the airplane for several hours now and not even one emergency had happened. The sky remained clear, and with a few hints and tips from Robbie, they continued the descent and approach and arrived five miles from the runway at 1500 feet and configured for landing. Kyle's palms were a little moist and his heart rate slightly elevated.

Robbie reminded him, "We're in approach mode, so just follow the flight director bars to maintain the localizer and glide slope. The auto throttles will respond to pitch changes to maintain the approach speed, so try to keep the corrections small. The nose will be slightly above level during the approach because of the slow speed, and when you're over the runway, the throttles will retard to idle automatically. When that happens, just flare the nose a little more and feel for the touchdown.

Kyle trimmed the stabilizer and the airplane felt solid. The seconds ticked by and the runway grew larger as the ground got closer. *I should have used the autopilot.*

The end of the runway passed beneath them as the throttles in his left hand moved all the way back. He held his breath and slowly raised the nose. Nothing happened so he pulled a little more. He felt a slight vibration in the rudder pedals and then the spoiler handle flew back to kill the wing's lift and announce that the main gear had touched down. *No way... It can't be that easy.*

He lowered the nose, added reverse thrust, and began braking. Some of the tension left his muscles and his body reminded him to start breathing again.

"Tri Con 806, take the high-speed exit if able and ground is 121.9."

Robbie answered and then said, "I've got the airplane, Kyle."

After turning off the runway, Robbie smiled, "I told you there was nothing to it. I'll just shut up now and sign you off."

"Don't do that. I think that was blind luck."

"It was very nice in any case. Enjoy it. Let's do the after landing checklist."

When they reached the gate and shut down the engines, Robbie said, "I should stand in the door and take credit for that landing, but I won't. Go take your bows."

When he opened the cockpit door, Alma was already telling people goodbye as they exited. The next gentlemen that walked by looked at Kyle and said, "Great landing, Captain. I wasn't sure we were down until you reversed the engines."

"Thanks for flying with us."

When the guy was gone Alma said, "Wow, first day on the job and you're already a captain."

"Glad he thinks so."

The next passenger approached and he and Alma both spoke at the same time, canceling each other out. She said, "The way this works is, you say goodbye to everyone over forty years old, and I say goodbye to everyone under forty."

"How do I know their age?"

"Have you forgotten already that you're a captain? Captains know everything. The reason God made captains was because he couldn't be everywhere at once."

An older gentleman approached and Kyle smiled and said, "Thanks for coming with us today."

"Great flight, Captain. Thank you."

Alma whispered, "See how it works?"

Surprisingly, there was only one other passenger they both told goodbye. Alma argued that the lady was at least two weeks shy of forty.

Robbie stepped out and put his uniform coat and hat on, "Let's stretch our legs and I'll show you where Flight Operations is located."

Kyle reached into the crew closet and took his coat off the hanger. There was no hat. *I know I left my hat on the shelf.*

He looked in the floor and behind the suitcases. *Could I have left it somewhere? Robbie's gonna think I'm an idiot. Phil James said you could be suspended for not wearing your hat in the terminal. Where could I have left my hat?*

Robbie called out, "You coming, Kyle?"

"I...uh...can't find my hat."

"You lost your hat?"

"I thought I left it in the closet."

Robbie looked around in the closet, "Sorry, I don't know what to tell you. We need to get down to Ops. We'll look when we get back."

Kyle put his coat on and Alma whispered, "Don't let the chief pilot see you without a hat."

He felt half naked as they walked through the terminal. *God, please don't let me get fired for losing my hat.*

Flight Operations in Houston was much smaller than Atlanta, but Robbie found a computer terminal and pulled up the flight plan and weather for their next flight to Cincinnati. "This should be fun—looks like we get to do a little wind and rain action in Cincy."

Kyle looked at the weather. *Moderate rain with a twenty knot crosswind. That's why he wanted me to fly the first leg and not the second. Thank you, Captain Jenner. Thank you very much. You're way ahead of me.*

Robbie didn't seem concerned, "Let's get out of here."

"I can't believe I lost my hat, and we've got three days to fly before I can get another one."

"Let's get back and preflight before they board the passengers. The flight attendants have a crew change here so we need to brief the new crew."

Walking through the terminal, Kyle knew everyone was looking at him and wondering why he was hatless. He hurried onto the airplane and was relieved to be out of public view. As he passed the crew closet, he stopped and stared at the shelf. His hat had a note pinned to it. *"Welcome aboard, Kyle Bennett. You have been initiated and judged worthy. From this point on, you will be known to all flight attendants as one of the good guys. By the way, Houston is not a crew base. There is no chief pilot. Have a great career."*

It was signed—*Flight 806, cabin crew.*

He was far too relieved to be angry.

Robbie chuckled, "I had a suspicion there was mischief involved. It just means they like you. Wear your hat when you go out to do the walk around."

Chapter Twenty Four

Cindy's enthusiasm for returning to flying status powered her through the day with a high energy level. All three flights were full, and pushing the heavy beverage cart up and down the aisle was challenging, but a task she happily accomplished. Now that the day was over, she was pleasantly fatigued and satisfied that she had performed well. She much preferred the physical exhaustion to the emotional chaos that had dominated her life recently. The high rise hotel in downtown San Francisco was one of her favorites and the perfect solution for tired feet and an aching back.

After opening the door, she parked her rolling bag against it to keep it open, and then inspected the room to make sure no one was lying in wait to attack her. Tri Con trained the flight attendants to take every safety precaution possible. The large bed looked comfortable, and the bathroom featured an oversized tub that appealed to her need to relax.

With her inspection complete, she found the ice bucket and left the room, carefully locking the door behind her. On the way to the ice machine, she noted the location of the nearest fire exit and counted the number of doors between her room and the emergency egress. She had reluctantly declined the crew's invitation to attend what they termed *Debriefing,* which was in reality cocktails and gossip, and opted for a warm bath and an early night instead.

After returning to her room, she unpacked her bag and started the warm water to prepare the relaxing soak. The uniform went on a hanger in the closet and her other garments formed a messy pile on the floor that could be dealt with later. Testing the water with her toes, she found it perfect and proceeded to slowly submerge herself, enjoying the warm sensation as if returning to the safety and security of the womb. A rolled towel beneath her head completed her comfort and she let her hands float free. The fatigue was soon forgotten and her mind drifted. She imagined floating in space and gazing down at the earth with all the little people and their petty problems. The solitude became therapeutic. The silence was glorious and interrupted only by the occasional drop of water falling from the faucet and impacting somewhere near her toes. The ambiance could not be more perfect and soon she was at the edge of consciousness.

The soft ding of her cell phone sounded more like a church bell clanging. Several expletives sprang to mind and almost escaped her lips, but there was no one to address them to. *Stark...if you're texting me in the tub, I'm going to light your little screen up with words even a sailor will have to look up. And you won't like the definitions either.*

She dried her hands and picked up the phone to read the text. *Welcome to San Francisco, Darling. I'm so glad to see you back to work and making money again...staying in your favorite hotel no less. I'm looking forward to seeing you...real soon. Can't wait to spend some quality time alone with you!*

She stared at the phone in disbelief. *Tommy... How could he know where I am? Is he here?* She almost fell as she jumped out of the tub and grabbed a towel to cover herself. The door was double locked and chained, but that didn't stop her heart from pounding. She was alone and terrified...staring into the abyss again. Tears flowed from her wide eyes onto the towel she held at her chest.

MJ didn't realize she would miss Kyle so much. He had only been gone two days and she found herself constantly wondering where he was and waiting for his next call. She knew he wanted to perform really well on his first trip, and it angered her that the flight attendants had stressed him with their prank. Every time she thought about the RCX-40, a shiver traveled the length of her spine.

She had just sat down at her desk to begin her morning routine when Cason appeared in her office door. The look on his face was not encouraging. "Morning, Cason. What can I do for you?"

"I'm looking for Ed and Harry."

"They're attending a conference in downtown Atlanta. Harry said they would be back after lunch."

"We've got a problem they need to know about."

"Can I help?"

"Tommy Lane is gone again. The locals sent a patrolman in civilian clothes to watch him and he fell asleep in his car in the motel parking lot during the night. I drove by there on the way to the office and found him snoring. Tommy's car is gone and when I checked with the night clerk, she said Tommy had checked out. He could be anywhere by now. I knew I should have stayed there to keep an eye on him."

MJ felt the tingle return to her spine, "I would have certainly preferred that, but even you have to sleep occasionally. Didn't you tell me you could track his car?"

"A lot of good that did. He left it in the rental return lot at the airport. He could be on foot, or in a taxi, or on a flight to anywhere."

"If he's on a flight we can find that info easy enough."

"I know…I'll text Harry and see what he wants to do. When I find this creep again, his only means of escape will be crawling on his belly."

"I'd like a shot at him myself. I keep telling Cindy not to worry and this slime ball keeps slithering off in the weeds. I've got to call and warn her and she'll probably never believe anything I tell her again."

Molly Jackson appeared in the doorway behind Cason. "MJ, I just got a call from Cindy, and she's in a panic. Her husband knows where she's staying in San Francisco and she's been up all night, barricaded in her room. She's terrified that he might break her door down."

"How could he know where she is?"

"I wondered the same thing and there were only a few possibilities. I found out he called the duty desk last night with a sob story about a family emergency and they gave him her schedule. I should have briefed crew scheduling and the duty desk not to give out anything about Cindy without clearing it with me. Please tell me you still have him under surveillance."

After returning the rental car, Tommy called one of his drinking buddies who owned a small van. His friend was happy to let Tommy use the van at fifty dollars a day for the next week. The RCX-40 fit nicely in the back of the van and the flying club was happy for members to use the runway for practice. Arriving at the field, he prepared the airplane for flight and simulated the payload by using lead weights for ballast.

The takeoff roll was a little erratic, but his skill was improving. Once airborne, the craft was much easier to maneuver and the onboard camera transmitted a clear video. He flew the airplane over the field and looked down at his laptop to see himself standing beside the van on the screen. He commanded a climb and practiced his maneuvers at 400 feet above the ground. In his mind, he could see an airliner on the video feed. The vision of a $500,000 life insurance check, spiraling down from the sky, brought a smile to his face. He only wished he could see the look on Cindy's face when the moment came. *Her reaction to the text last night must have been priceless.*

He landed the airplane and almost lost control, but finally got it stopped without damage. When it was safely loaded in the van, he drove away to meet the drug dealer, who promised he could produce plastic explosive for the right price. An investment Tommy was happy to make. The Cartel had discovered that drugs were not the only profitable export from Mexico. *A half million dollars will be a great return on my investment.*

Kyle began the last day of his trip with some regret. He now had seven landings to his credit and only one of them had been embarrassing. On his first night landing, he drove the main gear onto the concrete so hard it rattled his teeth. Robbie warned him that the runway in Knoxville had an upslope that was tricky to handle, and he found out the hard way that it was true. When two of the flight attendants claimed they had suffered broken bra straps, he tried to laugh it off, but his red face told a different story. Still, he was having the time of his life and didn't want the trip to end. He had actually even made a few PA announcements that were acceptable.

The last day of his schedule consisted of landings in Atlanta, Orlando, and then back to Atlanta. He planned to beg Carl Smail in scheduling to assign him another trip as soon as possible.

Chapter Twenty Five

Kyle's first landing in Atlanta came after a long approach behind a string of other arriving aircraft. In the clouds and surrounded by jet airliners, carrying an untold number of human beings, the radio produced a continuous dialog between approach controllers and arrivals that left little room for error. When they switched to the tower, they were cleared to land and broke out of the clouds at 800 feet with an open runway ahead. *What could possibly be better than this?*

The ramp area was also congested, but they eventually made their way to the assigned gate and listened to the engines spin down as they completed the checklist. Robbie said, "We have less than an hour to get to the Orlando departure gate and preflight the airplane. No time for lunch, but we'll grab something in Orlando. Make sure you put your headset and sunglasses in the brain bag. It's easy to leave something behind when you're in a hurry."

When they walked into the terminal, Robbie said, "I'm going to drop by Flight Ops for a minute. I'll see you at the gate."

Kyle hurried along the concourse, dodging people and wheelchairs, and almost collided with Lindbergh Walker. Lindbergh smiled, "Watch where you're going, cowboy. This ain't no Rodeo."

Kyle laughed, "Sorry...we're a little behind schedule and I've got to find the departure gate and do a preflight."

"Where you going?"

"Orlando, how about you?"

"Chicago. Did you hear what happened to Cam Horner?"

"No. Is he okay?"

"Yeah, he's fine, but the flight attendants removed the buttons on his uniform yesterday and he had to walk through the terminal with his double-breasted jacket flopping around like a slob. You know how prepared he likes to be. Must have been really embarrassing."

Kyle laughed, "I've heard they like to prank new guys."

"Well, I'm warning you to watch out for yourself. They're not going to pull any of that crap on me."

"I gotta run, Lindbergh. Have a good trip, buddy."

"You too. Look out for yourself."

Kyle watched his friend walk away and did a double take when he noticed the suitcase he was pulling behind him. Prominently displayed, and swinging back and forth, was a pair of pink lace panties hanging out of the zipper. *Yeah right, they won't pull anything over on you. Wish I had time to take a picture of that.*

He chuckled all the way to the Orlando departure gate.

Cindy struggled through the last day of her trip after getting very little sleep. She was a bundle of nerves and continuously looked over her shoulder, expecting Tommy to appear at any moment. She stayed on the airplane during the intermediate stop in Dallas, afraid if she went into the terminal he would be there. She was relieved when the flight departed Dallas on the last leg to Atlanta. *As soon as I get home, I'm calling the cops to let them know Tommy's harassing me again. I hope they put him under the jail.*

The day was almost done and she walked through the cabin checking seat belts and tray tables. When the landing signal came, she took her seat at the mid-cabin crew station and tried to relax. Lack of sleep and being on her feet all day had taken its toll, but she was happy to be flying again. She chatted with her fellow flight attendant and complimented her on the photos of her two children.

From experience, she knew that the varying engine sounds and the pitch angle of the cabin meant they would be touching down any second. From habit, she ran through her mental checklist for landing and any problems that might occur. She glanced at the emergency exit door and reviewed the Boeing 767 evacuation procedures in her mind. Sometimes she felt ridiculous for always following her habit pattern, since nothing ever went wrong, but it only took a few seconds and she did it anyway.

At first she thought the loud thump was the wheels touching down, but then the airplane seemed to slide sideways and roll to the left. She braced herself as the cabin began to swerve and roll. Someone screamed and a full blown panic ensued as passengers yelled and objects flew out of the overhead storage bins.

The engine noise increased and the jet whine was like a siren. The nose pitched up and she thought the pilots were abandoning the approach to go around. Another jolt caused the shoulder harness to dig into her chest as she sat in the aft facing seat. From pure reflex, she closed her eyes and braced again.

Her body was thrown against the belts once more, and when she opened her eyes, the entire tail section of the airplane was gone. The people were gone too. The last thing she remembered was feeling zero gravity as the seat broke free from the floor brackets and she became airborne.

MJ had lunch at her desk and hoped she would hear from Kyle when he passed through Atlanta. *He must be too busy or having too much fun to call.* She stood at her office window overlooking the north runway. A long string of airplanes moved along the taxiway awaiting departure. *I wonder if one of those is Kyle's flight. Maybe he's looking at my office and thinking about me. At least he'll be home tonight and full of stories about his great adventure. I've got to get back to work and find Tommy Lane…again.*

As she finished the last of her soft drink, she watched one of Tri Con's big Boeings pop out of the clouds on final approach. The 767 floated majestically down the glide slope with its nose pitched up and its wheels down and locked. The landing lights were bright against the cloudy sky, and Kyle had explained that they were always used below 10,000 feet, even in daytime, to make the airplane more visible to other aircraft. *That is a beautiful sight. No wonder Kyle loves it so much.*

She noticed a flash at the right side of the Boeing and thought the landing light had suddenly brightened for some reason. The flash died away, but the airplane's nose pitched up slightly and veered to the right. *What...*

She held her breath as the airplane began to sink faster than normal. Something fell away from the right wing and smoke appeared. Then something else fell away from the wing. *Come on...stay up...*

The nose fell and the sink rate increased. *Oh God no...climb...please climb...*

The airplane appeared to turn slightly back to the left as it neared the runway. She thought it might be under control again as the nose pitched back up, but then the Boeing settled into the approach lights short of the runway. MJ was frozen in time and place as the explosion rattled the office windows.

Dear God...no...

She couldn't move or think. The scene unfolded in slow motion. She watched in paralyzed horror as the airplane appeared once again, seeming to bounce up from the smoke and flames, but now the entire fuselage aft of the wing was missing. The broken wreckage crashed down on the threshold of the runway and turned sideways as it continued to slide forward.

She may have screamed but wasn't sure. The left engine broke free of the wing and rolled ahead of the cockpit. She watched it career toward the line of airplanes on the taxiway, and an MD-88 sat trapped with nowhere to go. The smoking engine crashed into the airplane just forward of the right wing and a new explosion erupted.

As the forward half of the burning 767 finally came to rest, a portion of its wing separated and tumbled through the grass, impacting a second MD-88 on the copilot's side of the cockpit. There was no explosion, but flames flared beneath the cockpit as fuel from the Boeing's wrecked wing ignited.

Still, she could not move. *How many...oh God...somebody...*

Fire trucks seemed to appear from every direction. Big yellow beasts with diesel smoke pouring from their exhaust stacks as they sped along the runway and through the grass.

Thank God...

Black smoke billowed up from the approach lights, across the runway, and then merged with the smoke from the stricken MD-88. From there, the wind carried it along the surface and over the terminal. The entire airport appeared to be burning.

Every phone in the building started ringing at once and she could hear people running in the hall. Cason ran past her door and yelled, "I'm going out there. You've got the office till Harry and Ed get back."

He was gone before she could respond. She was drawn back to the window, but now everything was hidden by smoke with the exception of a late arriving fire truck. Without hesitation, the truck drove into the smoke and disappeared. *Please God...don't let the firemen die too.*

She began to process what happened and remembered the emergency phone tree with numbers for all security personnel to be notified. *Ed will know what to do.*

Picking up the phone to dial, her brain began assimilating facts. She knew it was important to process as many details as possible about what she had witnessed. The method she used, when helping other witnesses remember, was to have them recall what they were thinking immediately before the incident. Her mind went back to standing at the window and seeing the line of airplanes waiting to depart. *I was wondering if...* The next word terminated the memory process...*Kyle!*

Chapter Twenty Six

She called Ed and got voice mail. Dialling Harry produced the same result. Harry's secretary rushed through her door. "He's on line two."

She picked up the phone and punched the button, "Harry…"

"Yeah, stay with the office, MJ, and monitor anything that comes in. I'll be there in twenty minutes. Ed's headed out to the runway. Where's Cason?"

"He's already out there. I'm working the emergency call list."

"Let my secretary do that. I want you to keep your eyes and ears open till I get there. There'll be some crank calls to the reservations numbers and other offices too. Take the details and get recordings if possible. No comment to the press."

A dial tone announced he was gone. She went back to the window. A few red flashing lights were visible in the smoke, but it was impossible to see if they were from emergency vehicles or the rotating beacons of airplanes still trapped on the taxiway.

She remembered the day she met Kyle Bennett. He had just landed the 767 after being held captive by terrorists for months. He had stopped the airplane on the runway and shut it down because he didn't know how to taxi it. She was there when he walked off the airplane, in ragged jeans and cowboy boots, and her life had not been the same since. *Yes, Kyle Bennett, I will marry you. I will marry you in the little church you like so well. Please, come home tonight. Please ask me again and I will say yes.*

She was relieved when Harry rushed into the office and took charge. He limped up and down the hallway barking orders and sending people scurrying. An hour later the chaos in the office began to subside, but the frantic pace on the runway would continue through the afternoon and into the night.

The freeway, just west of the airport, was closed and all the surface streets around the airport were blocked. Traffic backed up for miles and then hours. The cell phone towers near the airport were overloaded almost immediately and service ceased. The news media descended like vultures and began continuous broadcasts and speculation about negligence and terrorism. They had hours of air time to fill and no theory was too insane to proffer.

Harry scheduled a security staff briefing for six p.m. and everyone was just gathering when Ed walked in. His face was smudged with soot and his white shirt was a blend of gray and black. His Tri Con security badge was barely legible. He smelled toxic and coughed continuously.

Harry asked, "What's the story?"

"As bad as it gets. I think we lost almost everyone on the 767 and probably most of the people on one of the MD-88's. Airport fire and rescue is still searching, but all they're finding now is bodies. Where's Cason?"

"He went to the scene immediately. You didn't see him out there?"

"No, but you couldn't see ten feet in the smoke and chaos. He could have walked right by me and I wouldn't have seen him."

Ed's secretary appeared with two bottles of water and he downed the first one in two swallows and then covered his mouth to burp. She handed him the second bottle and said, "Mr. Haley is on the land line. Evidently the cell service is still out."

Ed downed the water and then picked up the phone. "Cason where are you?"

"I'm still at the scene, sir."

"When you call me sir, it usually means you did something bad. What happened?"

"One of the airplane's engines fell off before it crashed. I heard about it on the radio. It landed about a mile before the runway."

"You heard about it on the news?"

"No sir. It was on the radio in the fire truck."

"What fire truck?"

"I know some of the airport firemen and they let me suit up sometimes when they drill."

"Does the fire chief know about this?"

"I don't think so, sir."

"I knew it. Quit calling me sir."

"You want me to stay here or go check out the scene where the engine fell?"

"How are you calling me from the scene if your cell phone isn't working?"

"It's a patch to the land line from the fire truck radio."

"Cason, leave the fire truck alone and come back to the office."

"Yes, sir."

Ed hung up and finished his water, "Harry..."

"I know...I know...I'll talk to him."

"There's a general briefing in Harold Collins' conference room in an hour. I'm going down to the hangar locker room to clean up. Find out what Cason knows about the engine falling off when he gets here."

Ed disappeared and Harry turned to MJ. "Don't pay any attention to Ed and Cason. They feed off each other. If Ed had a chance to ride the fire truck, he'd want to drive it."

"I know. I'm on to their game. What do you want me to do next?"

"Take a break and have some coffee. It's going to be a long night. I can tell you're upset and I'm sorry you have to experience this before you've had all the training."

She held back the tears and said, "It's tragic and hard to comprehend, but I'm also worried about Kyle. He was due to take off about the time of the accident, and I haven't heard from him. He may have been on one of the MD-88's."

"My God, MJ, why didn't you say something? I had no idea. Where was he going?"

"Orlando."

"That's good news. South and east departures use the south runways. North and west departures use the north runway. Let's make sure anyway. What's the flight number?"

Harry picked up the phone and dialed crew scheduling. "Hey Carl, I know you guys are busy, but do you have a crew list of the three accident flights yet... Great, can you email it to me... You're a good man, also can you give me the status of flight 1242 from Atlanta to Orlando...Thanks, Carl, I owe you one."

"MJ, you can relax. Kyle arrived in Orlando on time, but he may not get back to Atlanta tonight. I don't know when they'll open the runways again."

She put her arms around him and hugged tight. "Thank you, Harry."

"Next time say something sooner."

Molly Jackson's heart was broken. She was responsible for the flight attendants on the three flights and she knew some of them had died under her supervision. She tried to focus on preparing for the general briefing and gathering as much information as possible for her report. *I'm going to have to stand in front of the room and be accountable. Flight attendants died on my watch. God help me.*

Molly looked up to see her secretary standing in her office door with tears in her eyes. "I've got the crew list you wanted."

"Thank you, Janie. I'll need that for the briefing."

The secretary sobbed as she handed her the papers, "Cindy was on the 767."

Molly grabbed the list and scanned the eight flight attendant names on the 767 crew list. Near the bottom, C. Lane appeared in cold uncaring black ink

.

Chapter Twenty Seven

MJ became more focused once she knew Kyle was safe. She felt like she had been shot at and missed. Once again, she tried to replay what she had witnessed while it was fresh in her mind. The phone call caused her brain to flush and begin to refill. "Thank you, Molly, and I am so sorry. Don't broadcast this till we talk to Ed."

She found Harry and Ed at the office window looking at the carnage on the runway. "Harry, did you get that crew list?"

"Yeah, but I haven't had time to print it."

"I think Cindy Lane was on the 767."

"What…"

Ed said, "Where's the list?"

Harry pulled the email up on his computer. Cindy's name and employee number jumped off the screen and hit them in the face.

Ed ran his fingers through his hair. "No sane person would believe this could all be caused by a domestic dispute."

Harry limped to the printer as it began spitting out the crew list. "You're talking to a guy who got shot in the knee by an irate housewife who was mad at her husband and couldn't even remember why."

"Sorry, Harry."

"MJ, how did you discover Cindy was on the airplane?"

"I didn't. Molly Jackson told me. Do we know how many flight attendants survived?"

Ed coughed and didn't answer. He sat down at his desk and said, "We need to let Harold Collins know this in private, but don't bring it up at the briefing. If the news media gets a sniff of this, it will be like wild dogs going after raw meat. Maybe it's a cruel coincidence."

The briefing became an exercise in futility because no one knew enough to be informative. Each of Tri Con's divisions was represented to receive their marching orders. Harold Collins opened the meeting and struggled to find the words of encouragement he thought was appropriate for the situation. His day had gone from bad to worse. After entertaining Senator Walker and members of the city's Airport Expansion Committee for most of the morning, the meeting was derailed because of a delay in the aerial survey Walker had ordered. Now that was the least of his problems. He turned the briefing over to Charlie Wells.

Charlie referred to notes he had written on scrap paper. "Here's what little I know so far. The 767 originated in San Francisco and made an intermediate stop in Dallas before continuing to Atlanta. The manifest shows 193 passengers aboard. In addition, the normal complement of eight Atlanta-based flight attendants were on duty. The two pilots were based in Dallas.

I'm sorry to report that the fatality rate is going to be very high. At this point, we expect few if any survivors. We know that the right engine separated from the wing on final approach. Fortunately, the engine fell in the parking lot of an abandoned shopping center about a mile short of the runway. I'm not aware of any injuries at that site.

The airplane continued its approach but impacted the approach light system prior to reaching the runway threshold. The tail section appears to have separated at that point, but the forward half of the fuselage, and most of the wings, carried onto runway Eight Right. The flight was dispatched with a fuel reserve for forecast weather delays and arrived with approximately 30,000 pounds of fuel in the wing tanks. The resulting fire completely destroyed what was left of the hull.

It gets worse. The left engine from the Boeing broke off and rolled into a MD-88 on the taxiway. It impacted the forward fuselage and the right wing, rupturing the fuel tanks. The subsequent explosion and fire destroyed that hull also. We expect moderate to high fatalities at that scene. I can tell you that we lost two flight attendants on that airplane. The remaining flight attendant and the two pilots suffered injuries but will survive. I talked to the captain of that flight and he praised his crew for their heroics. The copilot re-entered the burning airplane not once, but twice and saved many lives, including the captain and the surviving flight attendant.

Finally, a second MD-88 on the taxiway was struck by a portion of the Boeing's wing. It literally crushed the copilot's side of the cockpit and he was killed instantly. That flight was evacuated successfully and the copilot was the only fatality.

That's the status as I know it and don't even think about asking me what might have caused it. There will be a long investigation, and someday we will have answers, but not today. There will be plenty of speculation in the press and on TV and I suggest you ignore it all. I promise I will share the facts as they evolve, but wild unsubstantiated guesses and theories only muddy the water.

Other departments made brief reports, but the meeting ended with more questions than answers.

Ed waited until the conference room was almost empty and then caught the CEO's eye, signaling that he needed a word. When they were alone, he reminded Collins who Cindy Lane was and reviewed the investigation concerning her husband. Finally, he told him that Cindy was on the 767 involved in the accident. He was surprised at the reaction.

"Ed, I know exactly who Cindy Lane is. Can this day possibly get any worse? Are you telling me that she's dead?"

"I don't know that, but it may very well be true."

"And you think her husband may somehow be responsible for this accident?"

"I don't know that either, but I wanted you to know we're investigating the possibility."

"I want to know the answer to those questions. Don't say anything else about your suspicions for now, but make it your top priority, and call me immediately when you find Cindy Lane...anytime, day or night."

Ed's paranoia alerted, "Is there something more I need to know about Cindy?"

"It's something I need to know. A personal matter... Get on it."

Collins returned to his office to find a phone number for Miriam Latimer. *How do I tell someone that their only daughter is missing and presumed dead? How do I tell the board of directors that we've killed a major stock holder?*

Chapter Twenty Eight

The airport fire and rescue personnel were generally seasoned veterans. They trained and drilled almost daily and their state of the art equipment was tended to like new born babies. When there was nothing else to do, they could be seen gently caressing the exterior of the huge yellow trucks with a soft cloth. There were no sopranos in the squads, so the barely audible deep tones you might hear while they worked must be murmuring a favorite tune. No one would believe a highly professional grown man would be quietly conversing with a piece of fire-fighting equipment.

Neither would it occur to most observers that the seasoned veterans at the world's busiest airport had never actually experienced the scene of a major airline accident. Today, the fire-fighters would discover that the training film they watched did not remotely provide a sense of the reality. The sight of human bodies and parts of human bodies, some burned beyond recognition, could not be viewed dispassionately by a normal person. Tears secretly moistened the inside of every fire-fighter's full face oxygen mask. Most also contained varying amounts of vomit.

It seemed to Firefighter J.J. Klauss like he had been on scene for days. The flames, fed by jet fuel, and minor explosions, seemed invincible. And the rescue effort, powered by muscle and adrenalin, seemed to be endless, but fear and urgency drove fatigue from the equation. Now he was dehydrated and operating on nothing more than will power.

When the chief ordered him out for a short break, he consumed water until he felt like his eyeballs were floating. The adrenalin was used up, the fear replaced by depression, and urgency seemed less necessary by the minute. He cleaned the inside of his mask with alcohol wipes, whispered a couple of words of apology for puking in it, and struggled to his feet. The fireproof suit and gear seemed twice as heavy as before. He and his partner replaced their oxygen tanks, grabbed a body bag from the stack beside the truck, and walked through the grass between the burned out hulk of the 767 and the MD-88 that had been struck by the Boeing's engine.

Recovering human remains, and zipping them in body bags, caused him to question his belief that God is good, but it wouldn't be the first time his faith had been tested. Scores of body bags had been transported to a hangar, used as a temporary morgue, and scores remained to be loaded.

The only flames remaining were smoldering deep in the wreckage, but smoke persisted and lay low to the ground in the still air of late afternoon. Scouting the area for bodies reminded him of an Easter egg hunt, and he rebuked himself for the thought. Secretly, he hoped there were no more Easter eggs to be bagged, but his partner pointed to a jagged pile of aluminum and the human foot visible at the edge.

Careful not to let the sharp metal penetrate their gloves, they uncovered the female body and unzipped the black rubber bag. He planted a red numbered flag in the ground next to the woman's shoeless foot and marked the body bag with the corresponding number. *The red flags should be inscribed like a tombstone. Here lies the body of number 186.*

He chastised himself once again for such thoughts and then stumbled backward when the Easter egg's foot, in torn pantyhose, kicked the flag over.

Ed declared the urgency of determining Cindy's fate, and assigned his troops their task. "Harry, I need you to go to the hangar and look for Cindy in the temporary morgue. MJ, you've got the hospitals. I'll get you a list of where the injured were taken. Cason, I want you to do whatever is necessary to find Tommy Lane. If you can get him alone and express our displeasure, perhaps he'll be willing to answer your questions more readily than those of law enforcement. Everybody call me here with what you find.

Cason decided he wouldn't learn much at the crash site in the dark. Instead, he drove west of the airport to find the abandoned shopping mall where the engine fell. He found a huge parking lot surrounded by flashing blue lights and crime tape. He knew most of the local cops and spotted a familiar face standing beside a squad car.

"Hey Sleepy, where's Dopey and Sneezy?"

"Don't bust my chops, Cason. I know I screwed up, but I swear I only dozed off for a minute. The guy just picked a lucky time to check out."

"I'll talk to the chief and put in a good word for you."

"The chief thinks I'm an idiot and so do I. He'll probably never give me another important assignment. If I lose this job, my wife and kids will hate me."

"Don't panic, maybe he'll get over it. What's going on here?"

"What does it look like? I'm guarding a parking lot because the chief thinks I'm an idiot."

Cason laughed, "Did the engine cause any damage when it hit?"

"Busted up some asphalt, but that's about it."

"I need to take a look so I can let Tri Con know how much it's going to cost them."

"There's not much to see. The detectives, FBI, NTSB, and the military have all come and gone already."

"I'm going to take a look anyway. Try to stay awake."

"Maybe I'll put a parking ticket under your windshield wiper."

Cason chuckled, "See you in court, officer."

The Boeing's engine appeared to have hit the ground nose first and then flipped over and spun around before coming to a stop. A large area of pavement was busted up and cratered, and there were gouges dug out where it spun. There was no sign of the exterior cowling that normally covered the engine. He remembered the first accident when the kid's airplane caused the engine to explode and the cowling and other parts floated down over an area covering several blocks. *How many people would have been killed if this was an active shopping mall?*

He walked around the engine and noticed that the fan blades appeared to be intact. *Nothing was sucked into the engine to damage it. Why did it fall off?*

Looking around the parking lot, he noticed a group of about twenty cars parked near the main entrance. He walked back to the patrol car to find the cop sipping coffee. "Why are those cars parked here, Sleepy?"

"It's a car pool for commuters. They park their cars here in the morning and ride a van downtown to work. The van is probably stuck in the traffic jam caused by the accident, and they haven't been able to pick up their vehicles."

"Let's go check them out."

"Why?"

"So we can look for clues, Sherlock. We can pretend you're a policeman. Besides that, I need your flashlight."

Approaching the parked cars, Cason noticed pieces of rock and pavement scattered on the ground. The first car in line displayed dings and dents as well as a cracked window.

Cason said, "See, now you can put in your report that vehicles were damaged by flying rocks caused by the falling engine. The owners and insurance companies will love you and the chief will be proud."

"Yeah, and I'll get to do a lot of paperwork."

Cason noted a van, backed into a parking spot, about fifty feet from the other cars.

"Why is the white van par' ed so far away?"

"Probably wanted to avoid falling engines and flying rocks."

"I knew you would grow a sense of humor someday. Let's take a look."

Walking toward the lone vehicle, Cason noticed a long gouge in the pavement and followed it toward the van, which seemed to be lower on the left side. A large piece of the jet engine lay beside the front wheel which was tilted at a forty-five degree angle and had a flat tire.

The cop said, "Looks like this one has more than cosmetic damage. Nobody will be driving this home with a broken axle. Tri Con will have to shell out some bucks to have it towed and repaired."

"At this point, I think Tri Con has bigger problems than a busted wheel on a used work van. Shine your light on this piece of the engine that caused the damage."

"What is that?"

"Some sort of accessory that broke off...probably the generator. Let me borrow your flashlight."

Walking to the rear of the van, Cason beamed the light into the back window but saw nothing unusual. Moving to the passenger side, he looked into the front seat.

"Sleepy, I think you just got off the chief's crap list. Take a look at this."

The cover of the book on the seat displayed the title *Operators Manual RCX-40.*

Chapter Twenty Nine

MJ fought through the traffic jam around the airport, and when she was a few miles away, her cell phone began to ding with message alerts. *I never thought I'd be so happy to get cell service back.*

The hospital parking decks were crowded, but she finally found a spot on the fourth level and squeezed into it. She took the phone from her purse and found five messages from Kyle. He was stuck in Orlando. He wouldn't be home until tomorrow. Was she okay? Please call ASAP. MJ please let me know you're okay.

She thumbed a quick message as she walked through the parking lot and hit the send button. The lobby of the hospital consisted of a large waiting area, and people were crowded around a big screen TV with news reports from the crash scene. *I definitely don't want to see that!*

She headed for the reception desk and prepared to show her Tri Con ID in hopes of gaining information. As she walked past the elevators, Molly Jackson hurried out and almost bowled her over. "Molly, what have you found out?"

"Not much. They brought the survivors from the 767 here, but there's not very many."

"What about crew members?"

Molly's voice quivered, "There aren't any. No one made it out."

"I'm so sorry, Molly. I've been praying to find Cindy here safe and sound."

"Me too, but I guess answered prayers are at a premium tonight, and ours didn't make it. I can't bear the thought of going back to that little church and seeing Cindy's casket at the altar."

"Don't think about that right now."

"I know. I've got to get over to the other hospital where they took the victims from the two MD-88s. Charlie says all three flight attendants walked away from one of them, but he thinks only one of the cabin crew survived the other one. I hope she's still alive."

"Mind if I tag along?"

"MJ, I will love you forever if you come with me for moral support."

"Cindy would want us to do everything possible to help the others."

Tommy Lane was running scared. The vision of the airliner approaching on his laptop screen haunted him. He had been excited when he launched his airplane from the abandoned shopping mall's parking lot, but when he saw the landing lights of the 767 pop out of the clouds, he had second thoughts. He had tuned his VHF scanner to the tower frequency and waited patiently for the flight to be cleared to land, so he had no doubt it was Cindy's airplane he was looking at. He hated her, but still he was hesitant. He maneuvered the little airplane at 300 feet and knew it would be directly in the path of the airliner one mile from the runway, but as it grew larger on the screen, he was scared. He looked around to make sure no one was watching him and then it was too late.

The noise caused his heart to race and he looked up to see smoke streaming from the airplane as it continued toward the runway. He flipped the controller switch off, and then the engine hit the parking lot just fifty yards away. He wasn't expecting that, and it took his breath away. The ground shook like an earthquake, and he fell to his knees in panic. A few yards away, rocks and the airplane's generator whizzed past and hit the van. He got up to run, but fell to the ground again when he heard the horrific explosion of the airliner hitting the approach lights. When he got to his feet again, he saw the wrecked van and followed his basic instincts. He ran like a madman possessed.

He was a block away when he remembered the laptop and the airplane controller. He had to force himself to go back, but he couldn't leave evidence at the scene. He had an escape plan using the van, but now he was on foot and running with both hands full. He was several blocks into a nearby neighborhood and gasping for breath before he slowed to a walk. His knees were trembling, and his pulse was off the chart.

It was just an accident. No one will ever believe I could cause that...just a horrible and tragic accident. My buddy's insurance company will fix his van and I'll pay him to keep his mouth shut. I just have to lay low until Cindy's funeral and then make my claim for the insurance. I should sue Tri Con for almost hitting me with an airplane engine. I could have been seriously injured.

He cursed his luck for losing the van and continued to walk away from the sound of sirens and blaring horns. Twenty minutes later, he emerged from the neighborhood and found himself in an older commercial district. A couple of gas stations, a pawn shop, and a Goodwill store offered little refuge, but up ahead a neon sign identified a perfect place to hide out and think things through. *A couple of beers are just what I need. The place looks like a dive, but it will do in this situation.*

The neon sign announced, "Kitty Mac's Bar and Grill."

MJ and Molly identified themselves to the receptionist who promptly informed them that patient information could not be released due to the privacy act. Molly said, "I'm well aware of the privacy act, and I'm not asking for details. I only want to know if Tri Con employees are being treated here."

"The news people have been asking me that all day. I've been told not to release any information."

Molly's face reddened to match her hair, and she leaned forward to put her hands on the girl's desk, "I appreciate that, but I'm not with the news. How many of my employees do you have here?"

The receptionist shrunk back in her chair and without thinking said, "Three."

"Thank you, where are they?"

The girl looked around and then whispered, "I like Tri Con and I want to help, but you can't tell anyone I talked to you."

The girl wrote something on a notepad and handed it to Molly. "That's my name and I have an application on file with Tri Con. All three are on the fourth floor."

Molly looked at the note, "Thank you, Karen."

Approaching room 418, they were stopped by a hospital security guard. "Sorry ladies, no visitors allowed."

MJ held up her Tri Con Security ID. "We're in the same business. We just want to check the condition of our employee."

"I'm not a doctor, but the patient seems to be doing okay considering."

"Mind if we have a quick look for ourselves."

"Sorry, Ms. Jones, I'm sure you understand I have my orders."

MJ was about to turn on the charm when the door opened. Senator Walker emerged with one of his aides. "Ms. Jackson, are you here to check on our patient?"

Molly and MJ both immediately imagined Cindy's smiling face. "Yes sir, we're very concerned."

"Well, I think a short visit would be encouraging."

He opened the door and stood aside as Molly beat MJ to the entrance. Lying in bed with a foot elevated and in a cast, Lindbergh Walker looked up with a surprised expression. Molly could not hide the look of disappointment on her face and hoped it would be mistaken for concern. MJ stepped in to save her. "Lindbergh, are you okay?"

"Thanks for asking, MJ. I'm fine, just a sprained ankle."

The senator added, "Actually it's broken in two places."

"Whatever," Lindbergh replied.

Molly remembered Charlie's briefing about the heroics of one of the copilots and took Lindbergh's hand, "Charlie told us you were quite the hero today."

The senator beamed a big smile.

"Not really. I couldn't get two of our flight attendant's out. I'm sorry Ms. Jackson."

"Call me Molly, and the flight attendant you did save will always think you're a hero and so do I."

"I hope she's doing okay."

"We're just about to check on her, and we'll let you know."

"I would appreciate that."

MJ asked, "What can we do for you, Lindbergh? Do you need anything?"

"I don't think so. Captain Wells was by earlier and I appreciate ya'll checking on me, but I'm fine. Take care of everyone else."

"Okay, you know how to get in touch if we can help."

They walked out together, and Molly asked, "Senator, do you know which room my flight attendant is in?"

"No, but let's find out so we can let Lindbergh know."

When they approached the nurse's station, two ladies stood to greet them, "Senator Walker, what can we do for you?"

"You ladies have been so kind. My friends here are from Tri Con and we'd like to check on our flight attendant."

"I just looked in on her a few minutes ago. Come with me and let's see if she feels like visitors."

The nurse quietly opened the door and said, "Amy, you have some friends here to see you. Is that okay?"

When the girl saw Molly, she broke down in tears. Her voice was raspy, "Ms. Jackson, I'm so sorry. I don't know what happened. All of a sudden we were on fire and people were screaming. I was alone in the back cabin, and I deployed the escape slide, but people panicked and almost ran me over. I tried to help the injured passengers get to the door, but I guess I passed out from the smoke. There were two little kids clinging to their mommy, but I think she was dead."

The sobs became uncontrollable and Molly took the girl in her arms. "Amy, you did a wonderful job, and we're so proud of you. None of this is your fault and I'm so glad that you were there to help those people. You did what you were trained to do and people are alive because you did it so well. Don't cry, honey, we're here because we love you. Everything is going to be all right."

The nurse shook her head and made an adjustment to the girl's IV bag. "Amy, we're going to let you get some rest, sweetheart. Just push your call button if you need me."

The IV did its magic and Amy's eyes grew heavy and closed. In the hallway, Molly asked, "What kind of injuries does she have?"

"Just shock and respiratory distress from smoke inhalation, but she was rescued in the nick of time. A few more minutes and her lungs would have ceased to function. By the way, the senator's son not only carried her out, but several other people too, including the mother and two kids she was talking about. The kids are fine and the mother's going to make it too."

Senator Walker beamed and turned to his aide, "Are you getting this all down."

"Yes sir, the press release will go out tonight."

MJ couldn't restrain herself. "Senator, might I suggest you have Lindbergh approve any publicity concerning his actions. He will want to be judged by his peer group more than anyone else."

Walker looked at her and frowned. "Thank you, Ms....what was your name again?"

The nurse said, "The other pilot has been sedated and is asleep, and I'm not sure what the status of your second flight attendant is. The ICU is on the first floor if you want to check on her."

Molly stared at her, "What other flight attendant?"

"The second one that came in about an hour ago. The ER guys said she was found in the grass outside the airplane."

"Which airplane?"

"The same one Amy was on."

"Oh my God, I thought the other two died."

"That's possible, but she was still alive about an hour ago."

"Can we see her?"

The nurse looked to the senator. He asked, "Who's in charge of the ICU?"

"Dr. James Holland."

He turned to Molly. "Let's go see what we can do."

Dr. Holland was very happy to meet the famous Senator Walker, and was pleased to be of assistance. Looking at the patient's chart, he reported. "Critical condition...shock...unknown internal injuries...head trauma...unresponsive to stimuli...still being evaluated. She'll be on life support until we can contact next of kin and determine if there's a living will. With the chaos, we're a little behind."

Walker said, "Perhaps we can be of help in that regard. Do you have a name?"

Referring to the chart, "Let's see...tentative...pending verification...airline ID card in vest pocket...Cynthia L. Lane."

Chapter Thirty

Dee wasn't worried when Cindy didn't come home on time. She was still in disbelief that Tri Con had dropped an airplane, but the entire airport was shut down and Cindy was probably in a holding pattern or already diverted to another airport. It wasn't until the news began reporting the details of the accident that she began to worry. The airplane was a 767...the flight was inbound from Dallas...the crew was based in Atlanta.

When her phone rang, the hair on her arms stood up. "Dee, have you heard from Cindy?"

"No, she hasn't come home yet, Stark. The airport's closed and she's probably been diverted. She may not be home until tomorrow."

"She's not answering her phone and when I call I get an out of service message."

"The cell service is overloaded. Only the landlines are working."

"I'm talking to you on my cell. The service is back, but her phone's not working. Cindy was on that flight, Dee. I just know it."

Dee knew it too, but she had to make a phone call to confirm it. Cindy was, in fact, on the flight and there was a very low probability of survivors. When she called Stark back he said, "I'm coming over, Dee. You've got to help me find her."

Several hours later she and Stark had been through two pots of coffee and Dee had called everyone she knew. The rumor mill was buzzing, but no one knew anything for sure. The news reports just repeated the same story over and over like a continuous loop. Each

TV station had called upon a different *expert,* and each one put forth his or her theory as to what caused the crash and who was to blame. As time passed, the speculation became competitive.

It was getting late, and they were at their wits end when Stark's cell phone rang. He looked at the ID and answered, "Lindbergh, I've been calling you for hours...why do you carry a phone around if you're not going to answer it."

"I love you too, Stark. I'm fine, thanks for asking."

"You haven't been fine for a long time. You're mentally deficient. Where are you?"

"I was involved in an accident and broke my ankle. I'm locked up in a hospital room with a beautiful nurse who loves pilots."

"You idiot... Have you been drinking, Lindbergh? Did you wreck your car?"

"You're an idiot, Stark. I was on the MD-88 that blew up on the taxiway."

"Lindbergh...are you...if you..."

"Stop blathering and listen to me. I need you to bring me some things. My bag is still on the airplane."

Tommy Lane sat in a dark corner and watched the TV mounted on the wall above the bar. He dared not make eye contact with anyone around him and didn't notice Kitty watching him from a table in the opposite corner. Everyone's attention was glued to the news reports. There were no known survivors from the 767. There were almost 200 deaths from the Boeing and approximately thirty more on the MD-88. He had dreamed of Cindy's demise for weeks, but it had not occurred to him that so many other people would die. The TV station ran video of the smoking wreckage over and over, and each time he tried to shrink further into his corner. After a couple of beers, he changed to hard stuff and it became easier to deny his guilt.

He called his drinking buddy and told him what happened to the van. "If you play it cool, Tri Con will have to buy you a new van and throw in some cash. You can't tell them I was driving it though because I don't have insurance."

His buddy thought that sounded like a good plan and was happy to cut Tommy out of the deal.

Shortly after sunset, Tommy called a taxi and found a cheap motel in the suburbs. He was still scared and couldn't shake the feeling that he was being stalked. He had the cabbie drive around the block to make sure he wasn't being followed. He signed the register with a false name and paid cash. After staggering to the room, he double-locked the door and crawled into bed. He covered his head and let the alcohol overcome his guilt before he blissfully passed out.

MJ had only been in bed a couple of hours when her alarm went off at 6 a.m. She and Molly had been up most of the night after finding Cindy. A phone call to Ed had resulted in his arrival at the hospital along with Harold Collins and Cindy's mother. It was determined that Cindy did not have a living will or health care directive, and permission to remove life support would not be forthcoming. At Ed's suggestion, it was agreed that no information about Cindy should be released until further notice.

After a bowl of cereal and a quick shower, MJ drove to the office for the 8 a.m. security team meeting. She gathered with Harry and Cason in Ed's office, and the fact that he was wearing shoes announced that he was not in a good mood. He opened the meeting with a five-minute tirade about the incompetence of the local police and prosecutor's office for not keeping Tommy Lane locked up. When he finished venting, he added that Cindy's condition was unchanged and asked Cason if he had anything to report.

The answer was, "Yes sir."

"Well, get on with it and quit calling me sir."

"I gained access to the site where the engine fell in the parking lot of an abandoned shopping mall. The only damage, other than the parking lot pavement, was to a few cars parked there by commuters. The only vehicle with serious damage was a white van parked separate from the other cars. I did some snooping, and it looked like someone had been living in the van. There was an operator's manual for an RCX-40 lying on the front seat."

"Well, we only know one guy who recently expressed an interest in an RCX-40. Where is he?"

"I'm working on it, sir. The van was not registered to Lane."

"Why would he leave the van there to be found?"

"The front wheel was almost knocked off by a piece of the engine. It was disabled."

"Do the police know about this?"

"Yes sir. They interviewed the van's owner last night and he changed his story several times, but when they took the cuffs out, he admitted that Tommy Lane had borrowed his van. The police chief informed the FBI, and they're dusting the van for prints."

"I don't know if that will convict him, but it puts him at the scene. We've got to track him down."

Harry said, "I've been thinking about that, and it's possible he may come to us. I don't think he's entirely motivated by revenge. As long as he's legally married to Cindy, he stands to collect her life insurance and whatever other assets she owns."

Ed rubbed his chin, "MJ, why don't you check that out."

"I already did. She has a $500,000 accidental death policy, but Molly and I had her change the beneficiary from her husband to her mother."

"I'm so glad I had the good judgment to hire you."

Harry asked, "Does Tommy know that?"

"I doubt it. I don't think she's talked to him since it was changed. Other than the insurance policy, she's in debt up to her ears. There's nothing for him to inherit."

Harry said, "As long as he thinks she died in the crash, he'll have to come to us to collect the $500,000."

Ed said, "Then that's what we'll let him think. Cindy's listed as an unidentified survivor, and we're going to keep it that way until he's locked up. Meanwhile, we need to find him, and we need proof that he actually caused the accident. Everybody work your sources and report to me. I'll keep up with what the FBI is doing. We're going to nail this slime one way or another."

MJ sat down at her desk and tried to organize her thoughts. *Now that I've run my mouth about the insurance policy, I better double check to make sure the changes went into effect.* Harry had taught her how to access the personnel files and she brought Cindy's records up on her screen. She was relieved to see that Cindy's mother was now listed as the beneficiary. She also noticed that Cindy's grandfather had been removed as a relative.

This poor girl has been physically and mentally abused, forced into a horrendous financial situation, lost her grandfather, and now she's fighting for what's left of her miserable life. Dear God, she deserves a break. It should be her husband suffering instead of her. It would be obscene if he collected one dime. I wonder if there's any possibility…

She ran Cindy's mother's name through several search engines and was not surprised to find her net worth to be modest at best. A school teacher's pension and a small savings account were her life's earnings. Just to cover the details, she reopened the search engine and typed *Alexander Morgan.*

The screen filled with references and the arrow at the bottom indicated several more pages were available. She clicked on a few of the alerts and…*Holy crap.*

Ten minutes later, she and Ed were in Harold Collins' office. The CEO said, "I'm aware of Miss Lane's inheritance, but her mother asked that it be kept quiet for now. Ms. Jones I applaud your investigative skills, but I'm asking that you two honor her wishes as well. I spoke to Mrs. Latimer last night at the hospital and she informed me that she has not yet had the opportunity to discuss it with Cindy."

Ed said, "You're telling me that Cindy has no idea she's a multi-millionaire."

"That's what I'm telling you. Her mother didn't even know until very recently, therefore, there's no way Cindy's husband could know either."

MJ said, "You realize that if Cindy dies intestate, her inheritance will go to Tommy Lane as next of kin."

"Yes, that possibility has occurred to me. First of all, let's pray she doesn't die. Second, I'm counting on you two to make sure he doesn't benefit in any way if she does."

Ed added, "If I have my way, he'll die long before she does."

"Settle down, Ed. I'm not advocating that."

"I'm sorry, but stranger things have happened."

"I'm heartbroken enough about the accident, let's don't make things worse."

Ed stood to leave, "I'm just telling you that Tommy Lane will pay for what he's done and he won't collect a penny. That's a promise."

Dee and Stark stayed at the hospital with Lindbergh through the night. His facade of bravado was impressive, but they easily saw through it. He was distressed and couldn't sleep and didn't want to be alone. They didn't push him, but he needed to talk, and the story slowly came forth.

"We saw the 767 hit the approach lights. I don't want to ever see anything like that again. I've never felt more helpless...nothing we could do but watch. When it came up onto the runway and spun around, we saw the engine come off and roll right at us. We were trapped between two airplanes on the taxiway and had nowhere to go. When it hit us, I think we moved several feet sideways and I remember hoping the gear didn't collapse.

"The captain was really cool and didn't panic. He called for the shutdown and evacuation checklist, but he had already pulled the fire handles and discharged the extinguishers. By the time we opened the cockpit door the cabin was already filled with smoke and flames were showing through the windows on the right side.

"The flight attendants were nowhere in sight. He opened the door on the left side and sent me down the chute to help people when they came out. I could see people sliding out the rear door too. When the last person came down, I didn't see him in the door so I climbed back up the slide and looked for him. He was laying in the floor in first class passed out from the smoke. I was so scared I almost passed out from fear. I got him to the door and pushed him out and then slid down myself. I tried to avoid hitting him when I came down and I think that's when I hurt my ankle.

"I heard people screaming at the rear door and I ran back to see if I could help. I saw a flight attendant at the top of the slide and then she went back into the cabin. I used the re-entry rope and made like a monkey to climb up the escape slide and help her. We got a few people to the slide and then she passed out too. The smoke was horrible...I'll never forget the smell.

"I finally pushed her down the slide and then kept dragging people to the door and pushing them out. They were just piling up at the bottom like firewood. The next thing I remember was a fireman pushing me toward the door and taking charge. He had on a fireproof suit and an oxygen hood so I was happy to let him take over.

"They told me later...they found the other two flight attendants at mid-cabin right where the impact took place. Nobody survived that part of the cabin...if I could have got there sooner maybe...

Dee said, "You did all you could, Lindbergh. If the flight attendants had been alive, they would have been helping people themselves. No one could have saved them. They were already gone."

"Yeah, well… I want to get out of here and attend their funeral to pay my respects. I want to apologize to their family."

Stark said, "Don't think about it now. It will make more sense later when you have time to process it. You did great."

Telling his story seemed to sap whatever energy he had, and when he closed his eyes, they watched him sleep for an hour and then quietly left. The guard at the door promised to tell him they would be back.

When they reached the ground floor Stark said, "Dee, can you give me a few minutes before we go. I want to visit the hospital chapel and say a prayer for Cindy."

"I'll go with you if you don't mind. Prayer is all we have at this point."

The small chapel was empty and dimly lit, and they took a seat in the front row. After a few minutes of quiet reflection, Stark got down on his knees and lowered his head in silent prayer. Dee joined him and they both shed a few tears. When they were done, Stark helped her to her feet and they dabbed their eyes as they walked up the aisle between the wooden pews. Halfway to the exit, the door opened and an older woman entered alone.

Dee said, "Mrs. Latimer…"

Chapter Thirty One

After the meeting with Harold Collins, MJ went back to her office. Kyle was on his way back from Orlando and she wouldn't rest until he landed safely. *Am I going to spend the rest of my life worrying and waiting? That could have been Kyle instead of Lindbergh and if it had been, he would probably have killed himself evacuating people. He could have been in one of the other airplanes where the pilots died. When he gets home, he'll be miserable until he gets to fly again.*

She was actually happy when the intercom on her desk buzzed to change her train of thought. The receptionist informed her that someone named Kitty was on line three. *What now?*

On the off chance that there might be more than one Kitty, she answered, "Corporate Security, Madison Jones speaking."

"Is this Miss MJ?"

There was only one Kitty.

"Hi there, Kitty, how are you?"

"Don't want to bother you none, Miss MJ, but I caint get Miss Cindy on the phone."

"No bother at all, Kitty, what can I do for you dear."

"I'm word' 'bout Miss Cindy 'cause ya'll told me to leave her no 'count husband alone and I know he still on the loose."

"Well, we're looking out for her, Kitty. Why are you worried?"

"Cause I saw him last night and he was drinkin' heavy."

"You saw him?"

"He come walk in my place big as day and set in the corner boozin' like no tomorrow."

"What time was he there?"

"He come in the afternoon and stays till 'bout dark. I left him lone like you said."

"Do you know where he went when he left?"

"Sho do. I want to make sure he don't bother Miss Cindy. My boys follow him to motel, but they didn't hurt him or nothin. He so drunk when he left, he forgot his computer and left it on the chair."

"You've got his computer?"

"Sho do...a nice one too. Man at the pawn shop say he give me $300 if I want to sell it. I'm gone ask Miss Cindy if she wants the money or the computer."

"Kitty, I need to see that computer. It might help me have him arrested. Can I come there and take a look at it."

"Course you can, Miss MJ."

"Give me your address."

MJ rushed into Cason's office. "I got a lead on Lane, I need your help."

"Let's go."

When they saw Kitty's place, MJ said, "Good grief...I'm glad I didn't come alone."

"I've seen a lot worse, but don't ever go out alone, MJ. You don't even carry a gun."

"I know. Harry wants me to get one."

"So do I...I'll teach you how to use it safely."

"I don't think I could shoot anyone."

"It's not as hard as you think."

"You're scaring me, Cason."

He laughed, "Let's see what we can do about Mr. Lane."

They found Kitty sitting at a table with two large men. "Kitty, this is Cason. He's another friend of Cindy's."

The two large men sized Cason up, and he returned the favor with a bemused look on his face. Kitty said, "Ya'll brang me that computer behind the bar, then leave me 'lone."

One of her bouncers retrieved the computer and set it on the table. He nodded at Cason and then moved to the other side of the bar and folded his arms to watch.

While MJ and Kitty talked about *Miss Cindy*, Cason booted up the computer. When the screen illuminated, he made a few clicks and found the icon for *history*. He clicked on the top file and a video program appeared. One more click on the start arrow and the video began. He knew immediately what he was looking at. He had watched lots of recon video in Iraq. He moved the timeline to near the end of the video and stared at the screen before shutting it down.

He caught MJ's eye and then said, "Miss Kitty, I think this is just what we need to send Cindy's husband away for a long time. Would you trust us enough to let us take it with us to use as evidence."

The look on her face indicated she didn't trust him at all. She said, "I trust Miss MJ."

MJ intervened, "Kitty, we may have to turn this over to the police to get Tommy locked up, but I promise you we'll get it back and give it to Cindy. Cindy's going to love you more than she already does when we tell her how you helped nail him."

Kitty smiled big, "I owe Miss Cindy."

"She's had her problems, and I'm glad she has a good friend like you."

Kitty's smile got bigger. "He left another thang too…don't know what it is."

The bouncer retrieved the RCX-40 controller and set it on the table.

Cason stared at it. *This is too good to be true.* He said, "Miss Kitty, I'd really like to have a little time with Tommy Lane before we turn him over to the cops. Will you tell us where we can find him?"

"My boys been begging to go see him."

"They already had some fun when they put him on the train. I want to do something for Cindy too."

She thought it over, "You gone hurt him?"

"Yes ma'am."

Kitty signaled to her *boys,* "Ya'll tell Mr. Cason where the man is."

When they drove away from Kitty's bar, Cason said, "Put on a pair of evidence gloves and open the computer. Click on the video."

MJ watched in disbelief, "This will give me nightmares. What kind of animal would do this?"

"I'll introduce him to you if you want. Wipe down the computer and controller. We don't want our prints or Kitty's on the evidence."

Nearing the motel, Cason said, "Looks like we got company."

MJ said, "I know. Let's hope they don't interfere."

"I'll talk to them."

Cason pulled into the motel parking lot and said, "Wait here."

He walked over to the car that had been trailing them. "You gentlemen are not going to get in my way here, are you?"

The driver answered, "Not if you know what you're doing. Miss Kitty wants to make sure he doesn't get away again."

"He won't. I think we have the same previous employer. Did you play in the sand?"

"A couple of times...Army Ranger."

"Congratulations. Kitty must pay pretty good."

"Not really. She's my aunt. I just like to watch out for her."

"Thank you for your service…just stay put and cover my six. This won't take long."

"Don't screw up. We're tired of toying with this delinquent."

Cason walked back to the car. "Just wait here, MJ. I'll be back shortly."

"They don't pay me to sit in the car. What if something goes wrong?"

He laughed, "I think you've got a mean streak, MJ. You want to slap this guy around a little bit, don't you?"

"I've never slapped anyone around in my life, but I'm not going to sit out here with Kitty's goons staring at me. Why don't you just call the cops?"

"Because they screw up at every opportunity, and when they arrest the wife beater, he needs to have some incriminating items with him."

"Shouldn't we call Ed?"

"Well yeah, of course we should, and we will…in a little while. Come on…we're wasting time and Kitty's little boys are getting nervous. Bring the computer and controller with you."

When they approached the room, the door was open, but it was blocked by the maid's cart. She was placing dirty towels in a bag. Cason smiled at her, "Well, I guess we came to visit and our buddy's not home. He didn't check out did he?"

"No sir. He asked me where to get a newspaper. There's a Seven Eleven just down the block. I'm sure he'll be back in a few minutes."

"Well good, he'll be glad to see us."

The maid closed the door and pushed her cart away on the sidewalk humming a tune.

Cason said, "At least we won't have to worry about getting him to open the door. We passed a vending area a few doors back. Let's wait there."

"No need, here he comes."

Chapter Thirty Two

Cason glanced in the direction she was looking and then put his arms around MJ in a lover's embrace. He whispered, "Sorry, but we have to improvise."

MJ thought, *I've done some stupid things, but this has got to be the dumbest of all...ever.*

They were only five feet away when Tommy opened the door to his room. He never saw Cason's boot as it connected with the small of his back. Suddenly, his lungs emptied and he couldn't breathe.

He was propelled into the room and his brain registered the fact that the bedroom wall was approaching his face, but he was helpless to stop it. It didn't make sense that he was moving and not the wall.

Cason pulled MJ into the room and closed the door. Tommy slid down the wall after impact and gasped to get his breath back. When he finally wheezed and looked up, Cason said, "Mr. Lane, I've been looking forward to meeting you."

Tommy wanted to speak, but at the moment breathing was more important.

MJ stared in fascination and disbelief.

Cason turned to her, "Put the computer and the controller on the desk."

Placing his hand at the back of Tommy's neck, Cason squeezed a vertebra which produced a squeaky squeal between Tommy's gasps. "Get up on your feet like a good boy. You have a really high, girly sounding voice for a big guy."

Tommy was happy to follow orders and Cason sat him down at the desk. He managed to speak at last. "Who...are you?"

Cason squeezed a little harder, producing the squeal again. "You can think of us as your new mommy and daddy. I'll tell you when to open your filthy mouth. I brought your toys back to you. Pick up the controller and show me how you flew your airplane into the airliner."

"I didn't...eeeeiiiiiiieeee..."

"You're not listening to daddy. I didn't say speak. Pick up the controller."

Tommy picked up the box.

"Show me how to turn it on and make the airplane climb."

Tommy pushed buttons.

"Make it turn."

Tommy pushed buttons.

"Very nice. Open the computer and turn it on."

When the screen lit up, Cason said, "I want you to show us your little video of an airliner on a collision course."

"No...I eeeeeiiiiieeee..."

"You really need to listen more closely, Mr. Lane. I didn't ask for narration, just the video, please."

When the video started, Tommy tried to turn his head, which resulted in another squeal. "Mr. Lane, there were two hundred people on that airplane including your wife. Any one of them was worth a thousand of you...even the little children. Don't close your eyes. I want this burned into your soul, and I want the video to play in your head every time a neuron fires in your pathetic brain."

Tommy started crying and MJ almost felt sorry for him. Every time he sobbed Cason squeezed and turned it into a squeal. "Play it again."

Each time the video ran, it ended with a blank screen. "Look at that blank screen, Lane. Two hundred lives are now a blank screen. Why shouldn't your screen go blank? Do you know what it's like to burn to death? Do you know what it's like when your heart beats so fast it explodes? Why shouldn't I slowly demonstrate that for you? You don't deserve a quick death. Your screen should fade two hundred times while you beg for it to go blank."

Cason slid his hand around Lane's neck and found his windpipe. Lane began to struggle and make gurgling noises. His hands went to his neck and grasped at Cason's. Removing one hand, Cason squeezed Lanes's elbow and his entire arm fell slack. Squeezing the other elbow produced the same result. His feet began to kick, but there were fewer gurgling sounds now.

MJ finally found her voice. "Stop Cason…"

"I bet his wife begged him to stop when he was beating her."

"I hear you, but if you're going to kill him, I don't want to be a witness."

"I'm not going to kill him…not yet. But I might make him beg me to do it."

A soft knock at the door caused MJ to look for a hiding place.

Cason said, "Tell them to go back to the car and wait."

"How do you know it's them?"

"Tell them to wait."

When she cracked the door, Tommy tried to call for help.

"Help meeeeiiieee…"

Kitty's nephew laughed, "Sounds like a girl squealing. Let me in."

Cason nodded and she opened the door just enough to let him in. "I told you to wait in the car…what do you want?"

"You've been up here a long time. Kitty wants to know what's happening."

"I'll give her a full report when I'm done."

"What happened to his arms?"

"He's got a little nerve damage to his elbows. He won't be picking his nose for awhile."

"Sweet. Are you going to do him here or take him somewhere else? I know a place."

"He's not ready. He's got some debts to take care of first. I'm still explaining it to him."

"Man shouldn't beat his wife like that."

"He understands that part. Give me a few more minutes...wait in the car."

"How do you make him squeal like that?"

"Something I learned from a navy corpsman."

"Can I try it?"

"Didn't they teach you anything in Ranger school?"

"Come on man, show me the trick."

Cason showed him where to put his hand and where to press with his thumb. "Not too hard. I don't want him paralyzed yet."

MJ listened to the conversation in horror.

Tommy tried to move and then squealed when the thumb pressed down.

"That is so cool. Thanks for the tip. I'm going to try it on my brother-in-law."

MJ knew this wasn't real. *I'm going to wake up any minute now and no one will ever know I suffered this insanity.*

Cason asked, "How's the food at Kitty's place?"

"Best in town if you like fried chicken."

"This is making me hungry. You ready for lunch, MJ?"

"If it will get me out of here I am."

Cason took a plastic zip tie out of his pocket and placed Tommy's hands together. He looped the tie around Tommy's index fingers and pulled. As it tightened, there was a cracking noise and a scream MJ would never forget. "That's the fingers he used to manipulate the controller," Cason said.

Kitty's nephew asked, "What controller?"

"We'll explain it all at lunch. We need to make sure he stays put for a little while."

"Let me do it."

Tommy was laying in the floor moaning in pain and shock. The nephew placed a big foot on Tommy's knee and then balanced all

220 pounds on it like walking a tightrope. Tommy was barely conscious and only moaned a little louder. The nephew performed the same balancing act on the opposite ankle and said, "He'll stay put now. Let's go eat."

MJ wasn't sure she would ever have an appetite again, but she was happy to leave the room.

Walking across the parking lot, Cason made a phone call. "Sleepy, this is Cason. I have an anonymous tip for you."

"How can it be anonymous if I know who you are?"

"Should I have someone else call or will you take the tip from me?"

"Just tell me what you want…I'm trying to eat lunch."

"Would you like to redeem yourself for letting Tommy Lane sneak past you in the dark of night?"

"What's this going to cost me?"

"Who knows? I might need a favor in the future."

"That's what scares me."

"He's in room 134 at the James Street Motel. He has a laptop and an electronic controller with him that will put him on death row. The door is unlocked, and he won't give you any trouble."

"How do you know this?"

"The key word here is anonymous. Don't screw this up, Sleepy."

Six minutes later, two patrol cars entered the parking lot with lights, but no sirens. One officer approached the room from each direction. With guns drawn, they pushed the door open and peeked in. A few minutes later, two detective cars rolled up, followed by a fire-rescue EMT team.

Cason, MJ, and Kitty's two bouncers sat in their cars and watched from a strip mall across the street. They had parked side by side with the windows down so they could converse. They were discussing the attributes of fried chicken and collard greens when Tommy was loaded in the ambulance along with one of the detectives.

As they drove to Kitty's for lunch, thoughts of Tommy Lane were replaced with a vision of hot buttered biscuits dancing in their head.

Chapter Thirty Three

Harold Collins had very little appetite, but old habits are hard to break. He sat at his desk and picked at the food tray. He had not slept since the accident and his emotions varied from guilt, to anger, to frustration. He continually asked himself what could have been done differently to prevent such a tragedy. His doctor had reprimanded him numerous times for not taking time to relax and reduce the stress in his life. He had promised his wife a long vacation once he finished dealing with Senator Walker and completing the airport expansion approval. The word vacation was no longer included in his vocabulary.

He pushed the half eaten food tray away. His taste buds seemed to have ceased functioning. He was about to have his secretary remove the food tray when she opened the door as if reading his mind. "Mr. Collins, there's a news report you'll want to see."

He scavenged around his desk to find the remote for the TV mounted on the office wall. He adjusted the volume to hear the local news anchor.

"Once again, if you're just joining us, we have breaking news in yesterday's tragic crash of a Tri Con jet that killed over 200 people. We're trying to verify reports that authorities have arrested a suspect who may have been responsible for the crash. According to our source, who wishes to remain anonymous, Thomas Lane was arrested this morning at a motel near the airport. He is currently being treated for injuries at a local hospital and it is unknown if the injuries are related to the crash. Mr. Lane is a local resident and is believed to be an employee of Tri Con Airlines. We have several reporters working on this story and we will bring you details as soon as they become available."

Tommy Lane is not a Tri Con employee. Where do they come up with this crap? Your un-named source is an idiot.

He picked up the phone and dialed. "Ed, why wasn't I told Tommy Lane was arrested."

"I just found out myself. Some local cop grabbed him at a motel this morning. The FBI has him now, and they tell me he has injuries consistent with an interrogation. I don't think the local cop did that?"

"Where's Cason Haley?"

"I was just about to track him down. He and MJ rushed out of the office a couple of hours ago."

"Please don't tell me those two have collaborated on something illegal. We don't need more problems. I want a full briefing right away. I want you, Charlie Wells, and someone from the legal department in my office in thirty minutes."

Ed hung the phone up and redialed. Cason answered, "Yes sir."

"Where are you?"

"On the way back to the office, sir."

"Quit calling me sir. Is MJ with you?"

"Yes s...uh, yes she is."

"What do you know about Tommy Lane being arrested?"

"I believe a local cop picked him up."

"Don't play games with me, Cason. Did you interrogate him?"

"I met with him briefly before the cops came."

"Just spell it out. I don't have time for twenty questions."

"When the cops arrested him, he had the RCX-40 controller and a laptop with a video feed from his airplane on it. The video clearly shows that he flew the airplane directly into the path of the 767. Both devices have his fingerprints all over them."

"Did you see the video?"

"MJ downloaded it to a memory stick."

"Has anyone else seen the video?"

"Just the cops, as far as I know."

"Are they aware of the fact that you have a copy?"

"No sir."

"I've got a meeting in thirty minutes. I need that video."

Ed rushed into the meeting a couple of minutes late because he had waited for the video. Charlie was just beginning his briefing.

"The NTSB has recovered the Flight Data Recorder and the Cockpit Voice Recorder from the wreckage. Both devices have been downloaded and they both indicate that everything was perfectly normal and by the book until the airplane reached 350 feet. At that point, the right engine separated from the wing. The event is marked by the fact that the right electrical system failed, the right hydraulic system failed, the right pneumatic system failed, and so on.

"Control problems developed immediately and then began to compound. When the engine separated, the right side of the airplane became approximately 50,000 pounds lighter causing the airplane to roll to the left. At the same time, the loss of thrust caused the nose to yaw to the right. The captain had to cross control the airplane by using right aileron and left rudder. The result was an increase in the descent rate that they could not recover from even with the left engine firewalled.

"There is no procedure in the book for an engine falling off the wing. When all is said and done, I think we're going to find out the crew did a great job and almost saved it. The question now is why did the engine fall off?"

The lawyer from Tri Con's legal staff said, "If it was caused by a mechanical issue, our liability is going to go through the roof."

Ed said, "I may be able to shed some light on that."

Collins asked, "Does this have something to do with Tommy Lane?"

"Very much so."

"Then you better bring our attorney up to speed on that whole situation. Start from the beginning."

Ed gave a brief history of Cindy's troubled relationship with her husband and their domestic disputes. He then chronicled Tommy's escalating revenge tactics and what led them to investigate his motives. When he was done, the attorney remarked, "The man is insane and will probably plead so. What proof do you have?"

Ed plugged the memory stick into Collins' computer and started the video. It began with a bumpy takeoff from the mall parking lot and then an erratic flight path around the neighborhood. The airport was clearly in view and several airplanes could be seen on approach to the runway. The scenario remained the same for about fifteen minutes and the attorney glanced at his watch several times as if he needed to be somewhere else.

Then the airplane changed course and flew toward the airport. It appeared to be using the freeway as a navigational reference and the approach lights to the runway seemed to be the focal point. The landing lights of the 767 broke out of the clouds and flared on the screen. The airplane grew larger and the video camera seemed to make small flight path adjustments as the airliner came closer.

The four men watched in silence and held their breath. Ed wanted to push the pause button as if he could change history, but the 767 continued to grow larger. The airplane finally filled the entire screen and the bright landing lights distorted the image. Then the screen went black.

Silence filled the room and no one could find words. Collins slowly made his way to his desk and sat down with his face in his hands. Charlie began pacing back and forth in front of the desk in agitated anger.

The attorney broke the silence. "My God... Oh my God..."

Collins removed his hands from his face and wiped his eyes, "Two hundred people..."

The attorney said, "Oh my God..."

After another silent pause, Ed said, "Look, no one knows I have this video. The FBI has the original, but they don't know about the copy. We can't let anyone know we have this."

The attorney was recovering from the shock of what he had viewed and returned to character. "How did you get the video?"

"I just told you it doesn't exist."

"If you want my help, I have to know the facts."

"I didn't ask for your help, but here's a fact for you...it doesn't exist."

The attorney folded his arms and was about to respond when Collins intervened. "None of that matters. We know what happened and the FBI will sort it out." Addressing the attorney, he continued, "There is something else you can help us with."

He explained Cindy's inheritance and once again swore the lawyer to secrecy. "If she dies, what will be the ramifications?"

"Since she doesn't have a will, it will be a simple probate. Her assets will pass to her next of kin. In this case it will be her husband. The fact that he will be incarcerated as a convicted felon will be grounds to contest the probate, but in the end, he will inherit."

That was not what Collins wanted to hear. "You're telling me that he can murder his wife and still profit from her death?"

"We can fight it in court and probably delay it for years, but in the end he will not be the only one to profit. The government will be licking their chops to collect the estate taxes on that amount of inheritance."

"What if he gets the death penalty?"

"In that case he will be assigned to a cell where he will be fed and watered by the state for the next twenty years while his appeals playout. Once his inheritance becomes public knowledge, there will be high dollar attorneys lining up to take his case. If and when he's executed, the government will be anxious to once again collect estate taxes when the money passes to his next of kin."

"That scenario makes me sick."

"I'm sorry. Maybe we can find a better legal path in time, but for now, it's not a pretty picture."

Charlie had tuned out the discussion since he had no expertise in estate law. However, he knew airplanes and something didn't add up. He said, "Ed, I know what we just saw, whether you say it exists or not, but I don't see how a small model airplane could impact a 767 hard enough to knock a 50,000 pound engine off."

"I may have failed to mention that the model was loaded with explosive."

"Oh…"

Chapter Thirty Four

Cindy Lane had never been more at peace. She felt totally rested and worry free. She felt healthy and energetic. All her blemishes and faults had magically disappeared and she had never felt more beautiful. It was an amazing and wonderful feeling to know that she could simply walk away from all her problems.

She strolled leisurely along, and the warm surface caressed her bare feet. The path was so soft it felt like walking on puffy white clouds. She wanted to dance on her toes like a ballerina. The world seemed so bright and crisp, and she continued to walk toward the bright morning sun as it rose to dawn a new day and a new beginning. She could not see beyond the bright morning, but optimism soothed her and made her smile. Sweet music drifted with her, and she thought she could hear familiar voices in the distance ahead. *Grandfather?*

Miriam Latimer looked at her broken daughter and wondered if she felt pain. The doctors were still assessing her injuries, but the prognosis had not changed. Cindy had not moved or reacted to stimulus of any kind. The breathing machine expanded and contracted as if it was more alive than the body it provided oxygen to. The feeding tubes pumped nutrients and the heart monitor beeped. Ms. Latimer dabbed at her eyes with a wet handkerchief. She was only allowed a five minute visit each hour and the same thoughts occurred each time. *Am I doing the right thing? If she is in pain, am I prolonging her agony? My own health care directive refuses extraordinary measures to prolong life. She is so young...what would she want me to do? She's all I have left...God help me...*

The nurse signaled that time was up and Mrs. Latimer was filled with guilt as she walked back to the waiting room. Dee and Stark both stood and looked at her with hopeful eyes.

"There's no change. I don't know if she feels anything or if she's even aware of anything. She's so pale and lifeless." Tears began again, "They told me she must have been ejected from the airplane and thrown across the field. That may have saved her life. Other people were incinerated in the fire."

Dee put her arms around her. "Then God must have a purpose for her."

"God may be punishing me. The doctors say she has no chance of survival without the life support. How long should I let her suffer?"

"Give it some time. Meanwhile, we'll pray our hearts out."

"Mr. Stark, I remember you from the funeral, are you friends with Cindy?"

"Yes ma'am."

Her eyes narrowed a bit, "Have we spoken before, your voice sounds familiar."

I'm busted. "Yes ma'am, we spoke on the phone."

"I thought so. I believe you asked my daughter out."

"In a manner of speaking, but it was just a running joke between us. I know she's married, ma'am, and would not go out with anyone."

"Yes, she tried to explain that to me."

Dee wasn't comfortable with the discussion. "Can you tell us why we have to be secretive about Cindy's survival?"

"No, I can't, but you must not tell anyone that she's here. Can I trust you two?"

Dee answered, "Of course."

"Mr. Stark?"

"Yes ma'am. I'll do anything I can to help you and Cindy. All you have to do is ask."

Stark suddenly stood and faced the door. He almost came to attention and saluted when he saw Harold Collins walk in. Collins was surprised to see that Mrs. Latimer was not alone. *What is it with this new pilot class? They seem to turn up everywhere I go. Did she tell them about Cindy?*

Mrs. Latimer looked up. "Hello Harold. This is Dee Daniels and Mr. Stark. I believe we can trust them."

Collins didn't look so sure, but he shook hands with both of them. "Miriam, can we have a word in private?"

Dee spoke up, "We'll wait in the hall."

"Don't go far. I want to talk to the both of you later."

When they were alone, Collins asked, "How much do they know?"

"Only that Cindy is in critical condition."

"They don't know about the inheritance?"

"Of course not. They were here to see the copilot, and when they saw me, I couldn't lie to them."

"There have been some developments that you need to know about. Tommy Lane has been arrested and will be charged with causing the accident. I'm sorry to have to burden you with that news, and I don't want you or Cindy to feel any responsibility for his actions."

She sat down and buried her face in her hands. After a minute, she said, "I don't know if I can bear this, Harold. I hate myself because I'm angry. I'm angry at Cindy for marrying that man. I'm angry at myself for letting her marry him. I don't want to lose my daughter while I'm angry. I'll never forgive myself."

"Everyone makes mistakes, Miriam. God knows I have. Cindy was trying hard to make things right, and I respect her for that. Don't beat yourself up over something you had no control over. I was impressed with your pastor at the funeral, and I think you should talk to him. A little spiritual reflection might clear things up for you."

Mrs. Latimer closed her eyes and silently prayed, *God, please don't take her. Please let her live.*

Cindy continued her light-hearted journey and quickened her pace when she thought of her grandfather. She seemed to float on her feet, and the fragrance of fresh flowers filled the crisp morning. *This is wonderful. It is so peaceful and serene.*

The sound of someone calling her name told her she was not alone and her heart swelled with joy. *Mom, where are you?* The voice called again and Cindy turned to look behind her. She was horrified at what she saw. The sky was filled with black smoke and an acrid stench filled her nostrils. The smoke swirled and the burning tail section of an airplane became visible. *Noooo...* She turned and ran toward the crisp clear morning.

Chapter Thirty Five

Tommy Lane was treated and released from the hospital. He didn't require surgery and was prescribed painkillers and bed rest. His victims occupied all the available beds and it was decided he could rest in jail. He was unable to walk so he was perp rolled out of the hospital in a wheelchair. The news media was delighted that he was cuffed and shackled to the chair. The cameras rolled and the reporters shouted questions. Tommy's only response was an obscene gesture that no one noticed because he couldn't raise his hand. He was still wearing the hospital's examining gown and a second obscenity occurred when he was transferred from the chair to the jailer's van. The reporters were disappointed that the video techies at the station would have to blur Tommy's posterior for TV presentation. Of course, there was always YouTube.

Tommy was assigned a cell by himself and immediately clammed up. He knew his rights and wouldn't speak until he was represented. He demanded his phone call and contacted his attorney. "Tommy, I'm a divorce lawyer. I can't help you. The court will appoint a criminal defense attorney for you. Until then, keep your mouth shut."

Tommy exploded when the line went dead and cursed the useless phone. The jailers laughed at him as they wheeled him back to his cell. He asked for his pain pills and they laughed again.

Tommy's interrogation was scheduled for ten a.m. the following morning. He explained to his reluctant attorney that he was completely innocent and had been tortured before being arrested. He also wanted to file suit against the jail for withholding his medication.

"Mr. Lane, you've been charged with serious crimes…capital crimes. I can't help you unless you are completely honest with me."

"I'm telling the truth, I didn't do it. If you don't believe me…you're fired."

"Thank you. I will so inform the court, and a new attorney will be appointed for you. Have a good day, Mr. Lane."

The attorney exited post haste and Tommy went into a rage. The jailers ignored him.

Two hours later, a second attorney arrived. The attractive young woman sat her briefcase on the table and without introduction she said, "Shut up, Mr. Lane, and listen to me. You just fired an attorney who was much more qualified than I am. If you give me problems and ask for another lawyer, the judge will dislike you very much, and you will die of old age before he lets you go to trial. They don't pay me enough to put up with a bunch of your crap. Tell me what happened and I'll advise you what to do."

She remained standing until Tommy said, "Okay, tell me what you want to know."

Ed used his connections as a former FBI agent to gain permission to observe the interrogation. He watched through the one-way mirror as Tommy was wheeled into the room. His attorney sat beside him with a legal pad at the ready. The FBI agent informed them that the session was being videotaped and then introduced everyone present for the record.

"Mr. Lane, you have a long list of charges pending, and perhaps you can clear some things up for us that will allow some of those charges to be dropped. Where do you reside?"

"I don't have a place right now."

"Do you own a vehicle?"

"Uh…no."

"Do you have access to a vehicle?"

"No."

The agent handed Tommy a sheet of paper. "This is a statement from Mr. Joseph Craven indicating that you rented a white van from him. Is he lying to us?"

"Yes, he's lying."

"Okay. Do you own an RCX-40 radio controlled airplane?"

"No."

"Mr. Lane, where were you at the time of the recent air crash that resulted in over 200 deaths?"

The attorney intervened, "You don't have to answer that."

The agent continued and placed a clear plastic bag on the table. The RCX-40 controller was clearly visible inside the bag. "Mr. Lane, do you recognize this item?"

"No."

The agent handed the attorney an evidence sheet. "This verifies that Mr. Lane's fingerprints are found in several places on this item."

Tommy said, "Oh yeah, I think that's the thing I was forced to touch when I was tortured."

"Who tortured you, Mr. Lane?"

"I don't know. It was a man and woman I've never seen before."

"I see."

The agent placed Tommy's laptop on the table in a plastic bag. "Do you recognize this computer?"

"No."

"It has all your personal data on it, including emails addressed to you. It also has your fingerprints all over it."

"It may be the computer they forced me to touch."

"Who forced you to...?"

The attorney interrupted again, "He already answered that."

"Mr. Lane, is your wife currently employed by Tri Con Airlines as a flight attendant?"

"Yes."

"Was your wife on board the 767 when it crashed?"

Tommy lowered his head, "Yes."

"Are you and your wife in the process of being divorced, sir?"

"We were trying to get back together."

"Does your wife have a $500,000 accidental death insurance policy?"

The attorney glared at the agent and said, "If you want to fish, you need to get a boat. We're not going to sit here and listen to accusations and speculation. Do you have any more relevant questions?"

"Mr. Lane, did you fly your model airplane into the path of a Tri Con Airlines jet, causing it to crash?"

The attorney stood up and said, "My client declines to answer further questions at this time. He is in great pain and is on strong medication."

"Suit yourself, counselor. I think we have enough for now."

When Tommy and the attorney left the room, Ed walked in to debrief. The agent said, "This guy is toast. We have him three ways from Sunday. The van has his fingerprints all over it and there are traces of plastic explosive in the cargo area."

"Don't forget the RCX-40 owner's manual."

"Icing on the cake. I'm a little worried about the torture thing. Do you have your people under control, Ed?"

"Of course."

"Well, somebody definitely caused him bodily harm."

"I think he's had a few disputes with a local criminal element. Probably something unrelated."

"We'll look into that, but you better not let your people go rogue on this thing. It's looking good and I don't want anything to muddy the water."

"Looks like a slam dunk, I don't see a problem."

Chapter Thirty Six

The attorney looked across the table at Tommy. "Don't lie to me and don't withhold information. Why didn't you tell me your wife was on the airplane?"

"I was too upset to talk about it."

"Are you getting divorced?"

"No, I changed my mind about the divorce. I wanted to reconcile."

"Are you the beneficiary on her insurance policy?"

"We're still married."

"I have to tell you, their evidence is compelling. The only reason they would reveal their case like that is to encourage you to plead guilty and negotiate a deal. You're going to have to give me something to work with or we're looking at the death penalty. If you were there and flying your little airplane, we might be able to spin this as an accident."

"Can I collect the $500,000?"

"If you do, you'll no longer be eligible for a court-appointed attorney and your legal fees will be very expensive."

"My pain's getting worse. I need to rest…can we talk about this later?"

The gravel road was no challenge for the four wheel drive pick-up truck. The frame of the truck had been lifted to provide ground clearance and to accommodate the oversized tires. The loud rumble of the engine announced that the exhaust was not restricted by mufflers. The truck was the pride and joy of the two teenage brothers and the perfect vehicle to explore the Chattahoochee River west of the airport and look for isolated fishing spots. The driver turned to his brother who was looking at the map, "Where do we turn, dimwit?"

"Just keep driving, dufus—I'll let you know when we get there."

"What's the name of the next road?"

"Slow down, bozo, I think that's it coming up."

"Dude, look at that river!"

"Don't get excited, it runs all the way to the Gulf of Mexico."

The truck rumbled along the road and through the densely wooded area near the river bank. The driver rounded a curve and applied the brakes as a deer scampered into the trees. The brother in the passenger seat raised an imaginary rifle and pulled the trigger.

"Kapow, I could take that bad boy without a scope."

"You couldn't hit the side of a barn with a two by four, bubblehead."

"Yeah, but I can kick your spastic butt all day long."

"I wouldn't put a lot of money on that, girlie boy."

"You know, you're like a chicken house—extremely noisy and full of crap."

"Yeah, and you're like a lightning bug—you don't want to set the world on fire, you just want to show your butt."

"Slow down, speedo, I think we're getting close."

The road curved back and forth and the driver downshifted as they descended a small hill. "This road's a little unpredictable."

"Oh, kinda like your hand eye coordination."

"Why don't you concentrate on your mono-tasking skills, blubber brain. Let's find a place to park so we can hike and explore for awhile."

A few minutes and several insults later, they found a safe place to leave the truck and began checking their hiking equipment. They both loved the outdoors and considered themselves experts in the art of hiking and camping. Their backpacks contained plenty of food and water as well as first aid kits and other survival gear.

"Make sure the GPS is working, retardo. Did you put new batteries in it?"

"Does a cat have a tail?"

After writing down the coordinates of their starting point, they set off along the river traveling to the northwest. The terrain varied from gentle slopes to steep river banks, but it was what they expected and they enjoyed the challenge. After an hour, they found a level stretch of ground and declared a ten minute break. Sitting on a flat boulder and dangling their feet they both chewed beef jerky and drank from canteens.

"Dude, this is some serious wilderness. I hope a black bear don't smell the jerky and decide to take it from us."

"A bear would smell your putrid armpits long before the jerky and run the opposite direction. You're a natural repellant."

"That's because I don't use that lady's perfume like you do, Miss Alice."

"Do you think we should head back?"

"We've got plenty of daylight left—let's check out what's beyond that next bend in the river before we call it quits."

"I'm up for it, lead the way, Magellan."

They worked their way along the side of the river, taking a zig-zag path and watching for snakes. After thirty minutes, they had marked GPS coordinates for a few more fishing spots that looked promising.

"Dude, check that out!"

"Check what out?"

"Right over there. It looks like a wheel of some kind."

They made their way over to the object half covered by underbrush.

"Man, how did that get here? What is it?"

"Duh…it's a wheel, sewer breath. The cavemen invented them a couple of years ago. It was on all the news channels."

"It looks like it came off a kid's toy of some kind."

"Yeah, I can see that a lot of kids play with their toys out here in the wilderness."

"Well, it must have fell out of the sky then."

"Remind me to wear a helmet next time we go hiking in case a wheel falls on me."

"Why? There's nothing in your skull anyway."

"Let's look around and see if we find anything else."

"Should we take the wheel with us?"

"Yeah, you never know when you might need a toy wheel."

Leaving the wheel where it was, they scouted the area but found nothing else of interest. They were about to head back to the truck when the younger brother said, "It did fall from the sky."

"What are you obsessing about?"

"Look up stupid."

Resting in the limbs of a thick pine tree, they could see a large model airplane. Other than missing a wheel, it appeared to be largely intact. "Bro, that's probably worth a lot of money. I'll climb and lower it down to you with a rope."

Twenty minutes later, the airplane nestled onto the ground among the pine needles. They examined their treasure and decided the wheel could probably be fixed without a problem. The right wing featured a decal that identified the airplane as an RCX-40.

"It has a switch mounted on the nose. Wonder what that's for?"

With typical teenage curiosity and a thirst for adventure, he pushed the button.

Tommy's attorney was happy to get away from the jail. The place depressed her and she knew there was no help for Tommy Lane. *What a total and complete fool. As if my reputation hasn't been*

tarnished enough, I now represent an imbecile on his way to death row. An imbecile without a penny to his name or a brain in his head.

As she drove away, she listened to the traffic and weather report on the all-news station. As usual, traffic was a snarl in Atlanta, but the weather was beautiful. *I should be representing the victims of fender benders.* She turned the volume up when the breaking news trumpet sounded.

> "This news is just breaking as we speak, but it appears that a victim of the Tri Con Airlines crash had just inherited a fortune in the days preceding the accident. Cynthia Lane has been listed as a Tri Con crewmember on the 767 that crashed and took the lives of 200 people. It's believed that Ms. Lane was a flight attendant. Court records filed this week indicate that she was the Granddaughter of Alexander Morgan, who passed away recently, leaving an estate worth millions. It is not known at this time what, if any, relationship Ms. Lane might be with Thomas Lane who has been arrested in connection with the accident. Stay tuned for details on this breaking news."

The attorney smiled and accelerated. *Millions... Hello. Now we're talking, baby.* In her mind, she could see the cover sheet of the lawsuit, *Lane vs Estate of Alexander Morgan et al.* She hung a U-turn at the next intersection and headed back to the jail.

Chapter Thirty Seven

Harold Collins was livid. The Tri Con lawyer had explained to him that Miriam's estate attorney had no choice but to file the probate papers with the court and at that point it was a matter of public record. The news media had snitches in every office of government and it was inevitable that the word would leak. He also warned him that the reporters would soon find out that Cindy was not deceased.

When Collins finally got his temper under control, he asked, "Can the divorce be finalized at this point?"

"The short answer is no. It's a contested divorce, and the judge will not issue the decree without a hearing, and Cindy obviously can't be present to testify. This is going to be a fur ball, Harold. If she dies he's going to inherit, and if she lives, he's going to share the assets in the divorce."

Collins' secretary stuck her head in the door, "Sir, Senator Walker is on his way up."

Collins ushered the lawyer out of the office, "Keep digging. Hire outside counsel if you have to. There has to be a way to solve this."

Senator Walker and his aide entered the reception area as the lawyer left. Collins waited patiently while the senator campaigned with the office personnel and flashed his winning smile all around. *For God's sake, give it a rest.*

When they were finally seated in Collins' conference room, the Senator frowned and said, "Harold, this accident is a failure all around. This Lane woman and her idiotic husband are all over the news. If the press finds out I bailed her out of jail, and she is somehow culpable for this tragedy, I'm going to hold you responsible. Tri Con can forget about the fruits of airport expansion or anything else that comes through my committee. Do you realize my son almost died because of this fiasco?"

"Senator, I stand by my employees one hundred per cent. Cindy Lane is in no way responsible for the accident, and I'm extremely proud of the way your son performed his duties in the face of great danger. If he felt Cindy merited your help when she was in jail, then I'm sure his judgment was justified. My employees, including your son, are the best in the business and we're going to overcome this adversity and move Tri Con forward. If you have pressing political concerns at the moment, I'm happy to put the airport expansion, and anything else that comes through your committee, on the back burner until you're ready to proceed. You might consider that my employees in the state of Pennsylvania have generally supported you in the past. You might also consider that Cindy and her mother, both millionaires, might express their appreciation for your help in the form of a generous campaign contribution. Do we have business to discuss or should I call for your limo?"

The senator's aide coughed and covered his mouth, but his eyes displayed an expression of glee. The senator hesitated and then also smiled. "Settle down, Harold, I just want you to understand my position. Where are we in the investigation?"

"Due to the excellent work of some of my security personnel, Tommy Lane is in jail and will probably be there for the rest of his miserable life. All things considered, you'll probably be hailed as Cindy's guardian angel for rescuing her from her reviled husband. You may want to leak the story yourself."

Walker looked at his aide, who was giving the idea consideration. Opening his briefcase, the senator said, "There are just a few pieces of property that might pose a problem for the expansion. I suggest we try to purchase the land through a third party so the owners don't realize they're dealing with Daddy Deep Pockets. I finally received the aerial surveys I ordered a week ago. Let me point out the problem areas."

The aide used his laptop to Power Point the photos onto the conference room screen. After a discussion of the property in question, the senator said, "You know more about the local market, Harold. I'll email all the photos to you, and perhaps you can find out who owns the property and how we should proceed."

"I'll put someone on it right away. How is Lindbergh feeling?"

"He's doing pretty well. Is there going to be a problem with his medical bills and salary during his recovery?"

Collins smiled, "His only problem will be dealing with being a media darling. Maybe he'll endorse you."

Lindbergh's ankle itched and the cast prevented him from scratching it. He was further irritated by the fact that his appetite had returned and the food on his dinner tray did not excite his palate. *This must be leftovers from the local soup kitchen.*

He was feeling sorry for himself when the door opened and Kyle appeared with MJ by his side. "Lindbergh, I was hoping you could get through your first trip without getting your name in the newspaper."

"Look who's talking. You're the guy who generated national headlines by making your first landing with dead terrorists on board."

"That was before I became a real airline pilot."

"MJ, I'm happy to see you, but did you have to bring your 'pain in the butt' boyfriend with you?"

"He's been away for a few days, and now he's clinging. I think he missed me. Shall I have him wait in the hall?"

"No, the hospital requires more decorum in the public areas than he's capable of."

Kyle laughed, "Speaking of decorum, do you make it a practice to parade through the airport with ladies' panties hanging out of your suitcase?"

"MJ, tell him to wait in the hall."

"No way. I want to hear this story."

The door opened once again and Cam Horner appeared. "Lindbergh, are we going to have to assign an escort to keep you out of trouble?"

"Not a bad idea, Horner. See if you can find me an attractive blond chaperone."

Dee walked in followed by Stark. Dee asked, "Are ya'll talking about me?"

Lindbergh smiled, "No, we were talking about an *attractive* blond."

"Well, you must be feeling better. At least your sarcasm has recovered."

"Just kidding, Dee. You're the prettiest pilot I know."

"Other than yourself, of course."

Stark said, "Are you going to eat that dinner roll?"

"You're welcome to it…you and the dinner roll deserve each other."

"Can I have the butter?"

"Stark, your stomach must be as empty as your brain."

"Shut up, Lindbergh. Here, read this while I eat."

The newspaper featured a front page story about Lindbergh's heroism, along with a head and shoulder photo. His face turned red and he threw the paper at Stark. "Did you do that, you moron?"

Stark stopped chewing and swallowed, "Even I wouldn't stoop that low. Nice photo though, Mr. Hero."

Lindbergh had a thoughtful look on his face, "Kyle was your story on the front page?"

"Unfortunately, yes."

Lindbergh frowned, "Was it above the fold or below?"

"Below, I think."

Lindbergh smiled, "I'm above the fold. Maybe someday you'll be as famous as me."

"I certainly hope not. We're both lucky we didn't appear in the obituaries."

Dee said, "This is not about you two idiots. Look who made the news below the fold."

Lindbergh read the article. "Is this right? Cindy is a multi-millionaire?"

"Apparently so."

"I had no idea."

Dee said, "She didn't either. It's a long story."

"You're telling me the guy I kicked in the head caused the accident."

"It sure looks that way."

"I should have kicked him harder."

"You had your chance. Looks like he'll be in jail for the duration."

The older brother said, "Stop pushing the switch, stupid. I think the battery's dead."

"Maybe we can get a new one."

"It's getting dark. We better get back to the truck. Grab one end of this thing."

"How much do you think it's worth?"

"Probably a couple million dollars...maybe we can get the lobotomy you've always needed."

"Did it hurt when you got yours?"

"Shut up and let's go. I think I know a guy who can help us sell it."

The sun was almost down when they loaded the RCX-40 in the truck.

MJ watched the sun rise as she drove to work. *A new day and a new adventure...what a way to make a living.* She and Kyle had stayed late at the hospital and visited with Cindy's mom after cheering up Lindbergh. Stark was still there when they left at midnight.

She was into her second cup of coffee when the receptionist buzzed. "MJ, there's some guy named Andy on line two."

"Andy who?"

"Don't know. He said he would only talk to you."

Now what?

She punched the line two button. "Madison Jones speaking."

"Miss Jones, this is Andy. Do you remember me?"

"I'm sorry, can you refresh my memory?"

"You had me arrested when my airplane went out of control."

"Oh, of course, how are you Andy?"

"I want to thank you for putting in a good word for me with the police."

"I know you didn't mean any harm, Andy. You shouldn't let it ruin your life."

"Thank you. That's what my parents say too."

"You should listen to them. What can I do for you, Andy?"

"I saw a picture of the guy they arrested on the news, and he's the same guy I saw a few times at the Aero Club. He was learning how to fly a new airplane."

"The police have interviewed several people at the Aero Club, who also saw him there."

"Yes ma'am, I noticed him because he was flying a brand new RCX-40 which is a really cool airplane."

"I appreciate you calling, Andy, but I think the authorities have all the witnesses they need."

"That's not why I'm calling, Miss Jones. I think I know where his airplane is."

"So do I. I think it met the same fate yours did and was destroyed in the accident."

"No, it wasn't. I know where it is."

"Andy, I don't understand what you're trying to say."

"A couple of guys I know found an RCX-40 in the woods out by the river. It's just like the one the guy was flying at the Aero Club. They asked me to find out what it's worth and help them sell it."

"Well, there must be lots of airplanes like that. It probably belongs to someone else."

"I know you don't believe me, but I know a lot about model airplanes. I have the serial number if you want it."

"Okay, give me the number and I promise I'll check it out, Andy."

She wrote the number on a notepad and left it on her desk. "Thanks for calling, Andy. It was nice talking to you."

"Okay. The airplane is in the kid's garage next door to where I live if you want to see it. I told them they couldn't sell it until they try to return it to the owner."

"You're a good kid, Andy. I'm glad you're trying to do the right thing. Give me the address in case I hear of someone looking for an airplane."

After concluding the phone call, she refilled her coffee and headed to the conference room for the morning staff meeting. Ed gave a brief summation of the NTSB accident investigation so far and he also described his observations from Tommy's questioning the day before. "The authorities seem to have this matter under control now. I've recommended that the locals increase the patrols around the perimeter of all our airports and hopefully the FAA will finally enact

242 – HARRISON JONES

new rules on flying model airplanes. The fact that Tommy Lane is in jail is little consolation for what happened, but that's where we're at."

When the meeting concluded, he called Cason and MJ aside. "Mr. Collins has asked us to do a little research for the airport expansion project. There are several parcels of property that he would like us to research. I want you two to find out who owns the land and determine the best way to approach them about selling without telling them that the government is the buyer. I don't think they're concerned as much about the price as they are about expediting the process. It's not the kind of busy work I like for us to be involved in. But while you're doing it, I want you to file a report on how the expansion will affect the perimeter security of the airport."

He handed them a manila envelope. "This is the aerial surveys and photos of the expansion area. The property in question is outlined. Try to have something preliminary for Collins by the end of the day."

When everyone left, MJ and Cason spread the photos out on the conference table. Cason said, "I hate this kind of menial work."

MJ laughed, "That's because there are no bad guys involved. There's no challenge."

"There's no fun either."

"Don't worry…I can do most of this on the internet. Let me work on it and after lunch we can drive out there and take a look at it."

"What do you think Kitty's having for lunch today?"

"I'm not going to start hanging out at Kitty's bar."

"It was just a thought."

"Go clean your gun or something. Check with me in a couple of hours."

Chapter Thirty Eight

Researching property records and deeds on the internet was easy for MJ, and she soon had a list of owners and tax assessments for the property in question. She researched all the recent real estate closings and computed the average fair market price for land in the area. *Cason's right, this is grunt work.*

After typing her conclusions into report form, she sat back to study the aerial photographs. The photos were of extremely high quality and exhibited great detail. She decided Cason was better qualified to determine the security ramifications of the new airport perimeter and waited for him to show up before continuing.

She decided to call Kyle and see if he had any news on Lindbergh or Cindy. She could hear the excitement in his voice when he answered. She said, "You sound happy today. Did an airplane fly over or something?"

"You didn't get my text?"

"Sorry, I've been busy. Some of us have to work on a daily basis."

"I've got a trip assignment."

"That would explain it. When?"

"This afternoon. I'm laying over in Boston, and I'll be back tomorrow night."

"Try not to lose your hat this time."

"You're too funny. I'll call you tonight."

"Yes you will…behave yourself."

She ended the call and looked up to see Cason standing in her doorway. "It's not nice to spy on people."

"Sorry. I didn't want to interrupt your call."

"I think I've got everything we need. You want to take a look at these photos and then drive out there to see the property?"

"I owe you, MJ. I would have no clue how to get all this information."

"Oh, I'm sure you could have gone to the courthouse and beat it out of someone. Let me show you the lots we're supposed to check out."

Spreading the photos on her desk, she said, "Somebody did a great job mapping this property. The photographs even have time stamps and GPS fixes overlaid on them."

"The surveillance photos we used in Afghanistan were like this. We knew everything about the area before we infiltrated. There were no surprises."

"Do you miss the military?"

"I'm still on active reserve. Ed gives me time off to stay current with the Navy."

MJ began putting the photos away and noticed her notepad on the desk. "The weirdest thing happened this morning. Do you remember Andy, the kid that flew his airplane into the MD-88?"

"How could I forget?"

"He called me this morning and said that a couple of his buddies had found an RCX-40 and it was just like Tommy Lane's."

"That is weird."

"He somehow believes it's Tommy's airplane."

"Not possible."

"That's true. Do you know where Tommy bought the airplane?"

"He bought it at a hobby shop. I have a copy of the receipt. So do the police."

"Is there any way to find out the serial number of his airplane?"

"Sure. It's on the receipt. Why do you ask?"

"Because Andy gave me the serial number of the airplane his buddies found in the woods."

"You don't like loose ends, do you?"

"Keeps me awake at night."

"Let's check it out. We can drop by my desk on the way out and compare the serial numbers so you can sleep tonight."

When the two numbers were lying beside each other on Cason's desk, they were both speechless. After a moment, Cason said, "How could...there must be a..."

"Wait a...what if..."

Recovering, Cason said, "If that's Tommy's airplane it's loaded with explosives."

"Oh my God. What if those kids..."

"Give me the address."

Cason dialed 911 and reported a bomb at the address. "Let's go, MJ."

Fifteen minutes later they arrived to find flashing blue and red lights dominating the street. Two police cruisers, a fire truck, an EMT unit, and a bomb disposal squad idled in random order. The bomb tech was just suiting up. A cop Cason didn't recognize said, "You two need to get back in your vehicle and clear the area."

"I called it in. I need to talk to the bomb team and tell them what they're dealing with."

"Who are you?"

Cason and MJ both showed their Tri Con Security ID.

"Oh, it's you. I've heard stories about both of you. Wait here."

The bomb tech waddled over in his protective gear and Cason explained about the possibility of plastic explosives and the impact switch. "That sounds simple enough if it's stable. We'll know in a few minutes. You might want to stand behind the fire truck. In case I never see you again, it was nice to meet you."

Cason smiled, "Don't damage the merchandise. It's evidence in an FBI case. See you in a few minutes. We'll help you count your fingers and toes."

The bomb tech chuckled as he waddled away.

After listening to the conversation, the cop cocked his head to one side and talked to his shoulder. The shoulder responded with static and garbled verbiage. "The chief is on his way. He said to arrest you if you try to leave the scene."

"I'll behave, but you might need to cuff MJ."

"Don't listen to him officer, he's prone to fabricate facts."

Cason asked, "Was anybody home when you guys got here?"

"No, and the other homes in the neighborhood have been evacuated."

MJ sat down on the running board of the fire truck and took out her cell phone to call Ed.

Cason covered the phone with his paw. "MJ, please don't generate a cell phone signal in the vicinity of a bomb. We're only guessing at how it might be triggered."

She stared at the phone and then looked up at him. "Why do I go anywhere with you? You're like a ticking bomb yourself."

"And all this time I thought it was you who attracted trouble."

They were joined behind the fire truck by several cops and firefighters, and after several minutes of breathing diesel fumes, the bomb tech waddled out of the garage. He removed his heavy gloves and helmet and then gave the all clear signal. He assured everyone that the bomb was disarmed and then looked at Cason. "It was set up like you described it. Looks like it had a rough landing, but the impact switch never activated. One of the wires connecting the battery to the initiator came off, probably during the landing, and rendered it harmless. Good thing too, because it's loaded with enough plastic to demolish the house."

A siren could be heard in the distance and one of the patrolman sighed, "Here comes the chief. He loves to bully traffic out of his way with lights and siren."

The car rounded the corner and screeched to a stop with lights blazing. The siren diminished to a low growl before giving a final burp and going silent. The chief emerged putting his hat on his head before walking toward them with his hand on his holstered weapon.

One of the patrolman said, "Thank God he's arrived and we'll all be safe now."

The chuckles were just dissipating as he came within earshot. No one commented on the food stains adorning his tie.

He snarled, "I'd like to enjoy my lunch in peace at least once before I retire. Cason, you must be attracted to crime scenes like flies to a cow patty. Does Ed know you're here?"

"I don't think so, Chief. I was just about to call him."

"Sure you were. Tell me everything you know and make it fast before the FBI gets here."

"Do I need an attorney?"

"You're going to need a doctor if you don't start talking."

It was mid-afternoon before MJ and Cason made it back to the office. Ed was waiting. "Why am I always the last to know what you two are doing? This whole case is going down the toilet and I'm hearing about it third hand from the FBI. Both of you are going to check with me before you leave the office from now on."

They both started talking at once, and Ed held his hand up, "Stop it. MJ, I want to hear you first. I've heard all of Cason's colorful excuses before."

"I'm sorry, Ed. I got a tip this morning, and Cason and I started tracking it down. When it all came together, we had to move fast. I wish I could provide you with a different narrative, but the facts don't support that. I can't make chicken salad out of chicken crap. The bottom line is Tommy didn't do it."

Chapter Thirty Nine

Locked in his jail cell, Tommy had no access to the news media or events that were happening in the outside world. When his court-appointed attorney returned to the jail, with papers for him to sign, he thought she must truly be a lame-brained ditz. In his current condition, he had no interest what-so-ever in reading three pages of fine print or listening to her legal mumbo-jumbo. He didn't know he might inherit millions, he didn't know his divorce settlement might be worth millions, and he didn't know he had just signed an exclusive agreement for his female attorney to represent him in all matters. Her fees would be billed at an hourly rate and she anticipated the case, and the subsequent appeals, would last for years. He had also unknowingly authorized her to hire co-counsel, and she planned to employ the best legal minds in the country to feed off the pot at the end of the rainbow.

Neither of them knew Tommy's little airplane was now in FBI custody and that it would exonerate him of the most serious charges.

Miriam Latimer could no longer think clearly. She was mentally and physically spent after two days without sleep. The short naps in the waiting room chair only served to enhance her headache. Her pastor and her doctor begged her to go home and sleep. They convinced her she would be far more useful if she were rested, and she knew she must look terrible and smell worse. She had become immune to Advil, and the doctor gave her something stronger to help her rest. Dee promised to stand vigil and make the five minute visit each hour. If there were any news, she would call immediately.

Dee dug a novel out of her bag to pass the time and made herself semi-comfortable in the hard chair. She had only read a few chapters when Stark arrived. "Hey Dee, anything changed?"

"Afraid not. It breaks my heart to see her so lifeless. Her mom finally went home to rest for a few hours."

"I don't think her mom likes me."

"I assure you her mom is not thinking about you one way or the other."

"Dee, do you believe in love at first sight?"

"Assuming that I believed in love at all, the answer would be no."

"You've never been in love?"

"I've never had time to be in love."

"Me either, but the first time I saw Cindy, I knew I wanted to be in love."

"Did you feel the same way after her husband kicked your butt?"

"He didn't kick my butt, he sucker punched me. If I ever get the chance, I'm going to teach him what a butt kicking is all about."

"Good luck with that. For what it's worth, I think Cindy likes you too."

"She won't even go out with me."

"For God's sake, Stark, she's married and she's been abused. Do you expect all that to go away immediately just because you came along? Her ego and self-confidence have been destroyed. Tommy made her feel worthless. She's damaged goods."

"I don't care. I want to take her out anyway. Now that she's a millionaire, she probably won't even consider it."

"So far she doesn't know she's a millionaire, and if she did, I don't think it would change her very much. Her favorite meal is pizza, and she hates shopping."

Stark stared at his shoes, "Her husband deserves to die for what he did."

"If he's convicted, he will die. He'll be executed."

A thought occurred to Dee, and she made a quick decision. "It's time for the hourly visit. Walk me to the nurse's station."

The nurse recognized Dee as they approached. She asked, "You want to see our girl for a few minutes?"

"Actually I was hoping Gary could make the visit this time."

"Mrs. Latimer authorized you to visit in her absence, but other than that, it's family only."

"I know—Gary is Cindy's brother."

The nurse looked skeptical, "There's not much resemblance."

Dee answered, "That's true…Cindy got all the good looks in the family…the brains too."

The nurse stood up and looked up and down the hall as if a crime were about to take place. She turned back to Stark, "I'll take you in to see her. Five minutes, and I'll let you know when time's up."

He didn't know what to expect, and the hiss and beep of the machines were alarming, but her injuries were not visible. He was relieved to see that she looked peaceful. When the nurse left, he took Cindy's hand and leaned forward to softly talk to her. Her hand was cold and he rubbed it gently while choosing his words carefully.

Cindy loved the feeling of euphoria that surrounded her on her journey. It was intoxicating and addictive. Reaching her destination was her only goal. Time was not a consideration, and the world seemed to have stopped turning with the bright morning sun positioned for her continuous enjoyment. *If only I had someone to share this wonderful feeling with.*

The voices she heard ahead of her had slowly faded and she stopped to listen more carefully. The soft music remained, but the enchanting melody was the only sound to be heard. The rhythm seemed to soothe her soul, but there was no one to share it with, and somehow she knew it would be impossible to describe the emotion later. *Will I always be alone here?*

She tried to call out, but the music seemed to absorb her voice and render it silent. *I have to move on. There must be someone I can share with.*

Something brushed her hand and she looked to see nothing there. It was more an awareness than a feeling. She tried to speak again and realized the music had faded. "Hello…is anyone here?"

She knew she was speaking, but could not hear her own voice. Still she felt a presence.

She hesitated to look behind her, afraid of seeing the black smoke and burning airplane again, yet she was drawn to the awareness. She made the decision and slowly turned, expecting to see someone. There was no smoke and no airplane, just dim light fading to darkness and the feeling that whatever had been there might be ending forever.

The empty darkness was depressing, but somehow she sensed a presence. Her hand tingled and she longed for the touch of another human. She felt small and insignificant. Loneliness washed over her and a tear trickled down her cheek. She squeezed her fingers together to make the tingling stop and then took a couple of steps toward the fading light. *Someone is there…*

Stark didn't hear the nurse come in, and she couldn't make out the words he was whispering, but the five minutes had passed and she had her orders. She was touched by the fact that he was holding Cindy's hand and hesitated to disturb him. Then she noticed the whiteness of Cindy's knuckles and looked at her face. A tear made its way across her cheek and fell on the pillow. *Praise God...*

She gently touched Stark's shoulder and said, "Don't move. I'll be right back."

A minute later she returned with a doctor. He took Cindy's other hand and held it gently for a moment. Taking a small light from his lab coat, he opened her eyelid and examined her pupil. "She's crying…that's wonderful."

Stark wanted to punch the guy. "Crying is not wonderful. What's wrong with you?"

"Sir, you have to leave. This is the first response we've had from her and believe me it's wonderful. I'll come out to the waiting area and explain it to you in a few minutes. Please go now."

The nurse tugged on his arm and led him out. He said, "That guy's a whacko—don't leave him alone with her."

She smiled, "That man is the absolute best in the business. Go call Mrs. Latimer and tell her to come back to the hospital."

He walked back to the waiting room. *I'm not calling that woman. She hates me.*

Dee looked up when he came in and saw his confusion. "What did you do, Stark? If you screwed up they'll throw us out of here."

"I didn't screw up. Some doctor got his panties in a wad and made me leave."

"I knew better than to send you in there. What did he say?"

"He said it was wonderful that she was crying. I almost punched him. The nurse wants you to call Cindy's mom back to the hospital."

Dee grabbed her phone, "If Cindy's brain is telling her to cry, that means it's working again and communicating with her body. That *is* wonderful."

A light bulb seemed to come on behind Stark's eyes. "It told her to squeeze my hand too."

Dee finished dialling, "Miriam, it's Dee. I have good news…"

Stark paced the room and waited for the doctor. When Dee ended her conversation, her phone vibrated again immediately. She looked at the screen and said, "Oh great, perfect timing."

She answered, "Hello crew scheduling."

"Dee, we've got a no show. How soon can you get here?"

"Probably forty-five minutes."

"Drive carefully, but the flight will be on delay till you show. It's a three day with layovers in Kansas City and Toronto."

"I'm on the way."

She stood up and grabbed her purse. Stark said, "You're not leaving me here alone."

"You're a big boy now, Gary. Tell Cindy's mom what happened and stay with her until someone else gets here."

She noticed the beads of sweat on his forehead and almost laughed at the thought of a combat fighter pilot being terrified of being alone with a girl's mom. *I wish I had time to watch him squirm.*

Chapter Forty

MJ put the finishing touches on the real estate report and took it to Ed's office. The door was open and she found him talking to Charlie Wells. Ed said, "Have a seat, MJ. I was just explaining to Charlie that we're back at square one."

Charlie said, "I'm not really surprised. The NTSB has found no trace of explosives around the engine, and I don't think a model airplane could knock an engine off just from the impact."

Ed asked, "What have they found?"

"There's massive damage to the outboard side of the engine and also the pylon area between the engine and the wing. The mounting brackets that hold the engine in place are broken in half and it wasn't caused by a fifty pound model airplane. It would take a massive blunt force to break those brackets."

Ed replied, "I've always feared someone would eventually deploy a surface to air missile against a commercial airliner. Is that what we're looking at?"

"Maybe, but again, there's no evidence of an explosion. I'm sure they'll find something eventually to explain it. MJ, Ed tells me you witnessed the crash."

"I was looking out my office window when it happened. I hope I never see anything like that again."

"It must have been traumatic, but sometimes it helps to talk about it. It might help us to understand if you describe what you saw."

"I don't think I can add anything to what you already know. It looked like any other approach I've watched from the window, but then things started falling off the right wing. Something came off and started falling, and then the airplane turned and started to roll. Something else dropped and the airplane started descending faster than normal. I didn't know it was an engine at the time, but it seemed to come apart as it fell."

"That was probably the engine's cowling coming off. It was found some distance from where the engine hit the ground."

"The airplane hit the approach lights and you know what happened then."

"The crew almost saved it, but it would have been a miracle if they had. Please let me know if you think of anything else, MJ. Engines don't just fall off like that."

Tommy woke up in a cold cell. His knees were killing him and the breakfast tray looked like mud with pebbles in it. The orange jumpsuit was too big for him and the sandals hurt his feet. He was not in the best of moods when they wheeled him to the interrogation room to meet with his lawyer.

She was accompanied by an older gentleman. His distinguished gray hair indicated that he was experienced and his expensive suit was evidence of his success. He was introduced as a senior partner with the largest criminal defense firm in Atlanta.

"Mr. Lane, I've met with the prosecutor and examined the evidence against you. I requested, and have been granted, an immediate bail hearing. We'll be proceeding to the courtroom very shortly and you will say 'Yes sir' and 'No sir' as appropriate. Nothing more. Is that understood?"

"Okay."

"Good, I have some documents for you to sign and we'll be on our way."

I have nothing to lose. Of course, I'll sign your stupid documents. Tommy signed without hesitation. He had just agreed to an hourly fee, plus expenses, plus twenty percent of whatever was awarded in the inheritance or divorce settlement. As an afterthought, the attorney had included representation agreements for all book publishing and movie production contracts.

The attorney placed the signed documents into his briefcase and opened the door to notify the bailiff that they were ready. The jailer pushed Tommy's wheelchair down the hall and into the courtroom. He was placed at the defendant's table alongside his court-appointed lawyer and the new *hired gun* from downtown.

Everyone but Tommy stood when the judge took the bench. The charges were read and the prosecution presented its evidence without mention of the RCX-40. The presentation was full of accusations and condemnations and concluded with the request that the defendant be held without bail.

Tommy's attorney made a brief statement and pointed out that rhetoric was not evidence. He stipulated that his client owned a radio controlled airplane, but the state had no evidence that it had been used in a reckless manner. He further asserted that Tommy had no knowledge of plastic explosive and challenged the prosecutor to present evidence to the contrary. The judge asked the prosecutor if he would like to add to the argument. When he said no, Tommy's lawyer demanded that his client be released immediately with all charges dropped.

The judge considered his political position with the potential for millions of dollars being litigated in the divorce or inheritance contests. He rationalized that the defendant was not likely to leave town with that much money on the table and there was no real proof other than possibly motive.

He shuffled some papers and said, "The court will consider a motion to drop charges. I will rule within seven days. Meanwhile, the defendant will be released on his own recognizance. Mr. Lane you are not to leave town without the permission of the court, is that understood?"

Tommy tried to process what was happening. *I'm being released?* He cleared his throat and stared at the jailer, "Yes, your honor. I was beaten and tortured and may have some charges of my own…"

Tommy's high dollar attorney stood and interrupted the speech, "Thank you, your honor. We await your decision."

The judge gaveled the session closed and the attorney turned to Tommy, "Mr. Lane, you will be taken back to the jail and processed for release. We will be waiting for you and escort you safely away from the jail. Do not talk to anyone."

The two attorneys retreated from the courtroom and conferred in the hallway. The hired gun said, "This guy is a total imbecile. We're going to take him out the back door and hide him from the media. The firm owns a cabin on Lake Lanier north of Atlanta. We can stash him there until we educate him. I overplayed my hand this morning. I hoped the judge would keep him in custody, pending the motion to dismiss. Now we have to babysit."

Thirty minutes later, Tommy was escorted out the back door of the jail and into the attorney's limo. During the hour long ride to the remote cabin, he learned that his airplane had been found, proving that he didn't cause the accident. He was informed that his wife was in the hospital and he would be entitled to a fortune if she died and half a fortune if she didn't.

Tommy's reaction reminded the lawyer of a guppy in a fish bowl. His eyes were big and his lips silently moved up and down. When Tommy finally spoke, he said, "Can I get a beer?"

Chapter Forty One

Ed's fury was unprecedented. Tommy's release lit his fuse, and his temper was uncontrollably launched. MJ, Cason, and Harry sat at the conference table and waited for the tirade to cease. The local prosecutor and his staff were the targets of the largest blast and the highlight of the extended rant came when Ed listed all the anatomical orifices he intended to insert model airplanes into. Only Cason considered the possibility.

Ed concluded with, "He may not have caused the accident, but he certainly planned to. We're going to stay on him like stink on a Porta Potty until he goes to jail for good."

Harry said, "They should have stuck him with possession of the plastic explosive at least."

Ed finally settled down, "I think the new lawyer rushed them into a bail hearing before they were prepared. We need to give them plenty of ammunition before the judge rules on dismissing the charges."

When Ed finished venting, he dismissed the meeting with orders to bring him information. Cason and MJ retreated to the privacy of her office. She said, "Lane's going to accuse us of beating the crap out of him and framing him for the accident."

"I don't think so. I'll find him and explain the facts of life. This time I won't be subtle."

"We just got lucky last time when we found him. It might not be easy now."

"No worries mate. His lawyers will know where he is."

"And that helps us how?"

"Let's multi-task...I'll take care of Lane and you find out what caused the accident."

"Great plan, I'll see you in the unemployment line on payday."

She could hear Cason chuckling as he walked away.

Tommy's lawyers knew they were sitting on a gold mine and they planned to exploit it fully. On the way to the cabin, they stopped and rented a motorized wheelchair for his use while he was secluded. The firm's lake cabin was handicapped accessible and they wanted him to be happy while they plotted to relieve him of his good fortune. The kitchen was well stocked with food and beverage for his enjoyment. Once he was settled, they admonished him to stay inside and not to disclose his location to anyone.

When they drove away, Tommy placed a couple of cold beers in his chair's cup holders and motored out to the front porch to check out the view. The cabin sat on a hillside with a gentle slope down to a floating dock in a quiet cove. He could see other cabins around the cove, but they were isolated by at least a hundred yards. He listened to the birds chirping and watched a squirrel scamper up a tree. *This is the way a man should live, and no one deserves it more than me.*

The receptionist looked up when the good looking young man entered the lobby of the small law office. *Maybe the day isn't a total waste.* She showed white teeth, "Can I help you?"

Cason said, "I sure hope so. I'm trying to correct a mistake before my boss finds out."

"Well, we can't have you getting in trouble with the man. How can I be of assistance?"

"One of your clients was released from jail and when his personal property was returned to him somehow his watch was left in the bin. We don't have an address for him so I was hoping you could help me out."

"I would love to, but then I'd be in trouble with my boss."

"I definitely wouldn't want that to happen. You're much too nice to be in trouble. I know you can't give me the address, but I was hoping you could just send the watch to him. I have a pre-paid Fed Ex box to put it in."

He held up the cheap watch and dropped it in the box.

"What's the client's name?"

"Thomas Lane."

"Oh, I know that one. I was just updating his file. Let me see if I've got an address for him."

Her fingers skipped over the keyboard, making it click and clack. Cason said, "I hope you can pull my bacon out of the fire. I'm skating on thin ice already."

"You must be a bad boy."

"Of course not, but I am sometimes misunderstood."

She giggled, "Here we are. I think you're in luck. Let me put some paper in there so the watch won't rattle around."

"You are the best. I won't forget this."

"Give me the pre-paid label. I'll fill in the address before the Fed Ex guy shows up. He's not due for another hour."

"Thank you so much. I owe you one."

"Yes you do, and don't forget it."

"I won't. Just don't tell anyone else. I'll see you soon."

She smiled again, "That's the right answer. I'll be here."

Cason waved as he went out the door. He walked back to his truck and waited. Forty-five minutes later a Fed Ex truck parked on the street in front of the office and left the emergency flashers blinking while he ran inside the law office. Five minutes later the driver jogged out with several packages in his hands. He jumped up into the truck and Cason could see him scanning the packages into the system.

As the truck drove away, Cason opened his cell phone and pulled up the Fed Ex website. When he plugged in the tracking number from the pre-paid label, a pickup time appeared along with the address and expected delivery date.

Google Maps gave him directions as well as a satellite view of the cabin on the lake.

"Hello again, Tommy."

Kitty was not a patient woman and she was not accustomed to relying on someone else to take care of business. She sat her nephew down to express her displeasure. "That Tommy done got loose again. He gone make his lawyer try to take Miss Cindy's money. You gone find him and I don't want to hear no more about no Tommy Lane...no more ever."

"I told you not to let someone else deal with that."

She slapped him on his shaved head. "You don't sass me now. Go find him."

He laughed, "Yes ma'am."

"I don't want no scuses either."

"I don't need an excuse. I don't know where he is, but I know he's in a wheelchair and I'm betting he didn't leave the jail in their wheelchair."

He called seven medical equipment supply stores before he hit pay dirt. "The wheelchair you rented me this morning is giving me some problems."

"Is this Mr. Lane?"

"Yes."

"I'm sorry, Mr. Lane, that's our most popular and most expensive model. Of course, it's under warranty and I'll be happy to send someone out to take care of the problem."

"Do you have the right address?"

"Let me double check that. You're on Lake Lanier aren't you?"

"That's right."

The man read the address to confirm it and promised to send a technician out.

The nephew ended the call and said, "Hello again, Tommy."

Chapter Forty Two

M iriam Latimer rushed into the waiting room to find only Stark sitting there alone. He jumped to his feet and blushed.

"Where is Dee, Mr. Stark?"

"Tri Con called and sent her on a trip. She ordered me to stay and keep you company."

"She told me Cindy was responding."

"Yes ma'am. She squeezed my hand and started crying."

"And what were you doing in the room with Cindy."

"I'm sorry ma'am. Dee made me do it."

"That's ridiculous, Mr. Stark, but if Cindy is responding, I don't care why. Where is the doctor?"

"I'll let the nurse know you're here."

"I can do that myself. You come with me."

The nurse escorted them into the doctor's office and he rushed in a minute later. "Mrs. Latimer, I'm happy to tell you that Cindy had a brief response earlier. I readily admit that with all my degrees and training, I have no idea what causes a patient to begin responding. Sometimes it seems that a certain person can trigger an emotional reaction and it causes their brain to want to function again. In this case, it appears that Cindy's brother has broken that barrier and awakened her emotions."

Miriam said, "Cindy doesn't have..."

She turned and stared at Stark. "Cindy's brother can be very resourceful at times."

"At any rate, we would like to try to replicate the event and encourage further progress. This time we would like for both of you to be present. Sir, if you could just hold Cindy's hand like before, and repeat the same things you said last time, we can, hopefully, measure her reaction. If things go well, we can begin mapping a strategy."

Stark panicked. *Oh no...not in front of her mother. Not gonna happen.* "I don't remember what I said before."

Miriam said, "Doctor, could we have a moment to discuss this?"

"Of course you may, but it's important that we get started as soon as possible. I'll wait in Cindy's room."

He closed the door when he left, and Stark squirmed in his chair. Miriam faced him and took his hand in hers. "Look, that's my daughter and your friend in there. She's in trouble and needs all the help she can get. I don't know what your relationship with Cindy is and I don't care. If I have to beg you, I will, but I'm asking you to do exactly what the doctor wants. If you want to be Cindy's brother, that's fine with me. I'll adopt you. I just want my daughter back at any cost. Please don't deny me that possibility."

"Yes, ma'am. I want her back too."

Cindy felt like she had been rejected. She was suspended between two worlds and unwanted by both. She had been teased by the beautiful morning, but no one appeared to embrace her or welcome her. It was as if she had arrived unexpectedly, and no one was prepared to greet her. It reminded her of a passenger boarding a jet with no flight attendants to welcome him.

When she faced the twilight behind her, she briefly sensed the presence of someone beckoning to her. *Did I imagine the feel of a human touch on my hand in the darkness before?* Her mind wandered in confusion and she waited patiently in hopes of the presence returning. *Next time I won't let go. I'll hold on until I know. Please don't leave me alone. Please come back and take my hand. Say something. Anything. Anybody.*

She took a few more steps into the twilight and waited. At long last, her fingers tingled and she tried to cry out. "Who's there?" She could not force her lips to produce the words, and it was frustrating. Her hand felt warm and she squeezed tight to hold on to the hope of companionship. *Please don't go away again.*

A dim glow appeared in the distant twilight and she began slowly retreating toward it, determined to find answers. The combination of fear and hope propelled her, but progress seemed impossible. Frustration boiled in her and she could not stop the tears from trickling down her face. Both hands formed fists and she marched to the cadence of a strange beeping noise that seemed to echo her heartbeat. *Whoever or whatever you are, please don't go away again. Please...*

The beeping of the heart monitor increased its rhythm slightly when Stark took Cindy's hand. Miriam stood on the opposite side of the bed and held her daughter's other hand. The doctor nodded his head and signaled to continue. Stark leaned forward and spoke in a soft whisper that he hoped no one but Cindy could hear. The doctor grinned when he saw the whiteness of her knuckles. Miriam Latimer began to cry when her daughter fisted her hand in a tight grip.

The doctor folded his arms on his chest and observed without interference as tears rolled down Cindy's cheeks. *Medical science is a wonderful thing. If only we understood all we know about it.*

Stark lost himself in his monologue and didn't notice the increase in Cindy's heart rate or the compassion on her mother's face. He focused on the hand that held his tight and made promises to Cindy that he only hoped he could keep.

When the doctor determined that Cindy's response was sustainable, he uncovered her feet and ran a metal instrument along her instep. When she kicked the instrument away, he looked up to see her eyelids flutter.

A moment later, Cindy Lane reached the glow in the twilight. Her wet eyelashes separated and light poured in. The heart monitor beeped like a Geiger counter on a nuke, and her chest rose and fell with labored breaths. The blue eyes grew large and stared straight ahead. Her body trembled and she tried to speak, but the respirator made it impossible.

She struggled to grasp reality and when she did, the tears flowed more freely. She stared into the eyes of the person holding her left hand… *Mom… Oh mom, I love you…*

Her eyes shifted to the right. *Stark… Stark?*

The doctor punched the nurse call button and began his examination. He allowed Miriam and Stark to stay for an extended visit until he was sure Cindy understood the situation and began to relax. He instructed her to communicate by blinking her eyes and assured her that she would be able to speak soon.

When the time came, he walked the two visitors back to the waiting room and offered an optimistic prognosis before leaving them. Miriam looked Stark in the eyes and said, "That was quite an eloquent conversation with my daughter, Mr. Stark. How much of it was sincere?"

"Mrs. Latimer, Cindy and I are just friends. She knows I want to date her, but she always reminds me that she's married. I respect that and admire her principles, but I hope she won't be married much longer. To answer your question, everything I said was true, and I hope in time she will see me as more than a friend."

"I want to thank you for your help, and I wish you the best of luck. Cindy deserves so much more than the marriage she's had."

"I absolutely agree. The description for her husband is phonetically an Alpha Hotel, pardon the expression. If I can find him, I intend to see that he never mistreats her again."

"And just what is an Alpha Hotel?"

"I shouldn't have said that, ma'am. What I mean is he doesn't deserve to share the same earth as Cindy."

"Were you in combat, Mr. Stark?"

"Yes, ma'am."

"Did you ever kill anyone?"

Stark shifted from one foot to the other and back. "Yes, ma'am."

"I wish I were in combat and Tommy was the enemy."

"He has it coming, ma'am. Don't worry about him hurting Cindy again."

"Can you stay and help me with Cindy's recovery?"

"I'm on call at Tri Con, ma'am, but I'll be here until they assign me a trip."

"Thank you. Please call me Miriam until we decide the adoption issue. Mom would be awkward before then."

"Would you like a cup of coffee, Miriam?"

"Do you have a first name?"

"Gary."

"If you're buying, Gary, I would love a cup of coffee."

When he left to get the coffee, she took out her cell phone. "Harold, I have wonderful news. Cindy is responding and the doctor is very optimistic."

"Fantastic, I'll come right over."

"That's not necessary, but can you arrange to have Gary Stark taken off the pilot reserve list? I need his help for a few days."

"Who is Gary Stark?"

"You met him here earlier with Dee Daniels."

"The new pilot class...I should have known."

Chapter Forty Three

With Ed's help, MJ gathered information from as many sources as possible, consisting of police reports, fire rescue reports, FBI briefs, and a few eyewitness accounts. Charlie Wells had submitted a written summation of the NTSB preliminary brief including photos. At five o'clock, she packed it all in a bulging briefcase and drove home to begin the analysis.

Nuking a quick dinner only took a few minutes, and she changed into sweat pants and a much laundered *Don't Mess With Texas* Tee shirt. The tile of the kitchen floor felt good to her bare feet as she spread the impressive pile of paper on the table.

After an hour, she rubbed her eyes and refilled her coffee cup. She made a few notes and began a second trip through the pile, quickly discarding things that offered little hope of insight. The accident photos and fire rescue reports were gruesome and only served to anger her and increase her motivation to find answers.

Like a jigsaw puzzle, she treated undisputed facts as easy straight edged pieces and quickly assembled the outline of the problem. *All the answers are inside the square. I just have to find the pieces and fit them together. Sometimes the piece that doesn't fit is the most important.*

The police reports offered very little useful information since the accident was primarily contained to airport property and the patrolmen had been assigned to traffic control and perimeter security. The only ones she saved involved the scene where the engine fell in the parking lot. One in particular caught her eye because it listed personnel, and organizations they represented, who had been granted access to the scene. The name that caught her attention was *Cason Haley, Tri Con Security.* The list also included FAA, NTSB, FBI, and several people the patrolman identified as members of GANG. *What in God's name is GANG?*

She placed the report to the side with a note to discuss it with Cason. Removing the photos from the NTSB report and turning them face down—she began reading it once again. *Photos of dead bodies with missing parts are distracting and depressing.*

The transcript of the cockpit voice recorder provided a timeline along with the conversation on the flight deck. The recording began thirty minutes before the crash and gave her a creepy feeling. It was important that she remain open minded and objective, but reading the last words of dead men felt like a horrible invasion of their privacy and dignity. *Shouldn't they be remembered for more than their last conversation? Could the last few minutes of their life condemn them to being hated forever if they screwed up, or hailed as heroes if they faced death with courage and professionalism?*

The transcribed recording began at 12:18 local time and each entry indicated the time in seconds. The pilots conversed with each other and with air traffic control with the routine of thousands of hours of practice. The captain was flying the airplane and shortly after the recording began, he asked the copilot to make an arrival announcement to the passengers. The first officer spoke slowly and sounded calm and confident as he described the Atlanta weather and promised an on time arrival at the gate. He thanked the customers for choosing Tri Con and invited them to fly again soon and often. *I bet Kyle makes great PA announcements.*

MJ paused to clear her mind when it occurred to her that an airplane full of people were listening to the routine announcement, and in a few minutes they would all be dead. Suddenly she wished she were not reading this alone. *Cindy was almost home when she heard the arrival PA.*

There was nothing unusual on the tape until near the end, and it took her a minute to identify the players. CAPT and F/O were obvious and then she realized RDO was radio transmissions and

CAM was sounds picked up by the cockpit area microphone. The flight number was Tri Con 310 and also carried the *heavy* designation due to its high gross weight and the danger its wake turbulence created for aircraft behind it.

12:40 18 RDO *Tri Con 310 heavy, tower on 119.5*

12:40 22 F/O *Tower on 19.5, Tri Con 310 heavy, so long*

12:41 02 F/O *Tower, Tri Con 310 heavy is with you for Eight Left.*

12:41 12 RDO *Tri Con 310 heavy, Atlanta Tower, I need you to keep your speed up as long as possible, wind light and variable, you're cleared to land Runway Eight Left.*

12:41 20 F/O *Go fast, cleared to land Eight Left, Tri Con 310 heavy*

12:42 30 F/O *Glide slopes alive*

12:42 36 Capt *Imagine that. Gear down, before landing checklist*

12:42 45 F/O *Here come the Goodyears*

12:42 47 CAM *Sound of landing gear extending*

12:43 18 F/O *Down three green*

12:43 25 Capt *Flaps thirty*

12:43 28 F/O *Flaps coming to thirty*

12:44 19 F/O *Landing gear*

12:44 22 Capt *Down three green*

12:44 30 F/O *Flaps*

12:44 34 Capt *Thirty*

12:45 01 F/O *Spoilers*

12:45 11 Capt *Armed*

12:45 20 F/O *Auto brakes*

12:45 28 Capt *Off*

12:45 50 F/O *Checklist complete, cleared to land. Should break out about 800 feet*

12:47 00 Capt *Runway in sight*

12:47 12 F/O *It's a miracle*

12:48 01 F/O *500 feet looking good*

12:48 30 Capt *What the...*

12:48 33 F/O *Right engine fail. Losing hydraulics*

12:48 35 CAM *Glide slope...Glide slope...Sink rate...Sink rate* (continues until the end)

12:48 36 Capt *I can't...*

12:48 36 CAM *Whoop Whoop Pull Up Whoop Whoop Pull Up* (continues until the end)

12:48 40 F/O *Rudder...Sink rate*

12:48 48 Capt *Rudder's full...It won't...Oh sh...*

12:48 48 Cam *Sound of impact*

MJ sat with her face in her hands with the image of the crash emblazoned in her mind. *I wish I had never looked out that window.* Reading the transcript had only proved that she was standing at the window at 12:48 and forty-eight seconds on the day of the crash. The timeline seemed so cold and uncaring, as if it would go on regardless of how many people died. The timeline didn't care if widows and sons and daughters read the last words on the recording. It had no conscious and no compassion for the deceased or the survivors. The timeline was relentless and unstoppable. Sound of impact had no impact on the timeline.

She hated the timeline and she hated the thought of Kyle's voice being recorded in the cockpit. *Does he sound bored and professional in the cockpit or does his voice reflect the excitement I know he feels when he's flying.*

She tried to erase the timeline from her thoughts, but it kept haunting her. Hands on a clock, ticking, and tocking. Digits on a dial, silently changing. Thirty short minutes from 12:18 to 12:48. *What difference does it make what time it is when someone dies?*

Chapter Forty Four

Cason and Harry were having coffee in the conference room when MJ arrived at 6:30. She set her briefcase on the table and said, "Cason, you look like you've been up all night. Did you have any luck finding Tommy?"

He sipped the hot coffee, "I'm working on it."

"I've got a police report I need to ask you about."

She removed the paper from her briefcase. "Do you remember this?"

Reading the report, he said, "Sure, this was when I went out to see the engine."

"Do you remember the patrolman on duty?"

"His name's Joe Watson. We call him Sleepy because he's the guy that dozed off and let Tommy get away at the motel."

"Poor guy."

"A dumb mistake, but it all turned out okay."

"I was wondering about this list of people he gave access to. What in the world is GANG?"

"That's a new one on me. Knowing Sleepy, he probably just made up the acronym to save writing the words. You want me to find out?"

"If you don't mind."

"Loose ends keeping you awake again?"

"No, the cockpit voice recording is responsible for that."

Cason thumbed his cell phone and talked to the cop while MJ found her mug and poured coffee. When he ended the call, she asked, "Do you realize what time it is?"

"He owes me. Time to get up anyway."

"Did he remember the report?"

"When he stopped cursing and yawning he did. GANG was his version of Georgia Air National Guard."

Harry asked, "What were they doing there?"

"Good question. He said he assumed they were helping NTSB locate wreckage."

MJ said, "I guess it doesn't matter. I was just trying to fill in blank spots."

Harry said, "We've got plenty of those to deal with. Ed will be on the warpath until we figure something out. We need to get back to basics and see things from a new perspective. The three of us are going to the hangar for a dose of reality."

Tri Con occupied several huge hangars on the airport and one of them was now being used exclusively for the accident investigation. The remains of the 767 had been hauled into the space piece by piece and carefully laid out in the shape of an airplane. The forward half of the fuselage was largely recognizable, although a portion of the top had been consumed by fire. The tail section lay behind the fuselage with a gap between the two. Pieces of the wings were spread out on either side with the engines mounted on metal stands forward of the wing attach points.

The sight was sobering and MJ looked away to gather her resolve. An indescribable odor assaulted her senses and would remain long after she left the hangar. The smell of molten metal, charred fabric and melted plastic combined with other things she didn't care to think about. They approached the nose section and the cockpit windows were dark and smudged from the fire fighting foam. The haunting words from the cockpit voice recorder played over and over in her mind.

She followed Harry and Cason to the right wing and looked at the broken engine mounts where the engine was once attached. The engine itself was only a few feet away, and without the sleek cowling, it looked like a giant fan with tubes and wire bundles hanging from it in random patterns. No one spoke as they continued walking to the aft section of the wreck. The fuselage was ripped open where the tail section had separated and passenger seats could be seen scattered helter skelter in the cabin. *Two hundred people... The last thirty minutes... Cindy was ejected from that hell and somehow survived.*

They continued walking around the airplane and learned nothing of significance.

Harry said, "I guess this was a wasted trip. I was hoping we'd see something all the experts missed, but all I see is nightmares in my future."

The hangar doors were closed to conceal the ugly sight from public view. But as they prepared to leave, a loud warning bell rang and the doors opened wide enough for a flatbed eighteen wheeler to back in. The truck was loaded with more wreckage and continued backing toward the rear of the hangar. The air brakes hissed as the trailer neared an area where wreckage was being unloaded.

Harry asked, "Who are those men in military fatigues?"

Cason said, "Let's find out."

A hangar foreman supervised the unloading process and recognized Harry as they approached. "Harry, I'm surprised we haven't seen you here sooner. What can I do for you?"

"We're just trying to figure out the process."

"Our role is pretty simple. When the wreckage is brought in we unload it here and then the NTSB guys determine what section of the airplane it came from. Then we take it out to the hangar floor and place it where it goes."

"Who are the military guys?"

"Oh, they're from the Air National Guard. The NTSB is supposedly teaching them accident investigation procedures, but I don't know what they're learning from sorting through wreckage.

They're pretty tight lipped about their orders and I don't think the NTSB is very impressed either. There seems to be some question as to who is in charge."

"That's interesting. Are they giving you trouble?"

"Not at all. I just supervise my guys running the forklifts and give them what they ask for."

Harry noticed Cason talking to a couple of the guardsmen and continued making small talk with the foreman. MJ wandered around the area making mental notes, and as she neared a truck with National Guard markings and a canvas covered cargo area, she was stopped.

The man had sergeant stripes on his fatigues and said, "Ma'am, this is a secure area. It's dangerous with all the forklifts running around. You might want to move to a safer area."

"Thank you. It does look like dangerous work. Are you with the Air Force?"

"No, I'm with the Air National Guard."

"That must be exciting. Do the stripes on your sleeve mean you're an officer?"

"I'm a non-commissioned officer."

"That sounds important. Are you investigating the accident?"

"That's what we're here for."

"It's horrible isn't it? What do you think happened?"

"Well I…"

An officer walked over and said, "Sergeant, this is a secure area. Ma'am, I'm sorry, but I'll have to ask you to move outside the crime scene tape. It's much safer there."

When they left the hangar, Harry asked, "What did you two learn?"

Cason said, "The guys I talked to just bragged about being in the National Guard."

"Did you tell them about your service?"

"Of course not…I wanted to hear about theirs."

"How about you, MJ?"

"I was making progress until an officer threw me out. He didn't want me anywhere near that truck."

Harry took out his phone and called Ed.

The trip to the hangar disturbed MJ more than she wanted to admit, and she was depressed when she returned to the office and sat down at her desk. The pile of papers on the desk didn't help matters, and she tried to put things in order on the desk and in her mind.

The cockpit voice recorder transcript was on top of the pile. Reluctantly, she picked it up and ran her eyes down the page. *The last thirty minutes of a long day. The last thirty minutes of a long trip. The last thirty minutes of 200 lives. The last words of two pilots from 12:18 to 12:48, then the timeline ran out without warning. What's missing?*

She forced the timeline from her mind and stood to stretch, carefully avoiding the view from the office window. She needed to clear her head and reboot her brain and decided checking her email was a good way to accomplish that.

The computer screen filled with a long list of emails and she began culling the junk and deleting them. Halfway down the list, she came to the email containing the series of photos of the expansion property south of the airport. Deciding she should save them for future reference, she created an electronic folder and began transferring them one by one.

There were about a dozen images and as she clicked on each one, she noticed the time stamp in the corner. 12:27…12:29…12: 32…12:36.

Another timeline, that's just what I need. At least this one doesn't have doomed voices to haunt me. The date on the photographs caught her eye. *That's ironic…* She continued to click. 12:38…12:40…12:42.

Holy crap…

Chapter Forty Five

MJ typed *Georgia Air National Guard* into the search window on her computer. The screen filled with websites and publicity articles. The official website described the unit's primary mission as transporting cargo and troops and also listed the benefits of becoming a member of the guard. Finding nothing useful, she moved on to the news articles.

She learned the unit had been deployed to both Iraq and Afghanistan and had accomplished their missions with success. Many of the articles were redundant and described the same events. Determined not to miss anything, she continued to the third page where a newspaper article caught her attention.

Georgia ANG Assigned New Mission

The Georgia Air National Guard will begin training for new duties beginning next month. In cooperation with the Department of Defense, members of the unit will undergo training in the use of unmanned aerial vehicles (UAV). The unit will take delivery of military surplus Predator Drone aircraft for use in joint missions with the U.S. Air Force. The program is the brainchild of U.S. Senator Henry Walker, who was instrumental in appropriating the Predator Drone aircraft and forging the approval for domestic use. The drones will be assigned to guard units in the Senator's home state of Pennsylvania as well as several other states including Georgia. The FAA is in the process of determining what new rules will be applied for use of unmanned aerial vehicles in domestic airspace. The Predator will be operated in an unarmed configuration for domestic flights.

Looking at the date on the article, she realized the drones were delivered several months ago. She jotted notes on her legal pad. *Senator Walker, Air National Guard, Predator Drone, aerial photos, timeline 12:48. Pieces of a puzzle that form a horrible picture.*

She typed *Predator Drone* into the search engine and found pages of unclassified information. *Are there no secrets anymore?*

Manufactured by Boeing, the drone featured a length of 36 feet and a wingspan of 65 feet. The aircraft was capable of a maximum takeoff weight of 10,000 pounds, and the turboprop engine could produce a speed of up to 300 miles per hour. *That's bigger than the light airplanes Kyle flew in Corpus Christi. If Andy's toy airplane could destroy an engine, this thing could... Oh God.*

She jotted a few more notes and headed for Ed's office

✈

Ed's FBI contact finally returned his call. "What can I do for you, Ed?"

"You can tell me why the National Guard is snooping around this accident investigation."

After an awkward moment he answered, "I'm told they have a national security interest."

"That's what the FBI is for. What's going on?"

"Just drop it, Ed, and let them do their job."

"Don't give me that crap. They're ordering Tri Con employees around in our own hangar like they own the place. You can tell me what they're doing or I'll find out myself."

"I'm telling you not to go there, Ed. We have orders from the top to leave them alone. Their work is classified."

"No problem, I have a top secret clearance."

"So do I, but I've been told I don't have the need to know. Therefore, neither do you. Do yourself a favor and leave it alone."

"Are you going to leave it alone?"

"The official word is they're doing an internship with the NTSB to learn accident investigation, and there's a rumor that there was top secret cargo on board. That's all I know."

"You don't believe that. There was no government cargo manifested on the flight. This is some sort of political crap. It's an election year and somebody's covering their butt or trying to expose someone else's."

"I've got to go, Ed. My best advice is to prop your bare feet on the desk and forget about it. Nothing good will happen if you interfere."

Ed ended the call and tapped his fingers on his desk while MJ and Cason waited for him to calm down. Finally, he stood up and paced the room. "These people are not going to come on our property and take over. MJ, see what else you can dig up. Cason, I want you to find out what's in that truck and what they're doing with it. Try not to create a major incident while you're at it."

Cindy was comfortable with the fact that she had lost her mind. If her brain told her she was in a bright and beautiful place with pretty flowers and intoxicating music, she was at ease with that. If it told her she was gazing into smoky darkness with a dull glow in the distance, it no longer stressed her. If it told her she was in a hospital room with her mother, and of all people Stark, that was fine with her. None of it made sense, but who was she to argue with insanity. She was vaguely aware that she had made a choice, but insanity abdicated responsibility and she could not be held accountable.

There were also periods of blissful nothingness when she waited for her brain to tell her what to imagine next. This time the nothingness ended and she slowly opened her eyes to find herself in yet another new place. Horizontal sunbeams formed stripes in her view and made it difficult to distinguish what she was looking at. *That's too weird to try to rationalize.*

She closed her eyes and reopened them to try again. This time she found the source of the sunbeams. A window displayed partially opened blinds with sunlight streaming through. The beeping noise gave her hope that she might be in the hospital room again, but this was a different place. *Maybe I'm not totally insane. Sometimes things seem real and present. If I'm imagining this, why does my body ache all over? Why does my throat feel raw and irritated?*

An alien-sounding voice repeated her thoughts and she realized she was speaking out loud. *Yep...I'm nutty as a fruitcake and talking to myself. All I need is a mirror to have a real conversation.* She turned away from the window and looked around the room. Two of the sunbeams illuminated a reclining chair and someone sleeping under a blanket.

She heard the alien voice say, "Mom, are you really there? Mom...please wake up."

She watched the recliner pop upright and the blanket fall to the floor. Miriam took her hand and said, "Honey, don't try to talk. They removed a breathing tube from your throat and it's going to be sore for awhile. Everything's all right now. You're going to be fine."

"Mom...I...please don't go away."

"Shhh...just relax honey. I'm right here. I promise I'm not going anywhere."

"What happened to me?"

"You were in an accident, honey, but you're just fine now. Don't try to talk."

"What accident?"

"Nothing to worry about, Sweetie. It wasn't your fault. You just need to rest and everything will be normal in no time."

"Did Tommy do this?"

"No, honey, Tommy's out of your life for good. It was just an accident."

"I'm hungry."

Miriam smiled, "I'm glad to hear that. Let's talk to the doctor and see what we can do."

Chapter Forty Six

Cason was glad to get away from the office. He enjoyed working alone and he knew it took patience to get a good result. No one noticed as he wandered around the hangar looking busy, as if he belonged, but it made for a boring afternoon. The last of the wreckage had been moved from the runway into the hangar and he watched as the men in fatigues sorted through it. Most of it was unloaded and placed in the designated area to be identified and moved to the proper location on the hangar floor. It was the occasional piece that was loaded into the truck that drew his interest, and he used his camera phone to snap photos of that action.

The truck was under constant guard and he couldn't get close without being conspicuous, but he thought he knew what they were loading and where they would take it. *Dobbins Air Reserve Base is only twenty miles north of here. That's the nearest secure location. Fortunately, I have military ID and access to the base. It's just a matter of time gentlemen. Whoever's running this fiasco better have some serious horsepower.*

The day was fading fast and the hangar lights were already on when the men began preparing the truck for departure. The officer in charge had made and received several cell phone calls in the last half hour. *You're such a good boy, checking in and receiving orders. Let's put this show on the road, I'm missing dinner.*

The officer finally closed the cell phone and climbed into the passenger seat of the truck. The driver waited for the other four men to climb into the back before slamming the tailgate and closing the canvas flaps. He pulled himself up on the driver's side of the cab and the diesel fired up with a plume of black smoke.

Cason hurried to the parking lot behind the hangar and was waiting when the truck made its way around the huge structure and arrived at the security gate to exit. He gave them a nice head start and then pulled out to follow. The big green truck was easy to see well ahead, and he allowed several cars to get between him and his quarry. As they approached the freeway, Cason anticipated the turn north toward the air base, but found himself in the wrong lane when the truck entered the southbound entrance ramp. Horns honked as he threaded his way through traffic and made the turn. *These guys are lost.*

He continued to snap photos of the truck to record the route as he followed it into the countryside. The two-lane road wound its way through fields and forest for several miles and as the sun finally disappeared he followed the truck's lights.

He purposely left his headlights off and closed the distance between himself and the truck. He slowed to a crawl when the brake lights came on ahead and then disappeared. *Now what?* Creeping forward, he realized the truck had turned onto a gravel road and doused its lights.

He continued on for another quarter mile and then shifted his pickup into four wheel drive before leaving the road and concealing it among the trees. He shut the engine off and lowered the driver's window. He heard only silence in the dark. *They must have stopped or I would hear that big diesel rattling.*

He crawled out the window rather than opening the door and causing the interior light to illuminate. Picking his way through the trees, he had not gone far when he heard voices ahead. *They're making enough noise—I could drive up in a freight train without being detected.*

He continued to move silently forward until he was stopped by a pasture fence. He could not see cattle, but the aroma of fresh cow patties announced they were not far away. Across the moonlit field, he could see the truck at an open gate and men with flashlights moving around. Taking his cell phone out, he activated the camera, but there was not enough light to video the scene.

He began moving along the fence and circled the pasture in order to get closer. When he came to the gravel road, he was able to move to within thirty yards of the truck and still be concealed by the trees. He could clearly hear the voices now, but the phone camera was still useless in the dark. *Might as well video anyway...at least I can capture the audio.*

After fifteen minutes of listening to the men complain about having to unload the truck in the dark, he heard the officer say, "That's about it guys. Get ready to light it up. I'll call it in after we leave."

Several men walked into the field, each carrying a large can. The rich smell of kerosene began wafting across the area. The officer said, "Good job, men. Start the truck and load up, we're ready to move out."

The officer walked into the field and Cason watched him light several matches and throw them on the ground. When nothing happened, one of the men in the truck said, "Sir, it's hard to light jet fuel in the open air with a match. You either need to vaporize the fuel or create a hotter flame."

"Yeah, I know that. I just like to play with matches. Gather some twigs and pine straw and bring it over here."

Once the fire was started, the flames began to spread through the field at a rapid pace. The driver popped the truck into first gear and moved down the road past Cason's hiding place. Once it rounded a curve, and was out of sight, he jogged to the pasture. He surveyed some of the things that had been unloaded from the truck and were now burning in the grass. *This is a fine example of ineptness. I don't think this is gonna work guys.*

Dinner parties in Washington, DC were a nightly occurrence, although some gatherings were more formal than others. The residence was easily large enough to comfortably accommodate the

150 invitees. The ladies were happy to take advantage of the opportunity to display the latest trends in evening wear and their most expensive accessories. Imported footwear trod the floor of imported tile and neither scuffed the other.

As the room filled, the murmur of conversation threatened to become a roar, and the tinkle of champagne glasses rang like sleigh bells. The host and hostess would not appear for another hour. The crowd must be brought to the proper level of anticipation before the grand entrance.

The festivities did not deter the working staff from their duties, and when the phone rang in the office on the ground floor, it was answered promptly. The caller said, "You can relax, it's done."

"I never relax, especially when incompetents like you are involved."

"I'm not the incompetent. I made a simple request and the military screwed it up."

"How many people are involved in the clean up?"

"Only twelve."

"Give me their names and service numbers."

"They're good men. They won't talk."

"No they won't, because they're all being deployed to the Middle East tomorrow."

"There are a couple of other things I may need help with."

"I'm not surprised."

"The lead NTSB investigator is chapped about the military involvement in his investigation. He's whining about his authority being compromised."

"What else?"

"The Tri Con security staff keeps asking questions. They won't keep their nose out of it. The director is a former FBI guy. He needs to be put in his place."

"What's his name?"

"Ed White."

"Let me handle it."

Hanging the phone up, the man closed his briefcase and opened the office door. The party was going strong and it was not the time to bother the boss with details. He exited through the service area and stopped to pilfer a shrimp cocktail on his way out. When he reached the street, he looked back at the White House and the limousines at the portico. *Have a good evening, Mr. President. I'm not going to let some hick down in Georgia clog the wheels of the federal government.*

Ed sat down at his desk at seven a.m. and kicked his shoes off. He scanned the morning newspaper, as was his custom, to see if any news pertained to Tri Con. Two articles caught his attention. *Why would the lead NTSB investigator resign in the middle of an investigation?*

The second article reported that a military drone had crashed overnight thirty miles south of the city. The drone had gone down in a remote area with no reported injuries. The only property damage was a small forest fire that had been quickly contained. The article reiterated previous concerns about unmanned aircraft operating in domestic airspace and the reporter lambasted the FAA for lack of regulations involving drone flights.

Ed was discussing the two developments with Harry at eight a.m. when his secretary buzzed to inform him that the Secretary of Defense was on line one.

Chapter Forty Seven

When Ed answered the phone, he was not speaking to the Secretary of Defense, but rather an aide who asked him to hold for the Secretary. After listening to elevator music for eight minutes, Ed punched the off button and went back to his conversation with Harry. Ten minutes later Ed's secretary informed him that The Secretary of Defense was on line one again.

"This is Ed White."

The aide said, "I'm sorry Mr. White, we seem to have been disconnected. Please hold for the secretary."

"I'll be happy to talk to the secretary, but I'm not going to sit here listening to crappy music. Call back when he's ready to talk."

"Wait one, sir. I won't put you on hold."

Ed could hear voices in the background and then, "Mr. White, sorry about the delay. I'm hoping you can assist us with a national security issue."

"How so, Mr. Secretary?"

"As you know, some of our people are assisting the NTSB with the Tri Con accident investigation, and I understand some of your folks have been getting in the way. I'd like for you to stand back and let us handle the investigation."

"I've never known the NTSB to need assistance, and they haven't complained about my people getting in the way. I don't see the problem."

"You wouldn't understand the issues involved, Mr. White. Your interference could cause larger problems for Tri Con and yourself. You don't want that to happen. Just let us do our job and there won't be any blowback. Let's keep this simple."

"I think I hear what you're saying. You want to explain why I'm being threatened?"

"I don't have time to chat, Mr. White. Just stand down and everything will be fine."

"I can't do that without good cause. I need a better explanation."

"Well, that's the only explanation you're going to get. I'm sorry, but this is government business and you can't stand in the way."

"Tri Con security is my business and I won't shirk my duties and responsibilities."

"I was hoping you would be more reasonable, Mr. White. Good day."

Ed put the phone down and Harry looked at him with raised eyebrows.

Ed smiled, "We must be doing something right. The bureaucrats are getting nervous. We better circle the wagons and find out what Cason and MJ are doing to cause Washington to be concerned."

Ed waited for Harry to summon the troops and thought—*they're both going to walk in here looking innocent as newborn babies and I'm not sure I want to know what they've been up to.*

His suspicions were confirmed when MJ sat down and crossed her legs at the knees with a legal pad on her lap, and Cason looked as if his heart rate was barely above a sleeping condition. *They could both defeat a lie detector.*

Ed began, "Do either of you know why the lead NTSB investigator has resigned?"

MJ said, "He wasn't given a choice. He's being investigated for sexually assaulting one of the maids at his hotel."

"How do you know that?"

"It's in the overnight police reports. I check them first thing every morning. He wasn't arrested because it's just his word against hers, but he's been recalled to Washington to answer for his alleged indiscretions. The news people check the same police reports I do so I'm surprised it's not on TV."

"I'm sure it will be shortly. The other thing that concerns me is the military drone crash south of town last night."

Cason spoke up, "It didn't crash."

"You're telling me there's not a busted up drone in the middle of a burned out farmer's field."

No sir...it's there, but it didn't crash."

"Okay, would you care to explain that?"

"The military guys from the hangar hauled their secret wreckage to the field last night and scattered it. After that, they set the field on fire to imitate a crash."

"Can you prove that?"

"I've got photos of the truck being loaded in the hangar and driven to the alleged crash site. I videoed soldiers unloading the truck, but it was dark and the audio is the only thing that's usable."

"Let's hear it."

Cason placed his phone on the desk and activated the recording. When it ended, Ed said, "That's not much evidence, but it does mention names. Is everybody thinking what I'm thinking?"

Harry said, "I'm thinking they used the drone for the photo mission and somehow ran it into our airplane. They've been picking up the pieces and now they're going to account for the missing drone by simulating the crash."

Cason added, "It looks that way, but the military wouldn't try a cover up like that unless they were under orders."

Ed said, "I think you're both right. If they get away with it, Tri Con is going to be blamed for the accident and the loss of 200 lives. We can't let that happen."

The discussion was interrupted by Ed's intercom. The secretary informed him, "Mr. Collins is on line two."

The CEO was not happy. "Ed, what are you doing? Why did we just get a Cease and Desist order from the Federal Court?"

"I was afraid of that. Apparently we've gotten between the government and the voters. Someone in Washington wants us to be accountable for their mistake."

"What mistake?"

"I'll need to explain it face to face, Harold, whenever you can make time for me."

"Now."

"I'll be right there."

Putting the phone down, he fumbled under the desk for his shoes. "Here's what we're going to do…"

The White House Chief of Staff was not known for patience and with the upcoming election looming, he had no time for diplomacy. He hung up on the Secretary of Defense when he found out he had failed to dissuade Ed White. He immediately implemented his alternate plan and had the court issue the Cease and Desist order.

With that accomplished, he dialed a private number that was answered on the first ring. He asked, "Are you still in Atlanta?"

"Yes sir, what can I do for you?"

"More of the same. We may have to discredit a few more individuals before you leave town."

"I can do that. Who are they?"

"Several Tri Con employees that won't listen to reason. They all work in the corporate security office. I'll call you back with names later."

"Try to give me time to set something up. The thing with the hotel maid was a little sloppy, but the best I could do on short notice."

"Time is not something we have a lot of. There's an election coming up and we can't postpone that for you to work at your leisure. If the boss doesn't win, we'll all be out of work."

"What about Senator Walker?"

"I think I can handle that from here."

✈

Ed was surprised to find Senator Walker with Harold Collins in the CEO's office. Collins said, "Come in and have a seat Ed. The senator is about to enlighten us."

Walker began, "Gentlemen, I'm going to entrust you with information that can't be shared outside this room. There's a political storm brewing and I'm going to give you the opportunity to shelter yourselves and your company from the fallout. I strongly suggest you take advantage and don't get involved."

Collins said, "I can't make any promises, Senator. I won't sacrifice Tri Con's best interest for anyone's political agenda...including yours."

"Just hear me out, Harold, before you get your butt on your shoulders. The only agenda I have is what's best for the country."

Ed said, "Before you begin, let me ask you something. How long have you known that one of your drones caused our airplane to crash?"

Collins said, "What are you talking about..."

Walker said, "I only learned that this morning. It was an accident, but it should never have happened."

"Did you order the drone to take the airport expansion photos?"

"No, my aide did that without my knowledge. I should say my former aide, but that's just part of the problem."

Collins stood up and stared at the senator, "Are you telling me that a military drone took my airplane down?"

"I'm sorry, Harold, but I believe that's what happened. The governor's nephew is an officer in the Air National Guard, and he came to his uncle with an incredible story."

"What story?"

"The drones are being used illegally by the guard. My legislation authorized the drones for training purposes only. They were to be flown only in restricted airspace controlled by the military. Now I find out that someone in Washington has allowed them to be used by the EPA, the DEA, and even the IRS. Those orders obviously came from the Department of Defense, but they had to be authorized from someone higher in the food chain. You can use your imagination as to who has that much power. My aide just called in a favor, but the precedent had already been established."

"A Boeing 767 crashed because you wanted a few stupid photos?"

"Don't accuse me, Harold. I had nothing to do with it. My aide acted on his own and I fired him."

"So the buck stops with your aide?"

"No, the buck stops with the President of the United States, but he's running a massive cover-up of the drone's involvement. You're going to be left holding the bag and held responsible for the crash. We can sit here and snipe at each other as long as you want, but it won't solve anything. We need to expose the cover up and prove the drone caused the crash or we'll lose the blame game."

Ed said, "I can do that."

He explained how MJ had linked the drone photos to the accident and how Cason had discovered the staged drone crash.

The senator said, "That's exactly what we need, but if the government knows you have that evidence, you and your staff will be discredited. You'll be accused of deviant behavior and charged with crimes you never imagined. No one will believe anything you say."

Collins said, "What do you suggest?"

"We need to leak the evidence to the news media and let them do our job for us."

Ed smiled, "That's being accomplished as we speak."

Chapter Forty Eight

The evening newspaper featured a photo of a Predator drone above the fold. The headline read, "Military Drone May Have Caused Tri Con crash."

The local six o'clock TV News led with the story and the cable networks picked it up shortly thereafter. Government officials were not returning phone calls and the TV networks assembled their *on air* aviation experts to speculate on the evidence. They all agreed that the timeline on the cockpit voice recorder matched the drone photo's time stamps and put the two aircraft in close proximity. Photos of the National Guard truck being loaded in the hangar and driven to the drone crash site were analyzed on air.

Viewers around the nation wanted to believe there was a vast conspiracy being orchestrated and therefore it must be true. Once the players were identified, the news media would declare them guilty until proven innocent.

At noon the next day, the Secretary of Defense resigned for health reasons and his assistant was named as a temporary replacement. The daily White House press conference was delayed a half hour, but when it finally began the first question was, "Did the president have any knowledge of the illegal use of drones in domestic airspace?"

The press secretary looked into the camera and solemnly declared, "The president only learned about this when it was reported in the news media. He is outraged and appalled at the implications. A full investigation is being conducted and as you know, this administration expects to be fully transparent."

The question was asked and answered several more times, but no other insight was forthcoming. However, the president's opponent in the upcoming election was happy to elaborate extensively on this and other misconduct by the administration. The candidate offered several quotes from Senator Walker's select aviation committee concerning the legal restrictions placed on domestic drone use.

Posts began to appear on social media accusing Tri Con investigators of planting evidence and attempting to defraud their insurance carriers. Ed White, Madison Jones, and Cason Haley were mentioned by name. The anonymous posts implied that all three had been involved in shady dealings in the past and formal charges would soon be forthcoming. The news media was aware of, but not impressed by, the attempted character assassination. Ed received notice that his FBI pension was under review. Cason received notice that his military security clearance was suspended until further notice, and MJ opened a certified letter to learn that her tax returns for the last five years would be audited. All three were proud that their efforts would not go unrecognized.

Each day brought new revelations, accusations, and denials in the news cycle. The Tri Con crash was revisited over and over with video of the horrific scene. A human interest angle was needed and the story of Cindy's survival and a daily update on the progress of her recovery was reported as a miracle. When they couldn't get an interview with Cindy or comments from her family, they began speculating on her pending divorce and the millions of dollars that might be involved. Tommy's lawyers were happy to provide his side of the story, although they refused to make him available for comment.

Cindy's mother sheltered her from any controversy that might cause her to be upset. The private hospital room allowed her to convalesce in peace, and Miriam had disabled the TV. The only visitors she had allowed were Stark and Dee, and she carefully controlled what they could and could not discuss.

The doctors had Cindy on her feet several times a day for brief periods of exercise and her strength was rapidly improving. The best indication of her recovery was the onset of cabin fever. She informed Miriam that she was, "Happy as a pig in slop," but boredom had set in and she was ready to get on with her life. Miriam didn't think so. *Girl if you only knew how your life has changed.*

With the morning sun beaming through the window, Cindy chased the last bit of bacon around her breakfast tray with a fork. When she finally captured and consumed it, she looked longingly at her mother's tray which was only half eaten. The two of them made small talk and Miriam deflected questions she didn't want to answer.

"Mom, I lost my purse in the accident. I need you to go to the credit union and get me some blank checks so I can pay my bills. I also need to cancel my credit cards and find out what I have to do to get a new driver's license."

"Don't worry honey…we'll get Dee or Stark to help with all that."

"You do realize his name is Gary?"

"Then why do you call him Stark?"

"Because everybody else does."

"Then do I need to answer your question?"

"I've been wondering about something else. Was anyone else hurt in the accident?"

"I'm not going to eat my toast. Would you like for me to butter it for you and add some jelly?"

"The short answer is, oh yeah."

The door opened and a nurse pushed a wheelchair in. "Miss Lane, how would you like to go for a ride? The doctor has ordered a few routine X-rays. I'll wheel you downstairs to the lab and we'll be done in no time."

"I would kill to get out of this room. How about we go to the mall instead?"

The nurse laughed, "I'll check your chart, but I don't think the doctor mentioned the mall."

Miriam stood up, "I'll take her down to the lab."

"Sorry, ma'am, I have to check her in and sign the orders. We won't be gone long."

"Relax, Mom, I think we can trust her. Recline your chair and close your eyes. You look tired. Help me get into my robe."

Miriam walked into the hall and watched the nurse wheel Cindy to the elevator. When the doors opened, Cindy flashed a smile and a wave. The ride to the first floor was brief and then the nurse pushed the chair through several hallways, stopping to open sets of double doors along the way. Arriving at the X-ray lab, they were informed of a short delay and the nurse wheeled Cindy into a waiting area. "If I leave you here a few minutes will you behave yourself?"

"Yes ma'am, I'll be a good girl, but don't forget me. I don't think I can find my way back to the psych ward."

Looking around the room, the nurse asked, "Would you like something to read while you wait?"

"Something with pictures and little words would be nice."

"I know just the thing." She scrounged around the room until she gathered several sections of the morning paper and placed them in Cindy's lap.

Miriam waited anxiously for Cindy's return. Her daughter had not been out of her sight for days and the forty-five minutes seemed like hours. When the nurse wheeled Cindy back into the room, Miriam jumped to her feet.

"Oh my God…what happened?"

Cindy's face was as white as the terry cloth robe she wore and tears streaked her cheeks. Her lower lip quivered.

Miriam asked, "Did they hurt you, honey?"

Cindy pulled the newspaper from beside her and handed it to her mother. "You lied to me, Mom."

Miriam collapsed in the chair and covered her face.

"Over 200 people are dead and I'm still alive. Why didn't you tell me the truth?"

"Because I wanted you to focus on getting well...nothing else matters. I almost lost you, Cindy, and I couldn't handle that. Please try to understand."

"I can't understand what I don't know. Don't lie to me, Mom."

"I'm so sorry. I just love you too much to see you unhappy. Can you forgive me?"

"I don't want to go back to bed. Help me get in the recliner. I want some real clothes to wear...I'm sick of this hospital gown. In fact, I'm sick of this hospital and I want you to get me out of here."

"The doctor wants you to go to a rehab center for a couple of weeks to build up your strength and monitor your progress. We'll talk to him this afternoon."

"Is Stark coming today?"

"Well, he hasn't missed a day yet."

"Give me your phone."

Stark answered on the first ring.

"Stark are you sober enough to do me a favor?"

"All you have to do is ask."

"I want you to buy me some workout clothes. I need running shoes, sweat pants, and some tee shirts."

"Give me sizes and tell me what color you want."

"How much money do you have?"

"None, but I've got a credit card."

"My Mom will pay you back when you get here."

"How about some shorts and halter tops?"

"How about you just follow instructions and behave yourself?"

"You're getting mean again. You must be feeling better."

"I'm not sure how I feel. I just found out I survived a major crash and inherited a few million dollars."

"You did?"

"Yes, and when you get here, you're going to have one opportunity to explain why you haven't been truthful with me."

"I'm not feeling very well, maybe I should come tomorrow."

"Or maybe you should be here by lunch and smuggle me a burger and some fries in the bag with the clothes."

"Does this mean you're not mad at me?"

"No, it means I'm hungry. Get a move on."

Clicking the phone off, she handed it back to her mother. "I want you to get me a replacement for my cell phone."

"I'll take care of that."

"Why have you never told me that grandpa was rich?"

"Because he never told me. I've been waiting for the right time to explain it to you."

"Now would be the time. The newspaper says Tommy is suing me for my inheritance."

"Our lawyers think that can be settled out of court."

"I won't do that. I won't give him a penny."

"Don't get upset, Honey. That's why I didn't tell you."

"Mother, I'm not a child. You better start explaining everything you know."

Miriam was still explaining when Stark walked in an hour later and set several bags on the bed. Cindy said, "What took you so long?"

"Excuse me, I'm just a junior copilot and they wouldn't let me go to the front of the checkout line. Do you want your burger now?"

"No, I've changed my mind."

"You were easier to deal with when you were comatose."

"That's not funny, Stark. I want you to go find a wheelchair while I get dressed."

Miriam asked, "What are you doing?"

"I'm going on a lunch date with Gary, and you're going to be my chaperone. Do you have lipstick in your purse?"

"On my...we're going to break the rules. What if the doctor finds out and throws us out of the hospital?"

"That would be my hope."

Chapter Forty Nine

Ed decided the best course of action was to do nothing. The news media investigated and reported every inconsistency in the government's story. The White House daily press briefing became a classic demonstration of how to stonewall and deflect attention, but the story just wouldn't die. It was rumored that the administration was considering invading a small country somewhere to create a bigger story.

Ultimately, politicians began turning on each other in order to defend their own interests and reporters found threads to pull that unraveled the coverup. Resignations began to accumulate, but the White House staff built a wall of denial around the president that could not be breached.

Senator Walker eventually pressured enough sources to put the facts together. The drone assigned to the National Guard unit had last been flown in Afghanistan and the navigation database installed in the aircraft had not been updated for domestic airspace. The guard unit was flying the training missions using visual reference only. The remote pilots used the onboard camera transmissions to navigate by visual landmarks.

On the day of the crash, they had followed the perimeter interstate highway that circled Atlanta from the air base north of the city to a point south of the international airport. The perimeter interstate passed several miles west of the airport and well clear of the approach path of the airliners. After taking the photos, the drone was to return to base using the same interstate as a reference. The tragic mistake occurred when the remote pilot followed the interstate connector that passed right by the runways at the busy airport.

The senator leaked information to the news media to keep them on track and simultaneously fed sources to the NTSB. Within a week, the focus was shifted from Tri Con to the Department of Defense. Government officials continued to fall on their own swords, and the NTSB promised a full report within a year.

The warm sun cast sunbeams through the treetops surrounding the cabin and evaporated the dew drops on the soft pine needles covering the ground. With stealth and efficiency, the man crept to within fifty yards of the cabin without being detected. He had already scouted the other nearby cabins and found them uninhabited. *This is not much of a challenge. In and out, go have lunch.*

He continued moving slowly toward the cabin, using the tree line for cover. Going over his plan once again in his mind, he was confident there would be no problems. The sound of a distant boat motor caused him to pause. *Might as well rest and make sure the boat continues on its way.*

He sat with his back against a tree and sipped a bottle of water. The cabin was quiet, but he knew his quarry was inside.

Empty beer cans were accumulating rather rapidly in the cabin, and Tommy tossed them aside indiscriminately. When his public defender called to check on him, his speech was slightly slurred.

"Mr. Lane, are you settling in okay? Do you need anything?"

"I'm fine for now. How long do I have to stay here?"

"We haven't determined that yet. Just make yourself comfortable and enjoy the cabin. A nice rest will serve you well when the divorce case begins."

"There's plenty of food, but the beer supply is not all that great."

"I'll arrange a delivery for you. Have you talked to anyone?"

"Only the wheelchair technician that came by the day after I arrived."

"What?"

"The wheelchair guy showed up and checked the batteries to make sure everything was working okay."

"Did he ask you any questions?"

"Nope…just checked the chair and left."

"Okay, don't go anywhere and don't talk to anyone. We're going to be busy working on your case, but call me if you need anything. Otherwise, I'll check on you again in a few days."

When she hung up, he motored to the kitchen and opened a beer. *She's a little bossy, but not bad looking. I should invite her over for a beer.*

He nudged the joystick on the chair and motored out to the front porch. A light breeze rustled through the trees and reminded him of the sound of gentle surf at the beach. Crushing the beer can in his fist, he threw it over the rail and listened to it bounce down the slope. Nothing relaxed him more than the sound of a beer can opening, and he popped the top on another one. Looking out at the lake, he saw a small fishing boat moving around the cove. *Where did that come from?*

The boat's lone occupant sat at the stern and steered across the cove. A fishing hat shielded his face from the sun. The idling motor made gurgling noises and barely rippled the water as the boat chugged around the cove, slowly passing each cabin. *There's nobody home, mister. You might as well chug on out of here.*

The boat turned and moved toward the dock in front of Tommy's cabin. *Just keep on chugging, Dude.*

The boat gently bumped against the dock and the man stepped out to loop a mooring line over a post. Tommy thought about scooting inside to hide, but the man had already seen him and raised his hand in a friendly wave. *Probably some redneck country bumpkin looking for directions...I'll tell you where you can go buddy.*

The man slowly climbed the paved sidewalk from the dock until he reached the porch steps. When he raised his face, Tommy's half-full beer can clattered to the floor and he clumsily grabbed for the joystick. The chair responded by whirling in a circle and colliding with a wooden rocking chair. Tommy had accomplished his third DUI accident, but this one would not be adjudicated by the court system.

The man watching from the trees recognized the fisherman. *Can't you mind your own business? You better not screw this up.*

He continued to sip water as he watched Tommy motor down the handicapped ramp with the fisherman walking beside him. The paved path was not an obstacle for the motorized wheelchair, and it took less than a minute to reach the dock.

A week of daily therapy and exercise at the rehab center had Cindy eating everything placed before her and moving with a bounce in her step. Every night found several members of the pilot class visiting her and several times the management had reprimanded them for disturbing the residents. Lindbergh had been released from the hospital and hobbled around while Kyle, Stark, and Dee tried to restrain him.

Cindy's attorneys spent hours with her explaining that half her inheritance was in play if they went to court. She would not hear of a settlement and steadfastly declared that Tommy would not get a dime of her grandfather's money. They continued to lobby for settlement but to no avail.

Cindy argued for outpatient status, but the doctors insisted that she stay for the entire two weeks. Miriam convinced her to complete the program.

Drenched with sweat and sore from her morning therapy, she returned to her room to find her lead attorney waiting. With arms folded across her chest, she declared, "I'm not going to settle out of court, and I'm not going to delay my lunch talking about it."

"That's not why I'm here. Your husband's attorneys have asked for a delay in the hearing next week. It seems they've lost track of your husband and can't contact him. I'm concerned that he may find you and try to negotiate on his own behalf."

"There's a restraining order to prevent that."

"That doesn't lessen my concern. The man's unstable and I want to add some special security for you while you're staying here."

"Just get me a gun."

"Please be reasonable, Ms. Lane. Humor me for once."

"Whatever…I'm not afraid of Tommy anymore."

"It's just for a week and then we'll seclude you until this is all over."

When the attorney left, Cindy placed a phone call. "MJ, I need a favor."

"Let me guess…you want Stark back on flying status so he'll stop pestering you."

"I didn't know he was off flying status."

"In that case I probably shouldn't have mentioned it. Sometimes my mouth runs without the benefit of my brain. It's just temporary so he can be available if you need anything while you recover."

"You mean he gave up flying his precious airplane to help me?"

"Apparently so, but like I said it's only temporary. You know they're all addicted to airplanes."

"I'll reprimand him and send him back to work. My attorney tells me that Tommy has gone missing again. Have you heard anything about that?"

"No, but we probably should ask Kitty. She seems to serve as his travel agent."

"The attorney thinks I need extra security until they find him."

"Probably a good idea...let me talk to Cason about it. I'll drop by later to check on you."

She found Cason at his desk staring at a computer screen and tapping on the keyboard. "Cason, have you had any luck locating Tommy Lane?"

"Why do you ask?"

"His attorneys seem to have misplaced him and he may come after Cindy."

He continued to tap the keyboard, "I don't think that will happen."

"It doesn't concern you that no one's watching this maniac?"

"I'm sure he'll turn up. Cindy shouldn't be worried."

"What are you not telling me?"

He looked up from the computer screen, "I see nothing, I hear nothing, and I know nothing."

"You really don't think she should be worried?"

"I really don't."

I don't know why I believe that, but I do

Cindy tolerated the two female bodyguards for the next five days even though it was spooky seeing them lurking around the rehab facility in nurse's scrubs. They worked twelve-hour shifts and were never far away. *I wonder how much this is costing me in overtime, and why do they always wear those silly looking fanny packs.*

She only had one day of rehab left when MJ and Dee paid a surprise visit for lunch. "Surely you girls could find a better place to eat."

Dee answered, "That's true, but you're buying our lunch little rich girl."

"If we hurry we can get one of the good tables by the window. My bodyguards hate it when I sit there."

MJ handed her the morning newspaper, "I don't think they'll mind today."

The story was on page two.

Missing Man's Body Found In Lake

The search for a missing man has ended at Lake Lanier. The handicapped man was reported missing last week when his empty wheelchair was found on the dock of a cabin he was staying in. The body of Thomas Lane was discovered floating near a small island several miles from the cabin. Preliminary reports indicate that Mr. Lane's blood-alcohol level was very high and he probably accidentally fell from the dock and drowned. Park rangers believe the body was carried by currents from the Chattahoochee River, which flows into the lake near the cabin Mr. Lane was occupying. Lane was originally suspected of causing the recent crash of a Tri Con jet before it was discovered that a military drone collided with the airliner as it approached Atlanta. Police do not suspect foul play at this time.

Cindy read the article a second time before tossing it on her bed. "Let's go before all the good tables are taken."

Chapter Fifty

Kyle was the first member of the pilot class to log 500 hours in the right seat of the MD-88. The competition had been fierce among the classmates and Cam Horner protested the rules but was relegated to second place. Lindbergh was ridiculed without mercy for coming in last due to being grounded for two months with his foot injury. Each classmate received a daily text message from Kyle, which included a photo of his logbook. He ignored the disrespectful responses and vowed to win the award for logging 1000 hours.

The pilot class had successfully flown through the winter months, and they were no longer intimidated by snow, ice, high winds, or instrument approaches. Spring thunderstorms were now the challenge and color radar was their new best friend. The gold stripes on their jacket sleeves had dulled a bit and no longer announced to the world that they were rookies. The first seven months of their airline career just made them hungry for more.

Each classmate circled the sixth of June on their calendars and placed their trip bids to have the day off. Everyone had received formal invitations for the wedding ceremony with reception to follow. The little church south of town was overflowing and pilots were requested to attend in uniform.

The church's air conditioning system was taxed to the maximum to cool the standing room only crowd. The roar of conversation and laughter filled the room and spilled out into the yard. The first notes from the church organ signaled the crowd to sit down and shut up, and an anticipatory silence fell over the room. The nervous bride was escorted into the vestibule to await the wedding march.

Her father lifted the veil covering her face and gently kissed her on the cheek. "Elizabeth, you are absolutely the most beautiful woman on earth. I am so proud of you, and you will always be my little girl."

"I love you too, Dad. Please don't let me fall on my face."

The wedding march began and they walked arm in arm down the aisle. Cason Haley stood smiling at the altar to greet his bride.

The ceremony was eloquently brief, but the kiss was long and a few giggles could be heard in the audience. Applause erupted when they turned to face the congregation and held hands as they moved to take a seat in the first row.

The organ began playing once again and the pilot who took Cason's place at the altar stood nervously erect in his uniform and wished he had worn sunglasses to hide the fear in his eyes. When the vestibule doors opened and he saw the stunning white wedding dress, his knees trembled and he was thankful everyone had turned to see the beautiful bride being escorted to the altar by her mother. Miriam Latimer could see that her new son in law was dangerously close to passing out. She thought she heard her daughter giggle.

Stark was able to compose himself, buoyed largely by his determination to perform a longer kiss than the previous groom, which he accomplished by several seconds according to Dee, who had been appointed as the official judge.

Applause erupted once again as the newlyweds faced the crowd holding hands and smiling. Tears darkened the mascara in Cindy's eyes as Stark escorted her to join Cason and Elizabeth in the first row.

Kyle Bennett asked Dee how long Stark's kiss had lasted before taking his place at the altar. She refused to answer him. As he stood nervously waiting, he remembered exactly how he felt before making his first PA announcement. *Please God, don't punish me now.*

Harry Dade was almost as nervous as Kyle as he limped down the aisle arm in arm with MJ. The veil could not hide the smile on her face. The vows they expressed brought tears to many eyes and the kiss was heartfelt and beautiful.

Dee clicked the stopwatch on her cell phone. *Ladies and Gentlemen, we have a winner.*

OTHER BOOKS BY HARRISON JONES

"There has never been a mid ocean ditching by an air carrier jet." These are the words that haunt Captain Charlie Wells when he realizes that his jumbo jet has a problem over the Atlantic. None of the passengers or crew could know that a disgruntled airline mechanic has sentenced them to a night of terror. As the flight approaches the *Equal Time Point,* and is the most distant from land, Captain Wells and his crew of pilots and flight attendants struggle to avoid making history. While airline personnel, the FAA, and the FBI try to solve the mystery of Tri Con Flight Eleven, a small U.S. Navy ship may be the only hope for the 208 souls on board.

Visit the author's website at www.harrisonjones.org

OTHER BOOKS BY HARRISON JONES

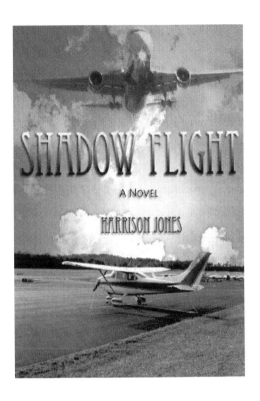

America's security may depend on a young flight instructor from rural south Texas. Kyle Bennett's charter flight disappears without a trace, along with a female student and the charter passenger. The mysterious disappearance cannot be solved despite the best efforts of the Civil Air Patrol, the Coast Guard and the FAA.

When a Tri Con captain, Bud Gibson, and one of the airline's mechanics, Matt Pierce, go missing, the two cases merge. A conspiracy to complete the 9-11 attack is underway and, the terrorists are sure they can defeat all of America's security measures. Only Kyle, Bud and Matt stand in their way.

Visit the author's website at www.harrisonjones.org

Made in the USA
Charleston, SC
11 February 2015